MAREK

Marek

Editor:
Hot Tree Editing

Cover Design:
CT Cover Creations

Marek/ S. Nelson. – 1st edition
ISBN-13: 9781734302332

MAREK

KNIGHTS CORRUPTION MC SERIES

S. NELSON

Dedication

This book is dedicated to my husband. Thank you so much for being patient with me while I lock myself in the office, writing for countless hours on end. I love you!

Prologue

Marek

Too many voices shouted demands, hands shoving me roughly forward until I was no longer standing on my own two feet. "Get on the ground!" was the one I heard the most. My knees hit hard off the gravel, my stomach kissing earth while my hands were jerked behind my back before I could utter a single word of protest. People in uniforms clambering to throw me and all my brothers down like we'd done something wrong. Don't make any mistake, we certainly weren't boy scouts, but the sudden invasion was most definitely unwarranted.

The DEA agent towering over me was none other than Sam Koritz, the most crooked motherfucker I knew, and that was saying a lot since I was the furthest from a straight arrow myself. He was forever trying to nail my club, even though it was because of us that his pockets were fattened to not only look the other way, but to forget we even existed.

Running my club, the Knights Corruption, was profitable but extremely dangerous. We were accountable for two-thirds of the cocaine supply smuggled into central California. The ports we utilized were run by us and people we paid hand-somely to keep the profit high and the risk low. But every now and then, someone became greedy—hence Koritz busting in like he owned the joint.

Fuck him if he thought he was gonna get away with this shit. I'd put one of my boys on him just as soon as we were able to. Maybe pay a visit to his house, have a little chat, remind him who paid for his kid's private school.

While I sucked the dirt into my lungs, my arms aching from the tightly coiled position, I dreamed up ways of paying back exactly who I knew was responsible—besides Koritz, of course.

The Savage fucking Reapers.

Koritz was most likely in bed with them as well, and whoever paid more won out every time. I had no doubt Henry 'Psych' Brooks, the president of the Savage Reapers, had put the DEA agent up to it. And why not? Killing two birds with one stone. If they found what they were looking for—drugs, guns and money—they'd profit. And if not, they'd been able to send a message by allowing us to witness Koritz's betrayal.

The continual war between our two clubs was coming to a head very soon. We'd already had casualties, and it would be over my dead body if any more of us were gonna meet the Devil any time soon.

"Where the hell is it, Marek?" Koritz shouted, stomping his boot down on top of my neck. *I'm gonna kill this sonofabitch as soon as I get the chance.*

Trying my best not to give him the reaction he wanted, I spit the soil from my mouth and laughed. As soon as the sound burst forth, he kicked me in the ribs before I could change positions to protect myself. I should have known it was coming, but I was too preoccupied with pissing the bastard off.

A rush of air flew from my lips, a low groan escaping before I could stop it. "Touch my prez one more fuckin' time, and you'll be meetin' your maker real soon," my VP, Stone, yelled. We faced each other on the ground, and as soon as his eyes met mine, I shot him a warning look for him to shut his mouth and lock it up. His reddened face told me he was seconds away from exploding.

Luckily, he did as I'd silently cautioned.

Loyalty.

Plain and simple.

His mouth and hot-ass temper were gonna land us in more trouble if he kept going. While I appreciated his undying allegiance to me and to the club, we needed to let this all play out.

Koritz didn't even pay Stone's threat any attention, keeping his focus on me the entire time instead. I saw his foot leave the ground, cock back then swing forward. I braced myself that time, but it didn't do any good—the fucker came wearing shit-kickers, and my ribs certainly felt the brunt of it. I wouldn't be surprised if he'd broken a couple in his attempt to make me talk. But that's okay, because when the opportunity presented itself to pay him back, I'd make sure to return the favor.

"I'm not gonna ask you again, *Prez*," he gritted, pacing back and forth, waiting for me to divulge the location of what they'd come here looking for—the product. But if he thought he would find it on our own goddamn compound, he was even stupider than I thought. We never kept that shit on site. The worst thing they would come across would be a few illegal handguns. That's it.

Lifting my head off the ground, I craned my neck to look up at him. Words fell from my lips, but he couldn't hear them. Which was done half on purpose, because I wanted him to squat down to my level. The other part was because I was having a hard time breathing. Finally, he did exactly what I wanted him to, leaning down so he could hear me.

"What was that, you piece of shit?" he yelled.

"Nothing," I replied, a drop of blood spraying from my mouth and hitting the dirt.

"What?" He was losing whatever patience he had left, and if I wasn't careful my ass was gonna really be hurtin' come morning.

He knew enough to make sure I was tied up and on the ground before he attacked me, otherwise, he'd have an up–close-and-personal relationship with my fists. He was no match for me, and the coward knew it. The man was in his late forties and ate too much garbage, the pot belly hanging over his belt proof of his overindulgences. His receding hairline was notice-able even though he tried to hide it with a laughable comb-over.

I was everything he wasn't and he knew it, so he exerted his authority, or whatever authority he thought he had. Once I found my opportunity, we'd see who the big man was then.

"Nothing," I said louder. "There's nothing here, so you assholes are wasting my precious tax dollars," I goaded.

"Tax dollars? As far as I'm aware, criminals don't pay taxes, or did that change? Oh, wait, I forgot all about the little strip club the Knights own," he chided. "Maybe that'll be our next stop. Maybe it accidently gets torched," he threatened, nodding as if he was truly pondering it.

I'd been venturing out to legal businesses, my main goal to turn my club legit. Simply put, the way we were doing things was way too dangerous, and I was tired of it all. I was only twenty-eight years old, but most days I felt twice my age. Physi-cally, I was as fit as could be, but mentally, I was drained. Stressed the fuck out. Sick of the bloodshed. I'd seen more in my short life than most men saw in their entire existence, and enough was enough. But there were debts which had to be repaid and vengeance that needed to be carried out before I called it legit for good. Once we went straight, we weren't gonna teeter back and forth between the two worlds, so we had to be sure everything was taken care of first.

Realizing Koritz wasn't gonna get anything out of us, he straightened up and yelled to his men, "Search it! Tear it apart if you have to. We have all night," he promised, his foot coming dangerously close to my face.

"Don't you need a warrant, asshole?" Ryder, my Sergeant-at-Arms, yelled, an outburst which earned him a swift blow to the stomach. He was fortunate—or unfortunate, depending on how one looked at it—to not be lying down. He was on his knees with his fingers interlocked and resting on the top of his head, his hands bound while one of the agents held him in place so he couldn't move. Cuffed or not, my men would run off at the mouth without a second's hesitation.

"Nope," Koritz's lapdog said, pulling back and sucker punching Ryder, that time in the face.

All these fuckers are goin' down.

After two very long hours, they finally deemed the compound all clear, only finding a few dime bags of weed. Nothing they were gonna waste their time over. They kept us locked in the same positions, my arms screaming in pain along with my possibly broken ribs. Koritz stalked my way, beyond pissed that he wasn't able to pin anything on me. For as crooked as he was, he wasn't stupid enough to plant evidence, though, probably out of fear of retaliation. Little did he know I was already plotting my revenge.

All in due time.

Reaching down, he took hold of my upper arm and pulled, but he was so weak he needed another man to help lift me. Once on my feet, I staggered a few steps, trying to find my footing all while doing my best to breathe. I masked the pain by clenching my teeth and trying to appear as pissed off as possible —which wasn't hard to do, given everything that'd happened.

"You lucked out this time, Marek," Koritz said, swiftly patting my side. The pain radiated through my entire body, and I held the air in my lungs, waiting to see what he was gonna do next. With my hands still cuffed behind my back, I knew I wasn't capable of doing shit until he released me. Roughly grabbing my wrists, he jerked them back, the muscles of my arms hollering in protest. "If you make a move on me or any of my men, I'll shoot you where you stand. You understand?" His putrid breath hit the side of my face, and I almost threw up.

When I nodded quickly, he withdrew the key to the restraints and popped them open. Normally, I would rub my wrists because of the tight pressure of the cuffs, but I simply flexed my fists at my sides, reminding myself that he would make good on his promise of killing me if I dared to strike back.

As soon as all my men were released, and all of the DEA agents left our compound, I vowed then and there to never be put into that situation ever again.

Everyone would feel the wrath of the Knights Corruption MC before we turned to the other side.

One

Sully

Turning his head in my direction, the man leading me down a dark, narrow hallway practically spit at me in anger. "If you don't hurry up, Sully, you're gonna regret being so goddamn slow." I knew that tone. I was petrified of that tone. But I was used to it and unfortunately, I was used to him and the way he treated me.

My tired legs tried to hurry, but I was extremely sluggish. Vex had woken me from a dead sleep, forced me to pleasure him, then tossed me out of bed. Throwing some dark-colored clothes at me, he ordered me to dress, hauled me from the compound and shoved me in the passenger side of a beat-up gray truck.

I didn't even need to ask where we were going. I already knew. Every now and again, he would drag me with him to be his lookout while he broke into people's homes and stole their drugs—cocaine, to be specific. He would snort as much of the nose candy as he could, then sell the rest to bring in a profit for our club, the Savage Reapers. Having a talent for bypassing even the most high-tech security systems, it was a shame he didn't put his talents to better use, but when it came right down to it, Vex Montale was a low-level criminal, never aspiring to be anything more than he was.

I took two more steps down the darkened space and ran smack-dab right into his back. He'd suddenly stopped, but I knew enough to keep my mouth shut instead of asking why. I learned long ago to know my place when it came to Vex, only speaking if he asked me a question. I was only fourteen years old when he claimed me from my father, Vex being all of eighteen himself. That was six years ago. At first, I was attracted to him, his sandy-brown hair and piercing green eyes were certainly head-turning. His square jaw and perfectly proportionate nose only added to his good looks, even with the slight bump in the middle. He'd broken it during one of the many fights he'd incited, never bothering to have it set properly. His lean, muscular build had enticed my awakening young hormones, but that quickly changed the first time his fist connected with my face. No matter how good-looking he was on the outside, the ugliness inside him had pushed through and repulsed me from then on.

I wasn't stupid enough to believe he was faithful to me either, witnessing him having sex with other girls on a few occasions. But did he care when he'd been caught? No. The times I'd accidentally walked in on him rutting like some kind of animal, he leered at me and continued on until he roared out his disgusting release.

Vex snatched my arm and pulled me closer, snarling at me like some sort of rabid dog. Hell, even a sick dog was nicer than he was, especially when he'd been snorting that shit up his nose, which happened more and more lately. "His room is the last one on the right. We have to get in and grab what we can," he sniffed, pinching his nose between his thumb and forefinger before starting to move again. "Don't fuck this up. Do you hear me?" he asked, squeezing my arm tight.

"Yes," I whimpered. Even though he'd asked me a direct question—my cue to speak—he didn't like it when I talked too much.

He was the second dangerous man I knew, my father trumping him and taking the title for the worst human being alive. At least Vex didn't keep me locked in a closet for days without food or water when I'd done or said something he didn't like. Don't get me wrong, I lived in Hell every single day, praying for a quick death each and every time he struck, raped and choked me unconscious. But because I was still breathing air into my lungs, my destiny obviously hadn't been fulfilled yet.

When we reached the room we were supposed to enter, he stilled on the threshold, peering inside and listening for anything that would tell him we weren't alone. Although the information he'd received from one of the other brothers told him the owner was out for the night—leaving his place unattended for the likes of us—he'd been given erroneous tips before.

I detested being dragged into situations I wanted nothing to do with. But I had no choice, just like I had no choice in anything that happened in my life.

It was better to go along than resist.

I had the scars to prove it.

Moving slower than I thought was possible while he was coked out of his mind, he shoved me forward into the dark bedroom. "Look in the closet." He pinched his nose again, making a sound with his throat before mumbling to himself, "He told me it was here."

Without answering, I did as I was told and headed for the closet in the far corner of the large room. The only light I had was from a small keychain flashlight. Anything bigger would pull too much attention—at least, that's what Vex told me.

While I searched for the kilos of cocaine that were supposed to have been hidden somewhere in the bedroom, Vex rummaged through drawers, opening and closing them before moving on to other areas of the expansive room.

Whoever lived here certainly had money. Not only was the house huge, but the furnishings looked expensive. The small light of my keychain had allowed me to see the king-sized bed, which took up the middle of the space, with four carved pillars the focal point. Two matching dressers and nightstands completed the bedroom set, the wood a rich mahogany color I itched to run my fingers over.

Living at the clubhouse, which was unheard of for a female, we only had old, ratty furniture. Most of it was rigged somehow, and the pieces that weren't would splinter apart with the slightest force. I wasn't a materialistic person, not by any stretch of the imagination, but just once I would like to own something new.

"Did you find anything yet?" he gritted, his warm breath hitting the side of my face while he crowded my personal area inside the closet. Before I could answer, he shoved me back into the bedroom and rooted through the space himself, cursing me every time he came up short, like it was my fault he couldn't find what he was looking for.

My head hung low, the tiny light slowly faded in and out while I waited for him to finish his search. Uneasiness ate me up the longer we invaded the stranger's house, the hairs on the back of my neck sticking up with each tick of the clock. With every second that passed, we were that much closer to getting caught. And if were spotted, it was somehow going to be my fault, and I would pay dearly because of it. As it stood, Vex was probably going to punish me anyway, if for nothing other than the frustration that he couldn't find more product to feed his nasty habit. Either way, my night was going to be less than ideal. But what else was new?

Lost in my own head, I never heard him approaching.

I never saw the light flick on in the hallway.

I never saw his hand reach into the bedroom where we were standing and pause by the light switch.

I never saw him until the room was immersed in brightness, instantly blinding me until my eyes focused on the scene around me.

"What the hell, Sully? Turn off the light before I knock some sense into you."

I didn't pay any attention to his ramblings; instead, my eyes were trained on the man standing in front of me, his gun pointed directly at my chest.

At first glance, the stranger appeared to be civil, dressed in a finely pressed suit matched with the most expensive shoes I'd ever seen. The light from above shone off his cleanly shaved head, his neatly trimmed beard a lie as to how dangerous he really was.

I thought for sure fear and panic would have imprisoned me, but unfortunately, it wasn't the first time a gun had been aimed at me. Shit, it wasn't even the second or third time my life had been threatened in such a way. But a stranger, a man whose home we'd broken into, was the one pointing the weapon at me. I should have been scared. But instead, I was numb inside.

"What do we have here?" the stranger yelled, instantly gaining Vex's attention. Stepping from the closet, he came to stand behind me as soon as he saw the man had a weapon. It didn't shock me that he chose to use me as a shield in case the guy went nuts and started firing. Come to think of it, I prayed for that exact scenario; then I would be set free from the invisible chains which bound me to this dreadful life.

"Don't do anything crazy, man," Vex warned, his grip on my arms tightening the more he realized how dangerous our situation had become when the owner of the house stepped forward without an ounce of reservation.

"You break into my house, scour through my things looking for God knows what, and *you* tell *me* not to do anything crazy. Do you know who I am?" Silence danced around the room. "Well... Do you?" he roared, scratching his cheek with the barrel of his gun, a deranged look on his face the closer he stepped toward us.

I knew that look.

Vex *just* had it on his face.

Cocaine is a hell of a drug.

"Yes," Vex admitted. "Look, we didn't take anything. No harm, right?" His nervous laugh hit a nerve with me. He never took anything seriously because he thought he was protected by the club, doing anything he wanted, treating everyone like shit just because he thought he could get away with it simply because he was with the president's daughter. But what he didn't realize was that he was a liability and his brothers were tired of coming to his rescue. He had no idea, but I'd accidentally overheard a few of the members discussing his future, or lack thereof. I kept my mouth shut because I prayed they would make their move sooner rather than later. But until then, I had to bide my time.

"How the hell did you even get in here?" the man asked, stepping perilously closer. "You must be some sort of electronics wiz to bypass my security system. Is that it?"

He hit the nail on the head.

"Never mind, what's done is done." He grinned dangerously. "And while you may not have taken anything, it doesn't mean I won't." His statement confused me, until he lunged forward, seized my arm and pulled me against his large frame. "I think I'll have a little taste," he promised, his tongue snaking out and licking the side of my face as I twitched in his hold.

Even though Vex treated me like a piece of property, less than human, someone he kept around solely to do with as he saw fit, I was still his. And any threat to that was a direct insult to him.

The blast of a gun pierced the air, my eardrums feeling as though they'd exploded from the close proximity. One minute, the strange man held me close and the next he was on the ground, a pool of blood surrounding him where he lay.

"Fuckin' cocksucker," Vex grumbled, kicking the man to make sure he wasn't getting back up. Once he was satisfied he'd killed him, he continued searching the room as if he hadn't just ended the man. I was left to stand there dumbfounded, not so much by the corpse lying at my feet, but that Vex could have easily killed me instead. There hadn't been much space between us, and that he'd been able to achieve such a clean shot was mind-boggling.

Or was he hoping I would have perished right along with the man?

Two

Sully

The ride back home was in silence. I never did find out who the man was. The less I knew, the better.

Vex found what he'd been looking for hidden in a faulty floorboard, ten kilos of coke his prize for the evening. After snorting a few lines, he packed up everything in the duffel bag he'd brought and ushered us from the home, not a care in the world that he'd left a body behind to be discovered.

Once we were finally inside the clubhouse, I walked toward the kitchen, needing to grab a drink before I headed off to the room Vex and I shared. A strange male voice stopped me in my tracks. I knew better than to pay attention to the goings on inside the place I unfortunately called home, but an uneasiness gripped me.

My father, Henry Brooks—aka Psych, aka president of the Savage Reapers—rounded the corner, followed closely by a man I'd never seen before.

I would have crashed right into them had it not been for my quick reflexes.

"Sully," my father greeted, his tone dripping with an indication that he was up to no good. As usual.

"Father," I answered, apprehension wrapping around me like the coil of a dangerous snake. I never referred to my father as Dad or Daddy. Not since I was a toddler. The man hated me; it was the only excuse I could come up with for the way he treated me. So I decided long ago to bury any fleeting feelings I had toward him as my kin, disguising the need for his approval with formalities.

"Who do we have here?" the man standing behind my father asked.

Stepping to the side to allow his guest to feast his eyes on me, he answered, "My daughter, Sully."

"Sully," the man repeated, stepping closer until he was only a few feet away from me. My breath twitched in my throat, my heart picking up pace the more he continued to leer at me. His beady, soulless eyes roved over my body, and right then I was grateful for the dark, baggy clothes Vex had made me wear. "Is she taken?"

"Yeah, but you can have her if you want. I'll handle Vex, explain it's good business and all."

What the hell is he talking about?

As if being summoned, Vex appeared out of thin air, walking up behind my father and the strange man who'd suddenly become enthralled with me.

"What are you doing out of our room, Sully?" he yelled, stalking toward me and roughly gripping my neck. While his touch was painful, I welcomed the familiar feeling. Better Vex than the bastard standing in front of me.

"Vex, I was just telling Yanez here he can have a go at Sully. What do ya think?" Looking back and forth between the man who'd given me life and the man I belonged to, I was stunned to find out Vex wasn't going to put up a fight. Which was extremely odd. I was his property, and any threat to that was always met with sheer force. Sometimes even resulting in death, exactly like what had happened earlier.

While he didn't voice his refusal, his face said it all. But that didn't matter. My father's word was law, and if he was going to give me to this man, then there wasn't a damn thing either one of us could do.

I still tried, however.

Slowly backing away, I prayed I had enough time to make it to my room before any of them caught me. I'd lock myself inside and count the minutes until they left me alone.

I knew I was being delusional, but an escape inside my head was all I had.

"Don't even think about it," my father sneered, lurching forward and snagging my wrist. "Do you know who this man is?" I remained silent because I had no idea. Shaking me, he said, "This is Rico Yanez, right-hand man to Rafael Carrillo. The head of Los Zappas cartel. We've just finished some business, and if he wants to fuck you then you'll let him. Do you understand me?"

"Nooooo," I whimpered, his bruising hold making me wince in pain. "I won't do it."

"You don't have a choice. If you don't give it up, he'll just take it. Actually, I think he prefers it rough. Don't you?" he asked, turning to look at Yanez.

The man nodded and smirked.

I struggled to break free from my father, but it was no use. Being forced to have sex with someone I'd been with for years was one thing, but to be forced by a complete stranger was something entirely different.

Rape was rape, right?

Wrong.

Better the devil I knew and all that shit.

My father passed me off, his fingers freeing me as Yanez's trapped me. "Where can I take her?"

"In that room back there. You'll find a perfectly good sofa as well as a sturdy desk. Just don't make too much of a mess," he warned.

Without another word, I was dragged away, seconds from being thrust inside a smoke-filled office.

My father's office.

He'd given me up to seal the deal with the cartel.

A prize for doing business.

Once we were alone, I tried to reason with the man, praying there was something human residing inside him which would allow him to let me go.

"Please, don't do this," I pleaded, yanking free and putting as much allowable space between us as possible.

"Don't worry, sweetheart. You'll enjoy this, I promise." His gaze creepily raked over me, looking like he wanted to devour me whole. He approached, a lock of his dark, gray-streaked hair falling over his left eye. For a man who was as high up in the cartel, he was shabby-looking, a bushy mustache hiding his otherwise thin lips. He was as big as he was tall, his stomach hanging over the belt of his pants proving he didn't care about himself in the least.

His fat hands captured me again, pulling me so close I shivered in disgust. His breath enveloped my face, the smell of alcohol and cigarette smoke strong as he crashed his lips to mine. I tried to turn away, but he snatched my chin roughly to keep my head still. Licking at my mouth, he became frustrated when I wouldn't open for him.

"This is gonna happen whether you like it or not." His voice was sinister. He walked me backward until we were close to the edge of the desk, the gun in his waistband suddenly apparent and pressing into my side. "Take off your clothes,"

Yanez demanded, taking a step back and licking his thin lips while waiting for me to do as I was told.

"Please," I begged, holding my hands up in surrender, shaking in fear. The seriousness of my situation hit me like a sledgehammer, and I was terrified of what was about to happen.

"Don't speak again," he ordered.

I kept my mouth shut, my body unable to move and do as instructed.

"I'm not gonna ask you again. Take off your clothes!" he shouted. When I still refused to move, that's when he struck, pain radiating across my cheek before I could even think about protecting myself. I hadn't even seen it coming, but I should have expected it. Holding my face, tears instantly welled behind my eyes. I chastised myself for appearing weak, but I was shocked. And hurt.

"Refuse again and I'll use the butt of my gun next time. And trust me, sweetheart, the pain will be unbearable." He smirked, finding it amusing that he was tormenting me into submission. His fingers rested on the handle of his gun, prepared to extract it if necessary.

In all my years of abuse at the hands of my father, he'd never given me to another man—with the exception of Vex, of course. No, this was something new. Would he do it again, though? To whomever he deemed worthy of receiving a *gift* due to the nature of whatever shady deals he'd procured? Would I become *good business sense* again in the future?

My hands shook as I reached for the hem of my shirt, drawing it up my body, taking a few precious seconds before pulling it over my head. My long black hair fell forward, covering my face from his view for the briefest of moments, and I cherished not having to look at him.

"Now the pants."

I quickly pulled the dark jeans down my legs, kicking them to the side to stand in silence once again.

A low whistle sounded as he stared at my entire body. While I couldn't see him right then, I could feel his leer, goose bumps breaking across my skin in fear.

"You've certainly got some body on you, don't ya?" His question was rhetorical, of course. "Take it *all* off."

Pleading was pointless.

Refusing proved to be dangerous.

I had no other choice but to obey.

But for some reason, all sense of survival left me, the sudden need to flee overwhelming beyond any sense of security. My body reacted before my mind caught up, darting left before closing in on the door of the office. If I could only make it through, I'd run as fast as I could. Not to my room because they'd only haul me back to Yanez, most likely battered and bruised. No, I had to try and make it outside. Nature would protect me if I begged hard enough.

Our compound was in the middle of nowhere, surrounded by acres of nothing but trees and hidden streams. I tried to escape once before, but I had obviously failed, the mental scars of being tortured outweighing the permanent marks on my body.

My feet propelled me forward, my heart skipping a beat while I choked on the stifling tension surrounding me. Before I reached the door, however, I was ripped backward, a large hand clutching my throat and forcing out the remaining air from my lungs. My chest burned from lack of oxygen, my eyes bulging with the thought that this could be it. And there was something disappointing in the thought of dying at the hands of a stranger. If anything, I thought I'd recognize the eyes of my killer before I took my last breath.

He released me before I succumbed to the darkness, a

raging coughing fit ensuing in order to draw air into my starved lungs.

"Where do you think you're goin'?" Yanez laughed, deliriously entertained with my need to protect myself. The man was cut from the same cloth as my father and Vex, their souls having been extinguished long ago.

Tossing me back toward the center of the room, he stood strong and blocked any further inclinations I had toward making it out of there before he'd had his fill of me.

"Strip."

I knew I was out of options so, with my head hung low, I finally complied.

My arms twisted behind my back and I slowly unhooked my bra, allowing it to slide off my shoulders before falling to the ground. I was tiny in stature; the only things out of proportion on my body were my breasts and my ass. Both attributes often drew unwanted attention from men, and I hated my body because of it.

His lust increased the more he stared, and it was only a matter of minutes until he would rip the last part of my soul from me. Hooking my fingers into the waistband of my panties, I drew them down my thighs until they were bunched at my feet. Stepping out of them, I moved to the side, brought my hands up and tried to cover myself.

"Drop your hands. Now," he commanded. I obeyed. Again. "Well, would you look at that?" He took a step closer. "Whose idea was it to have you shaved? No matter. All the better for me." Crossing the couple feet separating us, he turned me around and bent me over until my breasts hit the surface of the hard desk.

He didn't speak as he shoved my legs apart, unzipped his pants and pulled himself free. Of all the thoughts to race through my head, I was thinking how thankful I was that he left the rest of his clothes on, his massive gut something I most definitely didn't want to feel as it rubbed against me. Gripping my hip with his free hand, he shoved himself inside me with all the force he could muster. He wasn't small and, because I was completely dry, he tore through me, ripping me apart from the inside out. A cry erupted from my throat before I could stop it, my nails scouring the wood in agony.

Once he was fully sheathed, he rutted inside me, enjoying that he was fucking an unwilling participant. "Do you like that?" he panted. The only response I could muster was the frantic shaking of my head, tears soaking my cheeks and falling to the desk below.

If I remained still and let him get off then it would all be over with and I could return to my room. Hopefully, Vex would take pity on me and not beat me for allowing this man to rape me.

Yanez slowed his intrusion and without warning, fell from my body. I thought he was done so I tried to stand up, but he shoved me back down, pressing the side of my face against the hard surface.

"Not yet," he growled. "Gonna take that sweet ass." Before his words registered, he grabbed a fistful of my hair, yanking my head back until a cry tore from my lips. My anguish seduced him. He snatched my strands tighter, pain slicing through my poor head as he made me stand. "You know you want it," he threatened, pulling me so close my back hit his chest, his smoky breath making me sick.

"Put your hands on the desk." For a brief moment, there was no contact. He'd backed away, the chill of the room prickling my skin. But his absence was short-lived. Anchoring me to him, I heard him spit into his hand before he pressed himself against my tight, puckered hole. Instinct told me to struggle, but all that got me was an immobilizing grip to the neck, the sneer of his voice in my ear threatening to kill me if I resisted again.

Vex had repeatedly sodomized me, and for as many times as he forced himself there, it never felt any better. I braced myself, my paranoia pinning me in place. I tried desperately to mentally float off to a happier time, but I didn't have one. Yanez tangled his fingers in my hair once again, the pain of his grip shooting right through me.

"You're gonna love this," he rasped. Spreading my cheeks, he forced himself inside me, the unbearable pain causing my body to seize up. I stopped breathing, all while my heart slammed against my chest. Once he started to move, he ordered me to link my hands behind my back, releasing my hair to hold me in place by my wrists instead.

Fear and mortification flooded over me. Not only was this humiliating and degrading, the pain was indescribable.

My mind raced all over the place, pinging back and forth between the hell I was in and the hell I was going to find myself in once I returned to my room.

My wrists screamed under the weight of his pressure. I tried to wriggle them free, praying he was too distracted to notice. But he did. Instead of him yelling or gripping my hands tighter, he slammed his fist into the back of my head. Dots instantly invaded my vision, a searing pain slicing through my skull so fierce I almost passed out. Unfortunately for me, he hadn't hit me hard enough to knock me unconscious. At least then, I would have been saved from hearing him grunt out his release inside me.

When he finally finished, he withdrew from my body, zipped up his pants and disappeared from the room without a word.

I barely managed to clothe myself before I saw Vex striding straight toward me, the heat of rage dancing behind his eyes.

Realizing that bracing for his attack would only serve to piss him off even more, I stood there and waited for his punishment. He snatched my upper arm and dragged me from my father's office.

"You wait till I get you alone. You'll wish he'd killed you."

It was the last thing I remembered before darkness found me.

Three

Marek

Picturing Koritz's ugly face while I pummeled him to within an inch of his life made me smile. The thought of exacting my revenge made the cleanup somewhat bearable.

His men had trashed our clubhouse, and while some of the old ladies helped with the mess, they weren't allowed in the area where we met to talk private business. It was sacred, the one place we went to get away from it all, a separate suite inside the clubhouse.

Some clubs called it Church, but we called it Chambers. Mainly because it was where we talked about, then eventually delivered, justice.

The main room consisted of our meeting table and chairs, memorabilia plastered around the room for nostalgia. Off to the right was a bathroom linked to another room where the men chose to hide out if they were having issues with their women, or if they needed time to sort shit out that was rattling around inside their head. Since no one but the members were allowed in Chambers, they were safe for as long as it took for them to calm down enough to go back to their rooms, or any of the common areas.

"They sure made a mess, didn't they?" Stone grumbled, picking up pieces of broken glass from some of the dishes they tossed from the cupboards. *Really? What in the hell did they think we were hiding in there? Assholes.*

Stone and I had grown up together, and since the time we were young boys we knew someday we were going to run the KC. It was ingrained in us, our fathers pulling us into meetings early on to make sure we knew all the ins and outs of the club.

The politics.

The minute everyday details, from who was in our pockets to the best trade routes to what the dirt was on our biggest rival.

The fucking Savage Reapers.

Our clubs hated each other with a vengeance.

Their club was run with no rules, morals or consequences. They were heavily involved in human trafficking, selling women and children to the sickest, highest bidders. They beat and raped their own women, not a care in the world for another's life as long as they got what they wanted.

For all means and purposes, they certainly lived up to their name.

Savages.

And while we were no angels, exacting revenge when we felt it necessary, we at least lived by some sort of principle.

We didn't beat and rape our women, and we didn't kill innocent people. We ran drugs for the livelihood of the club, but they were forbidden to use. The strongest substances allowed at the compound were weed and alcohol. And although there had been many a time where some of the brothers went overboard and drank until they fell unconscious, they were easily controlled by the rest of us. All except for Ryder. When the club's Sergeant-at-Arms and head mechanic drank the hard shit, he was a mean motherfucker. Thank God he only partook when shit got bad, and since I'd taken over three years ago, I was able to control the shit that went down enough to ensure he'd only gotten out of pocket twice. Both times resulting in three of the brothers beating him into submission, locking him in his room until he finally calmed down.

Every man had his own room at the club, but they owned their own property away from the compound as well. I didn't require my men to stay together at all times, it mostly just worked out that way. Which was why most of them had problems in their relationships. But the women knew the life they were choosing when they shacked up with the guys, the men's first priority being the club above all else. Don't get me wrong, they loved their women and would kill to protect them and their families, but there was nothing like the brotherhood the club provided.

"Hey, Marek," Stone yelled across the room. "How about once we get shit right, we throw a ruckus?" That was code for an all-nighter, an 'anything goes' type of get-together. It also meant no wives or girlfriends allowed, only familiar party favors, aka club whores.

"Sure thing," I promised. "Get ahold of Zip and Hawke and tell them to make a liquor run. We're running low," I said, flipping the couch right-side up, cursing those DEA assholes with every flick of my eyes around the shambled room. "Then tell Ryder and Jagger to make their usual calls."

A ruckus was precisely what I needed right about then.

The clubhouse was a flurry of activity. Men chugging their favorite poison while barely clad women draped themselves around the member of their choice. Loud music and a cloud of smoke hung thick in the air while some snuck off to the back rooms for a quick fuck. It was exactly the kind of distraction I needed, and I welcomed it with open arms. I allowed my men to engage in a carefree night because, come tomorrow, we had to plan our revenge—on not only Koritz, but our biggest enemy.

The feud between the Knights Corruption and the Savage Reapers dated back to when I was a kid. But the real war began three years ago, and I was gonna be the president who finally put an end to those bastards, tearing them apart one by one. The reason for the battle was rooted in greed, mainly on the part of the Reapers, although my club wasn't innocent. We hadn't taken it to the extremes, however, killing off rival members solely for the purpose of getting rich.

No, they'd crossed the line.

Time and time again.

Swallowing the rest of my drink, I tapped the bar and signaled for Trigger to pour me another. "You sure you want to get shit-faced while there's plenty of pussy round here?" he teased, jerking his chin toward one of the wannabes walking straight for us. We referred to them as wannabes, amongst other things, because their ultimate agenda was to become someone's old lady. But the thing they didn't realize was there was no way a patched member was gonna make an honest woman out of someone who'd slept with half the club. The prospects, however, didn't know any better, until, of course, we explained the way things worked around here.

"Hi, Marek," Shelley cooed, kissing my cheek before whispering in my ear how she wanted to suck my dick until I shot my load down the back of her throat. She was attractive enough, her shoulder-length blonde hair cut into the latest trend, and a body made for a good time. Her tiny shirt showcased her perky tits and, although she wore a mini skirt, she was practically naked.

The attribute I liked most about Shelley was that, while I knew she wanted to be tied to me in the worst way, she didn't push too hard. Knowing damn well I'd replace her with someone who was only going to give me what I wanted. Sex. Nothing more.

I tended to stick with one piece of ass at a time, having no tolerance in my world for jealous bitches who could turn a good ruckus into an all-out brawl. Once I had my fill, I released them to have sex with whomever they wanted, never to be touched by me again.

Downing the shot Trigger placed in front of me, the slow burn of the liquor clouded my thoughts, quieting all the shit rattling around inside my head. After another two shots, I rose from my seat, grabbed Shelley's hand and dragged her back to my room, the sound of her satisfied laughter following me down the long, darkened hallway.

Her whispers in the common room were enough incentive for me to unzip my pants and give her what she wanted. Pulling myself from my jeans, I pushed down on her shoulders. "On your knees, sweetheart," I demanded, leaning my head back against the wall while I waited for her to wrap her plump lips around my cock.

"Can't I have a kiss first, Marek?" she whispered, leaning in until her mouth was a little too close to mine.

"You know I don't kiss, Shelley." Putting more pressure on her shoulders, she finally obeyed and sank to her knees, pulling me into her mouth immediately, sucking me off quicker than she normally did. I wasn't stupid. I realized she was pissed that I still wouldn't give in and kiss her, so if she wanted to take out her anger on my dick, then so be it. As long as she didn't bite me, it was all good.

There was no mystery behind me not wanting to kiss any of the women I fucked. I didn't have some weird phobia or

damaged reason why, I just didn't feel the need to be so intimate with someone I had no real connection with. I used them
like they used me, and that was the long and short of it.

Deciding to give her something to cool her temper, I
swiveled my hips and thrust into her mouth while blowing out
a breath of pleasure. "Fuck, sweetheart," I gritted out. "I love
that sweet little mouth of yours." Securing a chunk of her hair
in my fist, I held her still while languidly sliding past her lips,
her tongue swirling around the tip until I was pushing myself
further down her throat. Thank God she didn't have a gag
reflex or we'd have a big problem. "Love that cock, baby?" I
growled, knowing damn well her mouth was too full to answer.

As soon as she brought her hand up to aid her mouth, I
dropped away from her, pulled her off her knees and pushed
her against the wall, flipping her barely there skirt over her ass.
She didn't bother wearing anything underneath, and I was
truly grateful for the small things. Snatching a condom off a
nearby dresser, I quickly sheathed myself before spreading her
legs.

"You ready for me to fuck you now?"

Plunging quickly inside her pussy before she could answer,
I rocked my body into hers, taking her like I hadn't had it in
weeks.

Bracing herself against the wall while I took her hard from
behind, she purred while clinging to the wall for support. She
was still relatively tight, and it was mere minutes before I
charged down the path to explosion. Realizing I was close, I
found her clit with my fingers, expertly rubbing her until her
breathing picked up and she moaned my name over and over
again. "That's it. Come for me," I coaxed, my own orgasm
barreling down on me like a goddamn freight train.

As soon she threw her head back and screamed, I knew it
was my turn. I may not kiss, but I certainly made sure they

came before I did. Seizing her hips, I punished her body until I finally came inside her, the pleasure exploding from my body and leaving me in a haze of ecstasy for a few brief moments.

Then it was all over.

Discarding the condom in a nearby trash bin, I tucked myself away and zipped up my pants. Walking toward Shelley, I placed my hand on the small of her back to usher her from my room. There was no idle chitchat between us, even though I knew she was dying to engage me in some sort of conversation, hoping she could stay a little while longer. But once I came, I had no further use for her company. Never did. With any of them. She was invited to the clubhouse for one reason and one reason only, and she'd just fulfilled her duty for the evening.

Now it was time to go back out, drink some more and lose myself until I passed out, drunk off my ass.

As my hand circled the doorknob, I heard a shrill screech erupt from the front of the club. Pushing Shelley behind me, I snatched my gun from the end table and slowly opened the door. "Stay here," I instructed, pissed something was goin' down while I'd been too busy gettin' off.

Then I heard it again, the sound so ear piercing it cut right through me. The noise, which had me all amped up, was coming from a woman, and the more I ventured into the dark hallway, stealthily creeping forward, I realized a fight had erupted.

A cat fight.

Four

Marek

Fucking women.

No doubt they were fighting over dick. It happened some-times, especially when excessive drinking was involved. It seemed that was the time when people let go of all their sensi-bilities and overreacted to situations which would never have existed in the light of a sober day.

Retreating to my room, I escorted Shelley from my private area and forced her back out into the common area where all the action apparently was. She took a seat at the bar and watched on with curiosity. And, I had to admit, I was a bit inquisitive myself.

What I thought was a simple fight between two wannabes was anything but.

"I told you I'd cut a bitch the next time I found out," Hawke's woman, Edana, screamed so loud I thought glass was gonna shatter. Two prospects stood between her and the whore Hawke had apparently been fucking with, the look on the wannabe's face pure terror. Edana was a bit of a wild card, her temper notorious around our entire circle. Usually, Hawke could handle her, but there were times like this where she became uncontrollable. If fire could have shot from her eyes and disintegrated the wannabe on sight, it would have been less of a shock than what was about to happen.

How Hawke's woman even got in here was beyond me. She knew she wasn't supposed to show up, yet she chose to ignore club rules, which more than irked me, but I wanted to see how everything played out, so I was willing to let it go.

For now.

While the raving lunatic of a woman was focused on her man, the scared club whore grabbed her friend's hand and quickly headed toward the front entrance, realizing damn well that, if she stayed any longer, she was gonna regret it.

"Calm down, baby." Hawke laughed, his smile fueling the inferno that was Edana. He was clearly more than tipsy, and his brain wasn't registering the severity of what was about to pop off. He knew his woman better than anyone, and he of all people should have realized she was simply getting warmed up. They'd been together for years and their relationship had always been volatile. Sometimes they were lovin' on each other and other times... Well, other times were like this.

Full throttle all the way.

Simply because I craved a good show, I found an empty seat at the far end of the bar. Jerking my chin in Trigger's direction for another drink, I swiveled around to watch.

"*Calm down?*" she shrieked, quickly tying back her long auburn hair, indicating she meant business. Reaching for the closest weapon she could find, which just so happened to be a switchblade someone had left lying around, she aimed directly for his face and hurled it through the air. "We'll see how pretty you are when you have a nice cut down the side of your face," she seethed, trying to push past Jagger, one of the prospects doing his best to hold her back. "See how many sluts want your ass when your face is all fucked up!" she screamed.

Edana was a small woman, but she was strong as fuck. I'd gotten in the midst of one of their wars one too many times, so I knew what a handful she was. But, for some reason, Hawke loved her and kept her around, despite everything.

Luckily, the part of the knife that made contact with him was only the butt of the blade. It hit him right in the forehead, to be exact. The look of shock on his face was amusing, although I had no idea why he was stunned. He knew what she was like—fuck, he had the scars to prove it.

"Are you crazy, woman?" he growled, the stun of the metal handle knocking him back into sobriety. Well, a little bit at least. "You could have cut me." Hawke's long black hair was secured on top of his head into some sort of man bun, he called it. At least his vision wasn't obstructed for what she chose to do next.

Before anyone realized what was happening, she grabbed one of the heavy blades Jagger kept on his waistband, stepped around the prospect and threw it with all her might at the man she supposedly loved more than life itself. His eyes went wide when he realized what she'd thrown, thankfully stepping out of the way in time to allow the knife to hit the wall directly behind him.

She'd missed him by an inch.

Okay, now shit just got real.

I jumped off my chair and rushed forward, closing the distance until I reached Hawke. His face showed his rage, and he looked like he was ready to tear her apart.

"You fucking cunt! I'm gonna kill you!" he threatened right before he dove forward, the crazy look in his eyes unnerving even me. Luckily, I was in the way, my large body stopping him from making contact. From the look of pure terror on her face, a quick change from the fury which had resided there not a minute before, she knew she'd crossed the line. Yet again.

Stone stepped into play, replacing the other prospect who was stuck in the middle of their craziness, and forced her backward. "You better get the hell out of here, sweetheart," he said, his teeth clenched as he spoke, realizing Hawke could have been seriously hurt, and all over a piece of ass.

Gone was the psycho bitch, her lip trembling in instant regret. She realized what she'd done was wrong, but when she was in the throes of her jealous fits, it was as if she shut off all reasoning and fell into the trap of temporary insanity. Hawke struggled to reach her and, if she didn't leave in the next two seconds, I would seriously consider letting him go. Teach her a lesson and all. I'd never tolerate him beating the shit out of her, but sometimes a harsh shake or a quick throat snatch was called for. Especially after she could have seriously maimed him—or worse, killed him where he stood.

When she still remained, I decided it was time for me to finally say something. "Edana, get the hell out of here," I roared, the authority in my voice booming in everyone's ears. "And don't you ever come here again when you're not supposed to," I added, before turning back to watch Hawke relax a little, the ferocity in his eyes lessening to a tolerable level.

I nodded toward Stone, indicating he needed to take her outside. He seized her arm and quickly walked toward the door, disappearing quicker than I thought either one of them could walk.

Fucking ruckus. Never fails.

Five

Marek

"Prez!" I heard Stone shout from outside the Chamber doors. I'd been leaning back in my chair, shit going over and over in my head as to how I was gonna handle what I knew was going to be an all-out war. My VP's intrusion was definitely welcome, pushing my bloodthirsty thoughts aside. At least for the time being. There was no way I would be able to escape them forever, though. A decision had to be made, and it had to be made soon. My men were constantly caught in the middle, struggling between the thin line of decency and a new *legal* way of life.

I was on my way to taking the club in a new direction, all legit and shit. I still had to get everyone on board, some of the older members quite stubborn when it came to cutting into their weekly profits.

But when it came down to it, I was dog tired of constantly having to look over my shoulder, not only for the law but for the other clubs vying for our territory. There'd been a lot of bloodshed over the past two years, and the war was continuing to wage on with no end in sight. The Savage Reapers ambushed some of our crew a few months back, killing two of my brothers and badly wounding two more. We would exact our revenge, but we had to be smart and not attack blindly.

The Reapers were growing in numbers, and while they weren't as large, our charters spreading wide across the country, they were proving to be a massive pain in our ass.

While they took anyone willing to kill and move their product, we had a much more stringent process for accepting new members. You had to either be related or have grown up with someone in the KC before you would even be considered. If the person *was* from outside our inner circle, he had to prove himself loyal, sometimes taking years to be fully patched in.

Throwing open the door, Stone burst in with a wild look dancing in his eyes. As soon as he saw me, he hurried in my direction, his six-foot-two frame striding toward me with dire purpose.

"Fuck," he exclaimed, his hands running through his disheveled dark blond hair. "Why the hell didn't you answer your phone?" he asked, finally coming to a stop when he entered my personal space.

Pushing back from the table, I stood next to him, our eyes connecting while we silently passed information to each other. I'd come to read his expressions very well, and I knew something had just gone down.

A little too close to home.

Shaking my head slowly, I prayed it wasn't something that called for us to spring into action, endangering us all before we had time to properly prepare for retaliation. Smaller clubs often gave us a problem here and there, but they were easily dealt with. Usually, it was one or two renegades who thought they were the shit, testing our power from time to time. And every time, we reminded them who the big dog was.

"What happened?" I grumbled, plopping back in my chair to better brace myself for what was gonna come flying out of his damn mouth. Taking his seat next to me, he spouted off the information he'd just been privy to, his words tripping over themselves he was speaking so fast.

"Mother fuckin' Savages!" he blurted, hitting the table hard with his fist. "A few of those bastards dared to enter our turf and threaten us!" he shouted, his voice becoming louder with each barely controlled word. His eyes were wild, and I knew it was only a matter of time before my VP demanded we end this once and for all. Exert our power over those godless fucks.

"What happened, Stone? Tell me exactly what you know."

"Some of 'em came into The Underground earlier tonight, threatening to take us down one by one. One of them was certainly fucked out of his mind. That's for sure. Not sure if it was some sort of drug or if the asshole is messed up in the head —crazy like." He swirled his finger around in a circle by his ear.

Anger cut across my face, strong enough to force Stone back in his chair, putting some distance between the two of us. The fact that some of our enemies dared to set foot into a bar we owned infuriated me. No, that was too calm an emotion. Rage coursed through my veins, my heart picking up pace the more I thought of the balls those fuckers had.

"Where are they now?" I roared, the vein in my neck bulging strong enough for me to feel as if it were gonna pop through my goddamn skin. "Who was there when they came in?"

Before Stone answered, I shot out of my seat and raced toward the door, heading into the common area before my next breath. "Breck and Cut were there," he responded, his voice closer as he quickly walked behind me to keep up. Purpose fueled my steps. I needed to have a full table, and I needed it now.

Whipping around to face Stone, I stepped closer and cocked my head slightly to the side. "Where the hell are they now?" His brow creased until he realized I was still asking about the men who dared to enter our bar.

"Our guys *detained* them in the back room."

"Then let's go," I commanded as I led the way. "Trig," I called out, walking past the bar. "Get everybody here pronto."

His response was a simple nod.

"You seriously think you can walk into KC territory and come out alive?" Breck yelled, punching one of the assholes right in the face. The guy he was wailing on looked like he'd been to Hell and back, the far-off look in his eyes telling me he wasn't all the way present. If I had to guess, I would say he was coked out of his mind. But then again, so were half of their crew.

Like I said, no rules.

The other two fucks were tied to a chair, the frightened look in their eyes telling me they had no idea what they'd walked into. They both looked to be no older than eighteen, probably following the guy Breck was beating on simply because they were trying to prove themselves. But they weren't prospects. They were both full-fledged members, their cuts proving as much.

"Breck," I called out, placing my hand on his shoulder to stop him from decimating the man's face any further. If he knocked him out, we wouldn't be getting any kind of information. The dark look in his eyes told me he wanted to kill the guy simply for breathing the same air as us. Breck was a bit of a wild card, following after his old man, Cutter. Both were loyal to a fault, but let them loose and they could cause a lot of damage. That's where their similarities ended. Looking at both of them no one would guess they were related. While Cutter's graying hair was cut close to his head, Breck wore his dark hair down to his shoulders, his shaggy beard a big contrast to his father's clean shaven face.

"Why don't we just shoot 'em, Prez?" Cutter asked, circling around the enemy to intimidate them more than they already were. Figures the Savage Reapers would send in three weak assholes, knowing damn well they were replaceable if and when we chose to kill them. The only good thing was that they would probably sing like canaries if we pushed them hard enough.

I guess we'll see.

We had the privacy of the office to deal with these guys, the bass of the music outside fueling my aggression.

"Why did you come in here tonight?" I asked calmly. A little *too* calmly, judging by the increased unease in their eyes. The guy Breck was messin' with snapped his head to face his buddies and yelled for them not to open their mouths.

Hmm... Interesting.

"Well, we already know you threatened to take us out one by one," I offered, leaning against the desk, crossing my ankles while my hands gripped the wood behind me. "So, tell me, how do you expect to do that? And why in the hell would you warn us about it first? Only thing I can figure is that you think we're dumb enough to fall for that shit. So, what?" I asked. "Did you expect to flee and have us chase you down? Only to lead us into some sort of ambush?"

One of the younger guys' eyes popped wide, and I realized I had my answer.

"Shut the fuck up!" their buddy yelled, louder this time to make sure there was no mistaking his instruction.

Nodding toward Breck, he curled his fist again and sent it crashing against the guy's jaw, blood splattering over the guy next to him. The other two appeared to be unharmed, which only meant they went willingly when my men had grabbed them.

Had the roles been reversed, my guys would have been tortured, reinforcing yet again that although we were all bad men, we were nothing like the Savage Reapers. I would at least give them a quick death; I didn't condone torturing unless it was absolutely necessary.

Pulling me back toward the corner of the room, Stone whispered in my ear, "What are we gonna do with 'em?" Glancing between all three of them, I came up blank. I had no idea what I was gonna do, but I knew it had to be swift.

"Guess it depends on what they tell us, right?" I asked, stepping around Stone and walking back toward all the action. Standing directly in front of the one I thought would break first, I leaned over and placed my hands on the arms of his chair. He kept his head down, twisted to the side, probably hoping I would move on to one of his friends.

"Look at me," I commanded, my face dangerously close to his. Shaking his chair, I spoke again. "If you don't look at me and answer my questions, I'm gonna let my buddy here gut you like a fish." Cutter stepped up behind me, twirling a large knife and smiling big. My threat was enough to make him obey, the soft quiver of his bottom lip telling me he would be a quick confessor.

Once his full attention was on me, I saw the guy Breck was beating shift in his chair. Just as he was about to open his mouth and say God knows what, my man snapped his head back with a powerful punch, knocking his ass out instantly.

"Now," I grumbled. "Why did you guys come in here tonight, spoutin' off at the mouth about taking down the KC?" Waiting not-so-patiently for his response, I pulled a switchblade from my pocket, snapped it open so the blade glistened bright and trailed it down the length of his thigh. His eyes followed my every movement, glancing up into mine before swallowing hard. No words left his lips, which only meant I had to show him I was serious. I hated doing this shit, but it had to be done.

Without further warning, I tapped his leg three times with the knife, then withdrew the weapon. His brows creased in confusion, but before his brain registered a response, I plunged the blade deep into his flesh.

The bellow which erupted from him was most expected from such a weak bastard. It was obvious there was no training on his part.

Never show weakness.

Never allow your enemy to see the threads inside you unraveling.

His breaths came in quick succession, his face paling the more he focused on the blade sticking out of his leg. I flicked the protruding handle and he screamed again, the pain agonizing enough for him to fall apart completely.

"Please," he begged. "I'll tell you whatever you want to know. Just... Don't."

"Don't what?" I played with him.

"Don't kill me," he pleaded. Tears of fear coursed down his face and even though there was a twinge of sympathy for the weak fucker, I knew I couldn't let him live. I knew his club had sent him, sent them all here, not expecting them to live. They knowingly sacrificed some of their members, and if they returned, it would be detrimental to my club.

Show no weakness.

Pulling the knife from his thigh, I leaned in close so there was no mistaking his fate. "I can't let you live, boy. But I *can* promise you a quick death if you tell me what you know." The glaze in his eyes told me he was petrified, but he should have known this was going to be the outcome, right? Didn't he know whose territory he was entering? Hadn't his club warned him?

He continued to beg for his life, the guy next to him joining in when they realized their clock was about to run out.

"Man up, you pussies!" Breck shouted, his irritation coloring his face a light shade of red. "Die with some sort of goddamn dignity."

Surprisingly, my man's words stopped the flow of theirs, although their faces continued to give way to their obvious fear, glancing back and forth between all of us, just waiting for the end.

"Let's try this again," I prompted, pushing back a strand of hair which had fallen over my eye. "Why did you come into our bar tonight?"

A few seconds passed before the injured one spoke up. "We were told to lure as many of you out of the bar as possible. We knew our threats were enough to entice you to chase us," he sputtered, looking over to Breck before reining in his trembling expression. It was almost as if he were trying to prove to us that he was manning up.

"Who gave you the order?"

I thought there would have been some sort of hesitation, at least to prolong the inevitable, but he gave up the answer before his next breath. "Our prez."

Psych's audacity surprised me, although it shouldn't have. His name said it all. He'd earned the road name simply because he was unpredictable, his psychotic tendencies ruling his daily existence. There was no code the snake lived by, but one would have thought he would have been a little less obvious with his plans. *Or did he honestly think we were dumb enough to fall for it?*

"Why?" I walked back toward the desk to put some distance between us.

The boy's face paled, the loss of blood seeping from his wound taking a quick toll on him. Or it could have been that he knew he was gonna meet his maker very soon.

"He said the war... The war between us and the Knights was gonna en-end soon," he stuttered, "The bl-blood of your men coating the streets would seal our position with the cartel once and for all."

"Fucking hell," I cursed, stalking forward. "This has to do with the trade with the cartel?" I asked the question although I already knew the answer. Our feud had everything to do with drugs, territory and money—for them. For us, it was about revenge for what they'd done to our men for all these years.

Little did they know I was trying to get us away from the drugs, but I guessed that didn't matter too much now.

"Cutter." I gestured with a quick jerk of my chin. "Help Breck dispose of these three, then drop them off in front of their club." Locking eyes with the boy I'd stabbed, I finished with, "And make sure they receive a quick death. After all, I did promise as much." The boy's head hung in defeat, his conscious buddy expelling his fear with short cries. The other man was out cold, and I guessed it was for the best. If one was going to their death, better to not see it coming, right?

Six

Marek

I contemplated many things on the ride back to the compound. Ways to make our enemies pay for all they'd done, focusing more on Psych and the men he kept close. The roar of my bike helped calm me while thoughts of murder danced inside my head. I'd like to say I wasn't a violent man by nature, but it was how I was conditioned all my life, although I wasn't like most leaders. I didn't *crave* the kill. I didn't *live* for it, allowing it to rule every fucking move I made.

I killed only when and if I needed to.

My men knew we were on our way back, so it was no surprise when the large metal gate which protected the compound swung open upon our arrival. Nodding at Jagger, one of our best prospects, my bike roared on through, followed by Stone, Cutter and Breck. Everyone else had been gathered and was anxiously waiting for us in Chambers.

This is gonna be a long night.

"Why are we waitin' so long to attack?" Zip shouted, pounding his fist against the thick oak of our meeting table, rattling the gavel enough to jump and crash back down onto the wood surface. At just twenty years old, Zip had a fierce temper, one which should have only been warranted from someone who held a few more years of age and experience. From what I could gather, he'd had a pretty shitty upbringing, his father a KC rat who was disposed of after his deception had come to light. He'd been drugged out of his mind for years, hence the set-in-stone rule that none of my men were allowed to use. Couldn't ever trust a junkie. Zip's mother was a club whore who just got mixed up with the wrong guy. None of us really knew exactly what happened surrounding her death, but there were rumors that she was killed soon after her rat of a man. Even though she technically died in a car accident, there were thoughts it was simply a cover-up. My father had run the club during that time, and he never spoke about either one of them after they ceased to exist.

The club rules were a little different when my father was president, but when I took over, I made sure to ingrain in each and every one of the members that we were never to kill women or children, and we certainly didn't dispose of a fellow brother until we had irrefutable proof, which, thank God, wasn't an issue. All my guys were loyal to me and to their fellow brothers, Zip being right at the top of that list. I think he tried even harder than the rest because he didn't want anyone to think he was anything like his old man.

His dark hair was slicked away from his face, his green eyes glistening in anger and fueling a few of the other men's need for retaliation. His slight build became rigid while he waited for an answer.

"Zip," Stone warned, standing quickly and leaning over the

table, his dark eyes threatening Zip where he sat. "Calm down and show some goddamn respect."

Raising his hands in a display of surrender, Zip turned his head toward me, breaking away from Stone's fierce gaze. "Sorry, Prez, I just wanna get those fuckers already. Enough is enough."

I didn't take any offense to his outburst—I had my VP for that. Relaxing in my chair, I nodded at Zip before turning my focus back on the men surrounding the large oblong table. I really did have a great group of fierce, take-a-bullet-for-you, crazy-ass motherfuckers.

"We have to wait until we hear they're all there together. You know damn well," I said, my eyes falling back onto Zip, "Psych and his VP, Rabid, are hardly at the same place at the same time. No, we have to take them both out so their club is left in shambles." Glancing back to Stone, a hard look set on his face, I finished my spiel. "We wait."

Killing those bastards was at the forefront of my agenda, but just in case we failed, I had another plan in place. A plan which was carefully being orchestrated with someone even more powerful than me.

All in due time.

Throwing down the gavel, I left no room for argument. Our meeting was done. My word was law, and even if a few of them didn't agree, they didn't show it. I welcomed everyone's input, but once I had my say, there was to be no more discussion on the topic.

"Let's go get us some pussy!" Hawke yelled, following Ryder and Trigger from the room. Lucky for him, and for all of us, Edana was two states away visiting her mother.

A loud crash out front drew all of our attention. We'd only been two hours into an impromptu ruckus when the shit started to go down. Men scattered, yelling and reaching for their closest weapon of choice. Running toward the secured entrance of the clubhouse, some of the men waited to be ordered outside to find out what the hell was going on. Stone followed behind me as I walked into our surveillance room, staring at all the cameras to find out who or what was behind the loud noise. Each screen turned up blank, no activity as the camera slowly turned from side to side. We saw our bikes all lined up in a row, the lot otherwise empty, the door of our garage pulled shut, and the large metal gate, which kept us securely inside. Something quickly moved past the gate, a dark shadow passing in front of the camera before we could identify it.

Everything was all clear except for the ghost we'd seen on camera.

Headlights illuminated the lot before backing up from the gate, something falling to the ground in front of the car before it sped off. Running toward the front door, I pushed past my VP and reached for the handle.

"Marek, NO!" he shouted, but his plea fell on deaf ears. A sinking feeling gutted me, but I had no idea why. I couldn't see who had crashed into our gate, nor the body who was dumped on our property. But I knew it wasn't good.

There was a lot of commotion surrounding me as I stalked toward the gate, the compound security lights suddenly flooding the area so we could all see better. With every step I took closer, my heart picked up its pace and rammed against my chest. My adrenaline pumped through my veins and my vision became cloudy. At first, I only saw a crumpled male body, but the closer I stepped the more I could make out. He was certainly one of ours, his cut showcasing our club's emblem of a skull with a sword slicing through it. His short hair was greased with blood, his head turned to the side so I couldn't see who he was.

Yet.

Quickly scanning the street to make sure we weren't gonna be ambushed, I shouted, "Open the fucking gate!"

The slow creak of the metal was infuriating, my pulse quickening the longer it took to reach the man who'd been dropped off as a warning. I knew by who, but had to make sure before I lost my shit once and for all.

Gurgling sounded from the bloody man's throat and I breathed a sigh of relief, although it was short-lived once I turned him on his back. His pulse was weak, and it was only a matter of time before he exhaled his last breath. There was so much blood it was hard for me to see where his wounds were.

"Let me take a look," I soothed, the tremor in my voice certainly betraying my faux calm tone. His arms fell away from his stomach, his hands hitting the pavement beside him with a heavy thud. I lifted his shirt and saw he'd been shot four times, the holes gaping and seeping blood faster than was safe, although being shot just once wasn't safe. He was gonna bleed out right in front of us, and I still couldn't identify him.

When I finally turned his head, familiar eyes met mine, and I about had a heart attack.

I knew him.

We all knew him, although we hadn't seen him in years.

The bloody man I was staring at was none other than Hawke's older brother, Tripp. He'd joined our nomad charter four years earlier. Not belonging to any one charter suited him just fine. A loner lifestyle was more his thing, even though he showed up every now and again to see not only his club brothers, but his blood brother as well. They were close, and I was waiting for shit to erupt as soon as Hawke realized his sibling was lying on the cold pavement, dying with each struggled breath.

"Who the hell is it, Marek?" Everyone crowded around while I tried to decide the best way to break the news to Hawke, while still doing my best to try and drag Tripp into the compound without further injuring him. I heard you weren't supposed to move someone who was hurt, but was that when they'd been shot? Or was that when they'd hurt their neck? Goddamn it! Too many thoughts plagued me and before I could decide on one course of action, I saw the dying man's younger brother approach, furrowing his brow the closer he came.

He stopped ten feet from us and looked shocked, his brain actively trying to compute just who he was staring at. The simple fact that he recognized his brother from that far away was amazing, seeing as how I had been up close and personal before I'd identified him.

When I finally lifted my head to meet Hawke's stare, I gave him a simple nod, my indication that what he thought was true. It was enough to force him out of his own head, his legs bringing him to an abrupt halt once he'd reached us.

"Fuck!" he yelled, gripping his hair in fear. "What the fuck? Tripp?" he whispered, falling to his knees so his brother could hear him, if he was even still conscious. By his labored breathing, I wasn't sure how much longer he was gonna last, and I sure as shit didn't want his death on my hands simply because I had no idea what I was doing.

I knew we couldn't act like normal people and take him to the emergency room. Because of the gunshot wounds, the police would be called right away, and there was no way we were willingly going to include those pigs in our business.

Hawke gripped his brother's hand and held it in his lap, all the while watching me to give direction on what the hell we were gonna do. Time seemed to slow, the men's shouts lessened to whispers with every agonizing second that passed. In reality, the action around me was a flutter of curses and shouts, people moving around us quickly to decide what the hell the best course of action was.

It was then, during my mini freak-out, that I remembered Trigger's niece was a nurse. She'd helped us out quite a few times before and had done a bang-up job. No pun intended, of course.

"Trig!" I shouted over all the noise, whipping my head around and scanning the growing crowd to try and locate the one man I needed right then.

Pushing past Stone and Ryder, Trigger stepped forward, stopping to stand directly beside me. "What do you need?" he asked, obvious panic dancing in his voice.

Quickly glancing down into Tripp's pale, ashen face, I whipped my eyes back to Trigger and mumbled, "You need to call your niece, man. Tell her it's an emergency." I inhaled a deep breath. "Tell her to get here now!"

A simple nod and he was hurrying back into the clubhouse, a few of the club whores, who'd come out to see what all the commotion was, following directly behind him. They knew enough to know that curiosity of club business would get them banned for life.

Kneeling on the ground and holding a lifeless brother's body was gut-wrenching. No matter how many times I'd seen death, or impending death, up close, it never got easier. I thought I would have become numb to our way of life, but there was always an undercurrent of life pulsing through my veins. A hope for something better for not only me but for my brothers.

For my club.

A half hour later, I heard someone call out, "She's here," right before two bright headlights blinded me. We'd managed to carefully drag Tripp further into the compound, locking ourselves inside in case whoever had dumped him decided to return.

Slamming her door, Trigger's niece, Adelaide, quickly walked toward us, the sight of the blood-soaked pavement never once making her falter. Although she wasn't a part of our way of life, she knew enough about it from her uncle, and her visits to help us, to know we lived dangerously. She gave no indication that she wanted to know more, and her uncle made damn sure she wasn't exposed more than she had to be.

Pulling her long blonde hair on top of her head in a messy bun, she knelt down beside us, placing her black bag on the ground next to Tripp's thigh. Sensing help had arrived, a guttural moan exploded from his throat, the sound putting us all on alert. While his groan reminded us of his dire situation— like we needed a reminder—his pain also gave us hope, seeing as how he hadn't moved or made any other noises in quite some time.

"What happened?" Adelaide asked, gently pushing up his blood-soaked shirt so she could get a better look at the damage. Her almond-shaped eyes widened when she realized the poor guy had been shot four times. "I need you to help me," she said, looking between me and Hawke, who'd been a permanent fixture next to his brother.

"With what?" I asked, scooting back a little as she moved closer on her knees. I heard a noise come from above me, but it wasn't until I jerked my head to the right that I realized it had come from my VP. He was watching Adelaide with such intensity it instantly put me on edge. In all the years we'd known each other, I'd never seen him react to a woman like this. It was weird, and it was freaking me out. Since he was still crowding my personal space, I jabbed my elbow into his shin, directing his attention on me and not on the woman who'd been called in to help a fellow brother. Widening my eyes and flaring my nostrils was enough to make him back up a step, averting his eyes from Adelaide in the process. Although not gazing upon her lovely face seemed to be distressing him.

"I need to gently roll him over to see if there are exit wounds. If there are, I think there is a good chance I can help him. Possibly," she contemplated, her brows furrowing in thought. "If not, if the bullets are still stuck inside, he's going to need surgery. And although I've assisted in many an operation, I don't have the experience or necessary instruments to take on such a task."

I hadn't even thought about that shit. Her words caused my chest to deflate, the last reserve of hope I had swirling around inside escaping through the long breath I pushed from my lips. What were the chances all four bullets shot clean through his body? The answer was slim.

Preparing for the worst, Hawke and I cautiously rolled his brother off his back, all the while cushioning him as best we could. Tripp groaned, his hands clenching into loose fists the more we moved his lifeless body. "It's okay, man," Hawke mumbled near Tripp's ear. "We're just trying to patch you up." The pain in his voice just about undid me. He was trying to remain strong, all the while shoving his panic way deep down inside.

When Tripp was finally resting on his side, Adelaide brought out a pair of scissors and cut the material from his body. Luckily, we'd been able to remove his cut before she'd arrived, otherwise, she would have tried to slice through that as well. Once his back was exposed, she gingerly felt around his skin with the tips of her delicate fingers.

Searching for holes in his flesh.

She reached into her bag and pulled out gauze, wiping away as much blood as she could so she could better assess the damage. "Well, it looks like three of the four bullets have gone straight through, but there's still one stuck in there. And it looks like it might be close to his heart." She looked over at me first, then met Hawke's eyes before subtly shaking her head. "He needs surgery, and he needs it quick or else I don't think he's going to make it."

Hawke's voice shattered the otherwise silent air. "Fuck!" he screamed, leaning over the body of his dying brother. He whispered something in Tripp's ear, words no one but his sibling heard. As soon as he gathered his resolve, he jumped to his feet, walked around Tripp and pulled Adelaide to her feet. Everything happened so fast I barely had time to react. But Stone filled in for me, taking the few necessary steps to brace Adelaide on her other side. "You have to fix my brother," Hawke gritted through clenched teeth. I knew he was doing his best to hold his shit together, but in the process he was scaring the hell out of Trigger's niece. She didn't ask to be dragged into our mess, and the mere fact that she'd dropped whatever the hell she was doing and raced over to the club said a lot about her character.

"Hawke," Stone warned, a rare gesture of possessiveness brimming just underneath the surface. "She already told you she can't perform the surgery, if that was where this shit was headed." He pulled her to the side, Hawke's grip loosening until his hand fell to his side. Unspoken threats were whispered between the two men while I decided what the hell we needed to do.

Adelaide eyed both men cautiously before gently pulling

away from Stone, a strange look of hurt in his eyes when she moved. She smiled tightly before speaking again. "I think I may have another plan," she promised, pulling her cell phone from her purse and quickly punching the numbers. She took a few steps forward for some privacy, everyone watching after her in anticipation, the air suddenly thick with a mixture of hope and uneasiness.

Seven

Sully

A noise from the hallway jerked me awake—not that it took much, since I was an extremely light sleeper. I guess I'd been conditioned that way since I was a child, always wary of who was coming through my bedroom door. Sometimes it was my father, paying me one of his *special* visits, and other times it was Vex. Once my possessor declared me for himself, my father's visits ceased altogether, some kind of fucked-up code among club members.

There were some nights I wished whoever had walked through my door was there to do me in, to act in such a way which resulted in me taking my last breath.

To kill me.

Trust me, I realized it was morbid to put those kinds of wishes and dreams out into the universe, but if destiny proved anything thus far, it was that my life was not my own. Therefore, destiny was a goddamn liar. I had no control whatsoever over my own fate; I had to leave that in the hands of the men who surrounded me, stifling and suffocating me to the point I no longer saw any joy in the world. Granted, I hadn't seen much of it to begin with, but there were exceptions. Some days, at least. The soft song of a bird, the cool night breeze kissing my skin as the sun dipped below the horizon, the colors from the sunset embedding their awesomeness into my memory.

But the older I became, the less I saw these things as beauty, and the more I saw them as the universe's cruel joke at my expense. For as tempting as Mother Nature was, she spit in my face.

I could look but not touch.

I could feel but never experience.

While lost to the pity party for one, my bedroom door crashed open and slammed into the wall with such force I was convinced there was a gaping hole where there once was smooth plaster. One more distasteful thing to look at.

Vex rushed into the room, frantically searching for something he'd obviously hidden, but probably couldn't remember where. His eyes were as wide as saucers, his pupils dilated to an unhealthy level.

"What the hell are you looking at?" he yelled. His mood swings worsened the longer he snorted that poison. Thankfully, he didn't make me get high with him anymore. I hated every single second he forced the shit up my nose, but I didn't have a choice; it was either comply or endure some of the worst beatings of my young life. Truthfully, I think he stopped pressuring me because he'd become greedy. That and he was tired of hearing me complain, even though I gave in each and every time. Whatever the final reason was, I was grateful.

"Nothing," I muttered, quickly looking down at my trembling hands so as not to further aggravate him. Along with the mood swings, his paranoia heightened as well, forever accusing me of conspiring against him. As if I had anyone to even talk to, let alone plot against him with. Everyone in the club stayed clear of me, even the women. They knew Vex was unstable, and they chose not to have to deal with his crazy ass.

Normally, a young woman had her father to turn to for protection, but in my case my father was worse than Vex, simply because he held no love in his heart for me, which he proved over and over again. Rico Yanez being one such prime example. Never mind that he'd sanctioned the union between Vex and me when I was only fourteen years old, knowing damn well what a psychopath he was.

With the back of his hand, he swiped what few trinkets I'd been able to save over the years clear across the room. The glass from a snow globe shattered against the wall, tearing me apart because it was the last remaining item I had from my mother. Tears instantly welled behind my eyes, but I bit the inside of my cheek to distract myself from the pain building in my heart.

Vex knew exactly how much the trinket meant to me, and that it had not met with some sort of demise before was a miracle. For as cruel as he was, I thought there was a tiny piece inside him that wouldn't completely leave me with nothing.

But I was wrong. Of course I was wrong. What kind of stupid woman believed there was still some sort of humanity residing inside the likes of Vex, especially after all I had witnessed and experienced over the years?

"Fuck!" he shouted, walking quickly into the small closet we shared. Rooting through the mess, he yelled in frustration over and over again.

Even though my voice was not wanted, I needed to know what he was looking for. Maybe I'd seen the item, and the quicker he found it the quicker he would leave.

"What are you looking for?" I whispered, my voice loud enough for him to hear. He abruptly stopped all movement, turning on his heel so fast I thought he was going to trip over his own damn feet. Leering at me, he clenched his hands into tight fists, the craziness in his eyes coming out full force.

"You wanna know what I'm lookin' for?" he sneered. I remained quiet, silently berating myself for even opening my mouth to begin with. With every step he took closer, I braced myself, either for him to verbally berate me or for his fists to do the talkin'.

When I didn't respond, he reached for the book I'd left on a side table and whipped it at me. Thankfully, I'd been watching his every move and ducked at the very last second. Even if the book had hit me, it wouldn't have done much damage, seeing as it was a thin paperback. But still, any chance I could escape his wrath was a win, although it didn't happen often at all.

I knew it was in my best interest to answer him, even though my voice alone could cause him to fly off the handle even more. "Yes. I just… I just thought I could help you find it," I said dejectedly, looking back down at my lap.

"Well," he responded, "if you wanna help me so much, get off your lazy ass and help me look for my guns." He didn't wait for me to move before he tore the room apart, destroying the calm I'd tried so hard to create inside our bedroom. We didn't have much, but what we did have was neat and organized. I hated chaos. I couldn't stand a messy room, the scattered items instantly making me anxious. It's funny, I would give anything for a messy room to be my worst problem, but cleanliness was the only thing I could control, so I held on to it with everything I had still pumping inside me.

Knowing full well he was going to lash out at me if I didn't help him, I scrambled off the bed, the oversized T-shirt I had on falling down and hitting me mid-thigh. I had on boy shorts, but he couldn't see them under the shirt. I never purposely wore anything tight or revealing, mainly because I didn't wish to call any attention to myself, his possession of me casting over him in a near demonic way sometimes. Plus, the one time I wore clothing which actually fit me, he'd freaked out and accused me of wanting to have sex with every single one of his brothers.

It was the first time he'd raped me, but it certainly wasn't the last.

His eyes quickly grazed over my body before he resumed searching for his weapons. I breathed a sigh of relief that he wasn't focusing on me and helped him scour the small space.

Scrambling underneath the bed, I pulled out a small black duffel bag. Without looking inside, I called Vex's attention to me. "Is this what you're looking for?" I called out, taking a step back after placing the bag on top of the bed.

Whipping his head toward me, he eyed the bag before approaching. He was cautious not to appear thankful, or happy, or whatever emotion he thought would weaken him in front of me.

Pulling back the zipper, he peered inside, and I swore I saw a hint of a smirk trace over his lips before he closed the material. Without another word, he snatched the duffel and practically ran from the room, yelling for whoever was waiting for him.

A thin shield of fear enveloped me as soon as I was all alone. The only time Vex went in search of his extra guns was when they were preparing for a heavy defense or for retaliation.

And the only club we were truly at war with was the Knights Corruption. A club so vile they made ours sound like a walk in the park. At least that's what I'd been told my entire life. The fear of the devil had been drilled into me when it came to the KC MC. They were our most hated enemies and, although I was treated lower than the mud on their shoes, my club protected me from the outside world. Mainly, they protected me from the Knights. Contact with them in any way would prove detrimental to me. My father once told me he would rather see me dead than in the hands of the KC, threatening to pull the trigger himself if I ever found myself in such a predicament.

The biggest insult to the likes of our clubs was to be taken by the enemy. To be forced to live with them, to be integrated into their way of life and become one of them, for however long, was the worst kind of fate. Not only would my life be in ruins if the Knights ever got their hands on me, but I would no longer be accepted by the Savage Reapers.

They would hunt me down and kill me simply for breathing the same air as their nemesis.

Eight

Marek

Four days had passed since I'd found Tripp hanging on for dear life.

Four days of witnessing the touch-and-go status of a fellow brother, Hawke's actual blood brother.

Four days of planning our next move.

In our last meeting, I declared our retaliation would wait until we gathered enough intel, which would make our reprisal worth it. But things had since changed. They dared to spit at us, to taunt and harass us, jumping Tripp as he left The Underground. They knew enough not to go inside, the evidence of their last stupid mistake dumped in front of their club.

We had to move, and do it quickly, before anything else happened, or any more Knights' blood was spilled.

"That's it," I heard the soft tone of Adelaide say as I walked into Chambers. She was tending to Tripp with the utmost care, cleaning and re-dressing his many wounds, careful not to press too hard because of the amount of pain he was still reeling with. The call she'd made when we were in the thick of it was to a doctor friend of hers, someone she worked closely with at the hospital. She swore she trusted him but just in case, we put the fear of God into him as soon as he arrived. He looked none too pleased with the likes of us, his brows drawn and his face rigid, but luckily his features softened as soon as his eyes landed on Adelaide's face. And who could blame him? She was certainly the looker, her toned and tanned body nice and tight, her tits the perfect size with an ass that didn't quit. Her uncle had seen most of the men leering after her, and he'd made no qualms about threatening each of their lives if they even thought about touching her. A threat she found quite amusing, as was shown by the curvature of her full lips.

Our back room in Chambers had been turned into a makeshift operating room. Thankfully, the good doc, with the help of Adelaide, was able to remove the one remaining bullet from Tripp's chest. He'd given him a decent prognosis but warned us about infection, telling us the following twenty-four hours were going to be crucial.

My undying gratitude for Trigg's niece was not something I gave freely, but the woman was a miracle worker. Her gentleness with him was a welcome sight since we hardly witnessed such rare emotion in our lives. We lived hard, lived rough, so when an angel's touch was felt, it reminded me there was some good left in the world. Too bad I would never feel the effects of it. Not as far as I could see, at least.

"If you keep teasing me like that, sweetheart, you're gonna get a reaction you don't want," Tripp grumbled, his dry lips kicking up into a tiny smirk. His dark hair was clean, all the blood and dirt wiped from his face and body. She'd even given him a clean shave, ridding him of the slight stubble covering his jaw. He looked much better after she'd finished with him—pale, but much better. At least, that was what she proclaimed. Me? I could give two shits how my men looked. I only cared about how they acted.

Before Adelaide could respond, I spoke up, reminding him just who he was taunting. "Hey, buddy. You better watch yourself before Trigger comes in here and puts another bullet in you." I grinned, but he clearly looked confused. "Don't you know who you're hittin' on there?"

"My guardian angel." He chuckled, falling into a coughing fit and clutching his chest from the exertion.

"All right. All right. Let's not work him up too much. My patient has to rest, and I won't have the likes of you bothering him." She glanced back at me and smiled, not fearing me in the least. It was rare that someone spoke to me like she had, teasing or not. But my appreciation toward her gave her a pass; plus, I knew she meant nothing by it. She wasn't disrespecting me in any way and we both knew it, so I refused to make a big deal over it.

Another time and I'd throw the friendly warning at Tripp of just who his 'guardian angel' really was. I'd hate for the man not to be armed with the knowledge that she was a fellow brother's family, someone not to be messed with.

My demeanor changed as I approached them both. "Seriously, though, how is he doing?" I asked, stopping directly next to Adelaide and hovering over the recuperating form of our nomad member.

"He definitely has a hard road ahead of him, but I think he'll be fine. Luckily, none of the bullets did any major damage," she proclaimed, gripping his hand softly in hers. Tripp gave me a faint wink before drifting off to sleep. He was clearly exhausted, his body's fight to recover a tiresome one.

Once I was done checking up on Tripp, I thanked Adelaide once more and turned around to leave. It was then that I saw Stone hovering in the doorway. He looked unnerved, and I guessed it had something to do with one of the people behind me.

Walking closer so there was no mistaking my motive, I stopped two feet in front of him. His eyes instantly found mine and he relaxed a little. But there was some sort of fire burning in his eyes, and I had no idea why. As far as I was aware, there was no bad blood between my VP and the nomad. I couldn't pinpoint why he was so on edge until I heard her voice again, promising to care for Tripp until he was all better.

Then I saw it.

The tightening of his jaw.

His hands curling into fists.

His chest expanding and rigid.

His lips turning up into an unyielding sneer.

The look he shot their way was similar to the one he'd directed at Hawke when he put his hands on her while she was inspecting his brother.

It was an undying sign of possession. A rare emotion for Stone, for sure, but it was there nonetheless.

"Do we have a problem here, Stone?" I asked, preparing to physically remove him if I had to. The last thing we needed right then was a fight amongst brothers. I had enough to worry about with Trigger's threats for the men to stay away from his niece, never mind trying to figure out what the hell we were gonna do about payback. I didn't need to deal with Stone's weird reaction as well.

He looked past me when I spoke, so I shoved him back toward the threshold of the room. "Stone!" I shouted. As soon as his eyes found mine again, I repeated, "Do we have a problem here?"

His fiery gaze was his telltale sign that there was more going on than I knew. Countless tense seconds passed before he answered. Gritting his teeth, he unconvincingly said, "No. No problem here."

I obviously didn't believe him, but I wasn't gonna deal with whatever was up his ass right then. I had bigger issues to worry about. "Good. Now, go get everyone and tell them we're having an emergency meeting."

A fierce nod and he retreated from the room. When I looked behind me, I saw Adelaide's eyes following Stone, a strange look marring her features.

What the hell is going on with these two?

Nine

Sully

I hadn't seen Vex since the night he came storming into our bedroom. Having no idea where he'd gone, I'd kept to myself like I normally did. Women weren't allowed to wander the clubhouse unless they were called there for one particular reason—to be used and abused. Why most of them kept coming back for more was beyond me. They were free to live their lives outside of our MC, yet they craved the attention of the men. *Weird.*

I was the only exception to the rule simply because I was the president's daughter, although that didn't really mean much; they all knew how he treated me. But I was still allowed to wander the clubhouse at random, although I made sure to keep to the common areas, mainly because I knew Vex would accuse me of fucking someone if I wasn't in plain sight. Hell, he suspected it regardless, but I didn't want to encourage his paranoia any further than he already took it.

Pricking my ears toward a strange noise, I tried my best to listen for it again. Most of the men were retired to their rooms, only a few left to wander around the center room, drinking and laughing it up. It was a quiet night otherwise.

When all I heard were the sounds of the drunken club members, I resumed making myself a sandwich. The bread was but a whisper from my hungry lips when I heard what sounded like a car crash, the noise so explosive it drew the attention of the entire club. Men ran from their rooms in confusion, some of them tripping over items littered all over the common room floor. My need for cleanliness didn't expand past my bedroom.

"What the hell was that?" my father roared, appearing out of nowhere and zipping up his pants. Nancy, one of his many women, appeared but quickly hurried back inside the room he'd just come from.

His wild eyes found mine, his steps never faltering while he practically ran at me. "Get in your room, Sully. Lock and barricade the door and don't come out until I come and get you," he demanded, gripping my arm so tight I winced in pain. "Do you hear me?" he shouted.

"Yes," I whispered. He shoved me backward and once he saw me retreat down the long hallway toward my room, he ran for the front of the clubhouse, shouting for his men to get their guns ready.

There was so much commotion, so many people yelling indiscernible commands, it was hard to hear what was really going on. The only thing I knew was there was some kind of accident outside. It could have been deliberate or not. The men of our club were not the brightest bulbs, some of them downright stupid. While we were guarded by a tall, heavy fence, the men guarding it sometimes were so drunk off their asses, or coked out of their minds, they were utterly useless. On a sober day, they were ruthless and cunning, but get a little bit of poison in their veins and they were easy targets, making the entire place an easy target as well.

Once I'd successfully locked myself inside my room, I pushed a small dresser in front of the door. It was the only piece of furniture I could move myself, so I hoped it worked. I crouched in the corner, turning off the light so I was bathed in darkness. Shivering in fear of what was happening outside, I prayed to make it through unscathed. I was in mid-promise to God when I heard an endless spray of gunshots.

Reminding myself that I'd lived through this type of thing many times before, I tried my best to slow my thumping heart and calm myself with deep breaths, but nothing worked. Men continued to scream between unrelenting gunfire.

Minutes after bullets were discharged, I heard heavy foot-steps coming down the hallway, commands being given to the men barreling toward my room. I didn't recognize their voices. They weren't coming from any of the evil beasts who normally resided behind our club walls. No, these deep, dark voices came from whoever had just invaded the Savage Reapers' lair.

And the only club daring enough to pull off such a thing was the Knights Corruption.

Our biggest enemy.

"Back here!" I heard one of them shout. I prayed they were looking for someone or something else, but my hopes were dashed when the handle to my bedroom jiggled. As soon as they realized it was locked, someone started pounding on the door, so hard it was a wonder they didn't split the wood down the middle.

More shouts.

More pounding.

All of a sudden, the frame splintered and a small sliver of light from the hallway filtered into the room. From where I was hiding, I couldn't see who was out there, but I could certainly hear them.

"She has to be in here," I heard one of the intruders yell.

"There's no way they would leave her out of their sight." The second comment came from a different man, one whose voice was more gravelly and deeper than the first man. It was then I realized who they were talking about. They wouldn't be busting down the door for some common club whore.

No, they were coming for me.

Dreadful thoughts rampantly flitted through my mind. Thoughts of what they would do to me if they hauled me out of my room, and ugly thoughts of what my own club would do to me if they ever got me back.

Either way, I would be dead, but instead of welcoming the sweet lick of death to stroke my body, something I'd prayed for since I could remember, an innate need to survive kicked in from out of nowhere. Adrenaline pumped through me in waves, blurring my vision and hiccupping my breaths with each and every pound of the door, every shout directed toward and about me, and every gunshot that sliced through the thickening night air.

The room flooded with the hallway light, the door ripped from its hinges while I still tried to loose myself inside the small space. My room held no security for me, but as long as my ears were covered I could only hear muffled sounds, and stifled sounds were better than listening to what they were actually saying, what they had planned for me.

A loud crash jolted me back into the reality of the situation. I waited for more gunfire, but all that followed the toppling dresser was harsh, ragged breathing. I wasn't sure if the sounds were my own or from those who had just entered the room.

Then one of them spoke.

The man with the deep, gravelly voice. A voice which sent shivers of fear and fascination deep into my soul. The mixture of feelings confused me, but I had no time to delve into what they really meant. The only focus in the forefront of my disheveled mind was to figure out how to survive.

Would I beg for my life? Would I appear weak in the face of the enemy? I couldn't answer with certainty, and that alone was disarming. I had no idea what to do, what to say or how to feel.

Luckily, the decision was stolen from me the instant my eyes found him.

A tall, broad man stalked forward, every step closer deciding my fate. My head had instinctually risen so I could see who was coming for me, and what I saw stopped my heart. While my soon-to-be captor was covered in blood, no doubt from his up-close-and-personal bloodshed of my fellow Savages, his prowess shined through. His pale blue eyes pinned me defenseless, his hair short and cropped to his head, a trimmed beard covering his sharp jawline. Blood dripped from his cheeks, and I instantly wondered if he'd been hurt.

The man who had come to kidnap me was the most handsome man I'd ever laid eyes on. But I vowed then and there to never fall prey to his charms, if ever he decided to enchant me with them. Although I hated my club, my father and Vex, I wasn't a traitor. And falling for the enemy was the worst kind of sin to be committed in our ruthless, deadly world.

Shit, as far as I knew, he could be the Devil's nephew, just as brutal and evil as my father and Vex.

Reaching forward, his hand was suddenly thrust into my personal space. *Maybe if I close my eyes they'll all go away. Maybe it'll all be an awful dream, a nightmare I'll soon wake up from.* Shutting my lids tight, I squeezed my hands over my ears and drowned out the sounds in hope everything would return back to *normal.*

I'd never wished for my life more than I did right then, which was probably the saddest revelation I'd ever had.

While I rocked back and forth in my self-induced delirium, the man's hand gripped my wrist, the warmth of his skin setting me ablaze. My eyes flew open and before I could utter a single word, I was pulled to my feet so fast I tumbled forward. I would have fallen directly on my face had it not been for the man holding me upright.

His other hand shot to my side, stabilizing me so I wouldn't topple over and trip him up in the process, even though there was no way I would ever cause him to fall. His strength emanated off him in waves, and it was both frightening and intriguing. Caught in a whirlwind of unfamiliar emotions, I was utterly confused beyond my simple scope of reality. No words were exchanged between us. In fact, the other two men in the room never spoke either, watching intently to see what was going to take place between their fellow brother and the woman shaking in fear.

I started to tremble, cursing myself for being weak yet again. Luckily, my legs remained strong, and as soon as I found an opportunity I was going to put them to good use.

"Look at me," the man growled. I refused, keeping my head low. His impatience with me was evident, expletives falling freely from his lips as he shook me in frustration. "Fuckin' look at me," he repeated.

Very slowly, I found his eyes again, waiting for what he was going to do or say next.

"Are you the infamous daughter of the Savage Reapers?" His tone was mocking, the manner of his voice spurring me to defend myself, but I was indeed helpless. What could I do to protect myself? Fight? Argue with him? Plead for him to release me and pretend he'd never found me? I knew deep inside that whatever path I chose wouldn't matter. These men obviously had their minds made up, and the only thing I could do would be to follow suit. At least until I figured out my next move.

"Well, are you?" he gritted, his jaw pulsing with the weight of his impatience. It was then I reflected on his absurd question. *The infamous daughter of the Savage Reapers?* What an odd question. I was neither infamous nor the proclaimed daughter of the entire club. Still reeling in my confusion, he wrenched me forward until I was flush with his blood-soaked chest. "Answer me, woman!" he shouted. "Are you fuckin' Psych's daughter?" *Now, there's a question which makes sense to me, even though I wish it wasn't true.*

"Yes," I whispered, although I wasn't sure why I hadn't chosen to lie. I should have denied it, declaring to be just another club whore. But then, why would a common whore be barricaded in one of the back rooms?

"She's even more beautiful up close," one of the men standing near the door announced.

"Sure is," the man in front of me assured, holding me tighter against him. Turning his head to face his men, he asked a question I was curious about myself. "Have you found her father yet? And that crazy-ass fucker who's always attached to her?"

Vex. They were talking about Vex. I almost offered up the detail that he was gone, had been gone for the past four days, but I forced my lips to stay closed, my confession resting heavy in my throat.

Even though I hated Vex with every fiber of my being, he was familiar to me.

He was the devil I'd been accustomed to.

"Not yet, but we will. Then we'll burn every last mother-fucker in here," the tall, blond-haired man pronounced.

"Until then...," my captor said, pulling me toward the other two men blocking the entrance to the room. I wasn't quite sure what happened, but all of a sudden I flew into a rage, years of feeling helpless finally unleashing their grip, unbridled strength spilling forth which I had no idea was even nestled inside me. His grip on my wrists wasn't tight, so I was able to shrug free of him rather easily. Taking a step back, I startled him when I threw my tiny fist in the air and connected with his jaw. The look on his stupidly handsome face was most telling. He was stunned... and pissed. Taking advantage of his shock, I ran around his looming body and fled toward the bathroom.

My escape was futile, though. A large arm wrapped around my waist and hoisted me into the air, all the breath pushed from my lungs from the force. Stars danced in my eyes as I tried to regain some kind of footing, but it was useless. He tossed me over his shoulder before I could recover and rushed from the room behind his two men.

Now what the hell am I going to do?

Ten

Marek

Never before had a woman attempted to strike me, and that the first time it *did* happen was from the tiny spit-fire we'd abducted turned me inside out. Barging into her room hadn't prepared me for what or who I was going to find. Our main objective was to pay those fuckers back for all they'd done. Tripp was the final straw and we all knew it, even though I'd initially proclaimed I wanted to wait.

Well, four days was long enough this time around.

The goal was to destroy the Savage Reapers from the inside out, but because we weren't one hundred percent prepared, we'd only managed to wipe out half of the members present. Still a good hit, but it wasn't enough. We needed to wipe out Psych, take out his VP, Rabid, then destroy Vex, one of the most volatile members of the club. His crazy ass needed to be buried simply because he was one psychotic, soulless motherfucker.

I remembered hearing someone speak of Psych's daughter, her strange name something I'd never heard before. Her beauty was often whispered about, but then again I couldn't take stock in what a bunch of horny men said. Any pussy with a pair of tits and they would fall prey to their *beauty*.

There wasn't much information on her, always hidden away from the world, protected from the likes of rival clubs. To entice a woman from a rival club into your own was a big no-no. It was the epitome of insults to integrate them into your way of life, although it wasn't much different from their own, the biggest difference being the Savage Reapers were a den of devils. As far as dirty dealings, the Knights weren't much better, per se, but as far as morals and human decency went, we were ten times the men they were.

The ride back to the club was executed in silence. While I knew there was a chance of an extraction, I opted for taking the cage, aka van, instead of my bike, knowing full well I was gonna be the one escorting our *guest* back to our club. We only made it a habit of kidnapping people who needed to be reasoned with, and while this was a completely different turn of events, it couldn't be helped. We had to drive at least one nail into the SR's coffin, and stealing the president's daughter was the biggest 'fuck you' we could send.

Her hands and feet were bound tight enough so she couldn't wriggle free but not tight enough to cut into her lovely, creamy skin. Stone and Hawke were in the back with her, keeping an eye out just in case she chose to do something crazy. She'd already shocked the shit out of me once that day, and I wasn't taking any chances.

The rest of the men were in front of us, throwing the line of formation out of sorts with me and my VP riding behind everyone else. But the cage always held up the rear in case things jumped off and the riders fell into danger. There were enough weapons hidden behind secret panels to arm a small tribe, so it was up to whoever was riding in there to be sure we had our eyes peeled for anything. If we rode ahead of the others, we risked the lives of all the riding brothers in case they were ambushed.

A soft moan wafted through the otherwise silent vehicle. She'd drawn my attention immediately, and I couldn't help but inquire about her well-being. When I'd first laid eyes on her crouching in the corner of that small ass, dingy room, I felt my chest constrict. A shiver of something foreign shot through me, and I had this inexplicable need to comfort her. To tell her that, although we wouldn't harm her, she had to come with us. But, of course, I never uttered any of those words, instead choosing to confront her like the man she probably believed me to be.

An intruder.

A killer.

An invader who was there to snatch her away from the only world she'd ever known.

And she was right. I was there to take her, to integrate her into our club and never allow her to see any of the Savage Reapers ever again.

"Is she all right?" I queried, never taking my eyes from the road while I impatiently waited for them to answer.

I counted two deep inhales of breath before one of my men's voices cut through the building tension.

"What the fuck?" Hawke yelped.

"What?" I shouted, tightening my grip on the steering wheel. When he didn't answer, I yelled again, more authority cutting my tone and letting him know how serious I was. "What's the problem, Hawke?"

"She fuckin' bit me," he grumbled, Stone chuckling beside him in amusement.

"Why the hell did she bite you, man? What were you doing to her?" I growled, the thought of him touching her inappropriately instantly angering me.

"You asked if she was okay, so I pushed her hair off her face to see her eyes, and my fingers fell too close to her mouth. Then she goddamn bit me," he repeated, his disgust apparent in his tone.

"Did she hurt you?"

"Hell yeah, that hurt," he complained.

"Good. Think of it as payback for the little escapade your woman subjected us to." The lilt of my voice told him I was messing with him, even though he totally deserved it for not getting Edana out of the clubhouse before she started throwing knives and shit.

"How is that my fault?"

"You need to control your woman better, brother." Stone was still laughing about his buddy cradling his hand in his lap, a gesture I could clearly see from the rearview mirror.

"Fuck you," he murmured. "Just because you don't feel any pain, ever, doesn't mean shit to the rest of us." My eyes flitted to the woman lying between the two men and saw a fleeting look of confusion pass over her lovely face. "This shit hurts," Hawke continued to gripe.

"Man up, pussy," I demanded from the front, relaxing my grip on the leather of the wheel.

Over the next few miles, I envisioned gazing on our new captive until my heart was content. It'd been dark in her room and, although I could see she was beautiful, I couldn't wait to see her in the light of my private space. Sprawled on my bed or washing in my shower.

Get it together before you fall into more trouble than you know how to dig yourself out of.

Luckily, the clubhouse was directly ahead of us, pushing me from whatever wayward thoughts had invaded my sanity.

Once the van came to a stop, I hurriedly threw it in park and made my way toward the back. Stone had opened the door and filed out directly behind Hawke, pushing his shoulder in jest and continuing to tease him about his fingers. Thankfully, Hawke wasn't feeling the initial effects of the incident, but when I grabbed his hand to see the supposed damage, I was shocked to see she'd actually broken skin.

She sure is a feisty one.

Leaning close to her ear, I warned, "Don't think about biting me, sweetheart, because I won't be held accountable for my reaction." I was serious, although I doubted I could ever lay a hand on her in anger. Sexually was a completely different story—one I hadn't yet written, of course.

Her eyes scanned my face, landing on my mouth for longer than was normal for someone in her situation. Finally, I guessed when her curiosity had been sated, she connected with my eyes, and it was in those beautiful dark brown orbs of hers that I saw her complicity. She was scared, of course, but something else hid behind her gaze. Unfortunately, I didn't have any time right then to figure out what it was.

Escorting her from the back of the vehicle, I made sure she was stable before bending down to cut the ties around her feet. "Don't think about running either. Nowhere for you to go," I promised. That time I didn't wait for her to acknowledge me, clipping the ties effortlessly before standing in front of her once more.

She was a tiny thing, my own six-foot-one frame towering over her. From what I could see in the darkened lot of the club, she was slim. A little too slim for my taste. She wore a large gray T-shirt, which fell to just above her knees, and from what I gathered when I flung her over my shoulder, she was wearing tiny-ass shorts underneath. An old pair of slip-on shoes adorned her small feet, a hole in the side of the left one making me furrow my brow in irritation. Her eyes followed mine, and when she realized I was staring at her shoes, she shifted her feet, hiding the damaged one behind the other.

Ushering her to walk in front of me, I placed my large hand on the small of her back, the heat from her skin powering through her thin shirt and hitting me right where it counted. My dick twitched in my pants and before things got too *hard* for me, I adjusted myself, grateful she was facing forward and didn't see me grab my crotch.

I had no idea why I worried about what she saw, or felt for that matter. I wasn't a heartless man. Ruthless when I needed to be, but not heartless. But I never cared what women thought of me or my club before. Plenty of them had thrown themselves at me ever since I could remember, and not once did I ever apologize for my actions or words, never caring one way or the other if I ever saw them again.

But she was... different.

I knew it in my soul.

I knew she was going to ruin me, yet I had no idea how.

Eleven

Sully

Funny how life changes at the drop of a hat.

No warning.

No planning.

A simple prayer for my life as I knew it to cease... and in barged our biggest enemy.

Be careful what you wish for and all that shit. Isn't that the saying?

A sudden chill coursed through me. We were inside the Knights Corruption compound, leisurely walking toward what I assumed was their private bunker of sorts. The place they held meetings, threw wild parties and partook in unspeakable things. Well, if they were anything like my club, at least.

The only things I knew about the KC MC were what I'd heard over the years. So far, I hadn't witnessed any of their brutality. I certainly expected to be beaten after I'd attacked the man who snatched me from my room, then again when I bit the man with the long dark hair.

But nothing.

Neither one of them had laid a hand on me, which I found it very strange.

I was used to being punished for the simplest of things. Not having dinner ready on time, innocently glancing at one of the club members while they spoke, not cleaning up someone else's mess in a timely fashion. Those were the reasons I was punched and kicked. I couldn't even imagine what would have happened to me had I ever reacted and hit or bit Vex or my father, or anyone in the Reapers for that matter.

I would be dead. Of that, I was sure. So I was simply baffled why I'd chosen to react in such a manner with our most hated enemy.

Walking into what appeared to be a common room of sorts, I was instantly put on guard, ashamed of my appearance and what I looked like to the people suddenly swarming all around us. My hands were still restrained, my fingers interlocked and resting in front of me.

I quickly took in my surroundings, my eyes flitting over the beige-colored walls, neatly swept floor and array of various couches and chairs littered around the entire room. The area looked nothing like the common room back at my club. There were no dried bloodstains on the floor, no pile of used condoms strewn about and no liquor bottles cluttered into a massive mess in all four corners.

"Well, what do we have here, Prez?" an older man behind the bar asked as we continued to walk through. Keeping my head down, I heard the man who was guiding me speak up.

"We snagged us the SR princess," he responded. His voice was neither celebratory nor cocky; he was matter-of-fact, and it was even more unnerving than if he'd been boasting about his acquisition. We walked a few more paces before something dawned on me.

The man who'd stolen me from the only home I knew was

the *president* of our enemies? How was that even possible? My father would never barge into enemy territory, instead choosing to send his foot soldiers to do his dirty work for him.

An abrupt growl sounded to my left, drawing my attention right away.

The large man with the blond hair stood a few feet from us, his attention on the one and only other woman in sight, a beautiful blonde-haired woman who looked extremely out of place. She carried a small black medical bag, one I'd seen many a time back home when some of the men needed patching up. She was unaware the man was staring at her and she continued forging ahead, her head down and reading something on her phone. It wasn't until she walked right into him that she looked up. They were close enough that I could hear their conversation. Hell, anyone paying attention could hear them.

"Stone," she cried out, "you startled me." A light blush crept over her cheeks as she continued to stare up at him. Endless tense seconds passed before she spoke again. "Did you all just get back?" She hadn't seen me; it was apparent in the innocent way she tried to engage that Stone character.

She certainly wasn't a club whore. She could have been the man's old lady, but I didn't think so. Maybe she was someone they simply called in to help out whenever someone was injured. I had no idea, but I knew she wasn't integrated wholly into their... *our* way of life.

"Back to tend to him again, Adelaide?" he asked, stepping back so he could gain some distance. His posture was rigid, and I saw his hands curl into tight fists. Thankfully having something other than my own uncertainty to feast on, I leaned in so I could hear them better.

"You know damn well I have to check on him, to make sure he's okay. You don't want him to die, do you?" she asked. She gripped her bag tighter and appeared as if she was fighting the urge to tell him off, knowing she was outmatched with all the men milling around the room. If I dared to ever ask such a question, I would have been reminded of my place, and quickly. I waited with bated anticipation to see how he was going to react, bracing myself to witness a deplorable act.

"You don't have to constantly touch him the way you do," he seethed. Although their talk was quiet, it drew the attention of the man behind the bar. He stepped around and quickly walked toward the two of them.

Glancing around, I noticed everyone's focus was on the scene unfolding in front of us—the president of the club, the man standing behind me, was no exception. I heard him sigh loudly, his warm breath cascading over my cheek and making me feel something. I wasn't sure what, but it wasn't terror.

Pinning my gaze back on the couple across the room, I pricked my ears to make sure I didn't miss a word.

"What's going on here?" the older man asked, reaching for the woman's arm. Was he her old man? When she didn't answer, he turned his gaze onto the blond man. "Are you angry with my niece for some reason, Stone?"

Oh... she's his niece.

Biting his lip, Stone stalled to find the right answer, I was sure. "I just don't know why she's always here. That's all, Trigger."

"She's here tending to a fellow brother. You know he's not out of the woods yet." Her uncle, this *Trigger*, looked pensive for a moment. "Wait... Are you jealous?" Before Stone could utter a complacent reply, the man cut him off. "No, that couldn't be possible," he gritted, "because that would mean you feel something for my niece, and you know better. You know better than to mess with my family, don't you?" He continued on as if he hadn't just asked him question after question. "You might not be able to feel pain, you fucker, but that doesn't mean

I won't put a bullet in your ass if you touch one hair on her goddamn head." Stepping so close they were chest to chest, he practically spit in his face as he yelled, "Do you understand me?"

That's the second time someone made reference to this man not feeling pain. What the hell does that even mean?

"Uncle Trig," the woman interjected, "there's nothing going on between me and Stone. He's probably just pissy there's a woman constantly around, messing up the testosterone flow you all have going on up in here." She tried to joke to relieve some of the pulsating tension, but it was lost on her uncle. And on the irate man standing next to her.

The man behind me spoke up and his deep voice startled me. "Trig, Stone," he commanded. "Lock it up. Enough." His words were short and to the point. Both men glared at each other before moving aside. Stone gave the woman another hard leer before pushing past both of them, mumbling something incoherent under his breath.

At least the focus had been taken off me for a short time.

Twelve

Marek

I swear to Christ! If we didn't have enough shit to worry about, now I had to concern myself as to what the hell was goin' on with Stone and Adelaide... and Trigger, for fuck's sake. It wasn't enough that we'd just ambushed the Reapers' compound, kidnapped Psych's daughter, Vex's alleged woman, but then I had to worry about Trigger putting a bullet in my VP.

Can I not get one night of rest?

I ain't gonna lie. We were all intrigued to see what was gonna unfold between Stone and Adelaide, then Trigger stepping in, but I was tired and needed to get some sleep. But first, I had to take care of the woman still shackled in front of me.

My captive.

The newest permanent addition to the Knights Corruption.

Yeah, no way in hell I was releasing her back to them, no matter how much she begged, or how hard they came at us to retrieve her.

I ushered the tiny woman ahead, directing her down the

hallway and to my room, which was the last one on the left. Turning the handle, I guided her inside and turned on the light so I could finally gaze at her uninterrupted.

Spinning her around to face me, she hung her head low so she didn't have to acknowledge her current situation. Well, fuck that—I wanted her to watch me as I watched her. Pulling my knife from my waistband, I cut the ties from her wrists. As they fell to the ground, I saw her chest expand with a heavy exhale. Little did she realize those ties falling loose meant nothing. Going forward, she was property of the KC. She was my prize for all of the wrongs her club had committed against ours.

She rubbed at her wrists even though I knew the restraints hadn't cut into her flesh or stopped the blood flow, although they did leave a slight red mark on her skin. It was while looking at the faint lines that I noticed a bruise higher up on her arm, then another... and another. Without warning, I reached for her chin and jerked her head upright so she had no choice but to look at me. A faded yellow contusion covered the right side of her cheekbone. If I had to guess, I would have said someone had clocked her about a week ago, judging from the color of the mark.

Something inside me snapped and before I realized what I was doing, I yanked her shirt up and over her head, tossing it to the ground before she could protest. Her hands instantly covered herself, but because her tits were so large she spilled over her tiny fingers. I had no idea she had all that hidden underneath the damn shirt. To say I was pleasantly surprised was an understatement. While she did her best to conceal herself from my view, I raked my eyes down the rest of her, stopping when I saw the first scar. It was four inches in length across her lower abdomen, jagged and raised. Then I saw another one just underneath where her left hand was currently covering her tit. That one was smaller, but just as rough. She was littered with marks, some dark and fresh, while others appeared faint, her body healing itself and discarding the evidence of obvious abuse.

The majority of her torture was on her torso, although there were a few marks on her thighs. As my eyes moved lower, they stopped on those tiny-ass black shorts she wore. Lower still, I took in the remainder of her front. For as small as she was, her legs were long and lean, her body trembling the longer the silence lingered between us. Making a circling motion with my finger, I silently told her to turn around. She shook her head no —it was subtle, but I saw it.

Gripping her shoulders, I forcefully turned her around so her back was facing me, a small gasp falling from her pouty lips and quickly distracting me. Ignoring her disbelief, I inspected her further and discovered what looked like two small burn marks on her lower back. Fury coursed through me that someone could do that to a fragile woman. Granted, I had no idea what kind of strength she possessed, but she was a woman nonetheless, no match for the likes of a man.

My gut told me that fucker Vex had something to do with the way she looked. His reputation preceded him, and I had no doubt he thought he owned her, marking her as he saw fit.

With my hands still resting on her trembling shoulders, I tried my best to calm the anger raging in my throat. I didn't want to scare her any more than she already was. "Sully, is it?" I asked, sure that was the odd name I'd heard was attached to the woman standing before me.

She nodded once.

"Who did these things to you?"

Silence.

I tried to remain calm, but the more she chose to ignore my question the more irate I became. Before I could stop myself, I yelled for her to answer me.

"Tell me right now who did this to you!" I whipped her back around so I could see her. Her lip quivered when her eyes landed on mine. She possessed the darkest brown eyes, the color so rich it was like nothing I'd ever seen. I knew she held back her tears, no doubt internally demanding she not cry in front of the big bad man, who'd stolen her. Her jet-black hair was long, a tangled mess from the night's events. She was a little dirty as well, definitely in need of a shower very soon.

If I didn't know any better, I would have thought she was homeless, had suffered from bouts of hunger and abuse at the hands of strangers on the street. The longer she stood before me, in all her pitiful beauty, the more she intrigued me. I longed to know her story but I also knew I had to keep my distance, my inner voice warning me about getting too close.

I shook her shoulders. "Tell me or so help me God..." I warned.

As her lips parted to speak, there was a loud knock on the door. "Prez, you better get out here!" Zip yelled from the hallway.

"Why?"

"Trigger and Stone are about to come to blows." *Fuck! I can't handle this shit right now.*

"Sully, you need to go take a shower. Everything you'll need is in the bathroom." Her body never moved, but her eyes followed me when I walked to my dresser and pulled out a pair of boxer shorts and a Knights T-shirt. "I know these are gonna be big on you, but it's all I have until I send someone to buy you a few things."

Zip banged on the door again. "Marek, you need to get out here. Now!" he hollered.

"Jesus Christ! I'm coming." I looked away from her sadness and opened the door, staring at Zip so harshly he backed up a step. "What the fuck?" I mumbled, pushing past him to walk down the hall.

When I entered the common area, I saw all the men huddling around a commotion. As I moved closer, I saw Trigger and Stone standing toe to toe, both of them looking as if they were gonna kill the other. Adelaide stood off to the side, desperately trying to convince her uncle to back away. Trigger had a good twenty years on both Stone and me, but the man had a right hook that had knocked out many a man. Stone, however, was not your typical opponent. The man was skilled in not only boxing but some mixed martial arts as well. What can I say? My VP was a badass, although I would never admit that to him. His head was already swollen enough.

Then there was the little thing about him never feeling any pain. It was true. I'd heard all sorts of rumors about him before, everything from he was immortal to he'd been shot a thousand times and never once flinched. All of it was bullshit, although there was *some* truth to the tales.

Stone had what was referred to as a congenital insensitivity to pain. The only reason I knew the medical term was because he'd told me, otherwise, I would've probably fallen into the trap of believing some of the rumors. The man had been in some nasty wrecks, his leg dangling behind him as he crawled off to the side of the road on one of those occasions, and he never even balked. Instead, he was pissed off because he knew he had to wear a cast and couldn't ride until he was completely healed. I'd also seen him take the brunt of a blade as well as a bullet—twice. Luckily never hitting any major organs. Although the man laughed it off when that shit happened, he could still die if the damage was extensive enough. Though sometimes, I thought he bought into his whole immortal bullshit himself.

"What the hell is going on?" I demanded, pushing through

the crowd of men and coming to stand right next to the both of them.

"I saw your VP with his hands all over my niece," Trigger spit, shoving Stone as the last word left his angry mouth.

"Don't put your fuckin' hands on me, Trigger. You don't know what you saw, so just calm the hell down." The look in Stone's eyes was volatile, and I would surely have a mess to clean up if they decided to tear each other apart.

We should be fighting our enemies out there, not fighting each other in here.

"Uncle Trig, please... You don't understand. It's not what you think. Really," Adelaide cried, taking a step toward her family. "I tripped and Stone was simply holding me until I regained my balance." She tugged on his arm. "Please, don't do anything stupid."

"Is that right? Is she telling the truth?" Trigger asked Stone, careful not to back down until he confessed. Adelaide had given Stone an out, yet he hesitated to take it. The flaring of his nostrils and the tick in his jaw told me he was about to make a stupid mistake. But before he opened his mouth, a high-pitched yelp from down the hallway pulled all of our attention.

"*Now* what the hell?" I yelled.

Zip appeared out of nowhere, but instead of walking toward us like a normal fucking human being, he crawled along the floor, cursing and screaming with every slow inch of surface he covered. It was then I realized he'd come out of *my* room. The same room Sully was in, practically naked.

I swear to God, if he touched her, I'm gonna kill him.

Stalking toward him, I reached down and yanked him to his feet, his hands covering his crotch and continuing to double over in pain. Seething, I growled in his ear, "What did you do?"

"I... I didn't... do anything," he spurted, his breaths not fully carrying his words. They were short and choppy, probably because of the pain he was in. It didn't take a genius to see he'd obviously been kicked in the balls, but why? What had he done to warrant such a viscous attack? And I said vicious because it was one of the most excruciating, painful things to happen to a man. Although, getting shot was no walk in the park either.

"Well, you must have done something."

"I... I just... was trying to convince her to kiss me. That's all. I... I swear." Shoving him back down to the ground, I abruptly turned toward my entire club, most of the men still present after our little retaliation trip.

"Hear me now," I roared. "If anyone so much as touches a hair on Sully's head, you're gonna have to answer to me. And it won't be goddamn pretty. Trust me on that shit!"

Kicking Zip in the leg on my way back toward my room to check on her, I heard a few of the men grumble under their breaths. I didn't care if they thought she was gonna be passed around for their own amusement. She'd been through enough.

The evidence was scarred all over her body.

Thirteen

Sully

I heard shouting in the hallway, and I thought I heard my name, but I'd shut the bathroom door soon after I'd defended myself against one of the club members. He wasn't doing anything different than any other man in my life had done—always wanting to touch me, to taste me—but, for some reason, I'd snapped. Again. The only explanation for my bouts of bravery must be that I was still in shock, not in my right frame of mind. Because if I were, I would have never done any of the things I had since I'd been kidnapped.

There was no way I was going to get away with fighting these men as much as I had been. Maybe they were gearing up for something awful, counting my insolent acts up to warrant the attack which was surely coming at me.

Maybe I'd finally fought back *because* I didn't know them. I had no frame of reference of how they would react, therefore leaving me to my own self-justified—or delusional—world of denial.

The bathroom I was now trapped in boasted nothing special. A cream color washed over the walls of the small room. There was a silver rack next to the toilet, a beige towel hanging haphazardly from it. A single vanity with an accompanying wooden mirror was set in the middle of the intimate space.

Like I said, nothing to write home about, but it was the most enticing room to me. It allowed me a sliver of solitude, and after being ripped from the only life I'd known, it was comforting to be alone.

Turning on the shower, I waited patiently while the water heated up, steam quickly fogging the small mirror. Stripping off my shorts, I slid the shower door open and stepped inside, instantly feeling a smidge better. The power of hot water cascading all over my tired, worn-out body was the best thera- peutic release. All my demons were put to rest, all my self- loathing taking a backseat to the warmth I suddenly found myself enveloped in.

Reaching for the combined shampoo and conditioner bottle, I squeezed a healthy size into my palm before massaging it into my tangled hair. The soft repetition of my fingers on my scalp was quite relaxing, making me forget for a brief moment just where I was.

In the Knights Corruption's compound.

Naked in the president's shower.

My captor.

Once my long hair was rinsed free, I grabbed the shower gel and spread an ample amount on a washcloth, scrubbing my body clean. The masculine scent filled my nose and while it should have put me on guard, I noticed it had the reverse effect. The aroma calmed me. I'd smelled it before... on *him*. I first noticed it when he was standing behind me, guiding me toward his bedroom. Then again when he was inspecting my body, his hands holding me close to him as if he feared I was going to flee. And why shouldn't he think such a thing? Any normal person who'd been stolen away from her family—no matter how abusive and dysfunctional—would try and run given the opportunity to do so.

So, why wasn't I devising a plan to escape?

Focusing back on the task at hand, I almost didn't hear the bathroom door open, then close; the soft click of the handle was swallowed by the heavy flow of the water.

My head was immersed under the spray when I suddenly heard a gruff voice slice through the otherwise silent air.

"If you stay in there any longer you're gonna turn into a damn prune."

His deep voice startled me, my body's reaction completely involuntary. I jumped and slipped on the shower floor, my arms bracing myself against the tile so I didn't fall on my ass. Before I could reply, he quickly slid the door open and stood in front of me, a brief worried look passing over his handsome features.

I'm learning there's absolutely no sense of privacy when it comes to this man.

Reaching to take my hand, he pulled me toward the edge of the shower, keeping his eyes on my face and not my naked body. Not in the beginning, at least. His touch was soothing, but he also made me extremely self-conscious. Not simply because I was nude, but I felt he could see into the deepest parts of my soul. His blue eyes entranced me, blinking in slow motion as he seemed to memorize every aspect of my face. He stared so intently at my mouth that I could do nothing but lick my lips out of nervousness, biting down on the corner to sate my thumping heart. A low growl erupted from his throat, his hand tightening over mine as his gaze flew back up to meet my own.

Soon, he raked his eyes over the rest of me, being sure to take in his fill rather quickly.

"Are you all right?" he asked, licking his own lips while he waited for my answer. But I'd become mute all of a sudden. The chill of the room hardened my nipples, making them painfully erect. An ache shot through me while my heart pounded against my chest. But all I could focus on was his eyes... and that delectable mouth of his. He had the most perfect Cupid's bow, his lips full and inviting. A neatly trimmed beard coated his strong jaw, and the flare of his nostrils told me he was excited, although it was the only reaction which indicated so.

Instinctually, my fingers traced over the scar on my stomach, shielding the ugly, puckered skin from his view, in case he chanced a look down there again. But instead of hiding, he saw me—*all* of me—and it was quite unnerving.

"I still want answers," he demanded, quirking his brow while he continued to stand in the open doorway of the shower.

"About what?" I mumbled, knowing damn well what he was talking about.

Leaning closer, he said, "About who did that to you." He gestured toward my body with his finger. "I'll give you the night to settle in, seeing as how this is your home now. Then we'll talk, and you'll tell me everything I want to know. Got it?" he asked.

I remained silent, trying to process what I knew to be true, but it was somehow different when the words were spoken out loud. *This is your home now.* It couldn't be further from the truth, but I didn't know quite how to voice that without angering him. I'd been through such a whirlwind that evening; all I wanted to do was finish washing up and crawl into bed.

His bed.

But I didn't have another choice.

Did I?

His posture became rigid, as if he expected a fight, but I said nothing. I simply nodded, hoping he would close the door and leave me in peace.

Peace. What a funny word, one which had never pertained to me a day in my life.

Finally, after giving my body a once-over again, he closed the door and it was seconds before I heard another click, indicating he had vacated the one small room I wanted to spend the rest of my life in. I had no desire to ever see another person for as long as I could stand it, although the man who'd kidnapped me was different. I saw something in his eyes, a nature he tried his hardest to hide from people. Maybe it was because he was the leader of a notorious biker club, making sure no one questioned his power—hell, maybe even his sanity. Or maybe it was for a different reason altogether, but I knew I wasn't going to stick around long enough to find out.

While I had no set plan of escaping, I knew I had to do something eventually. I mean, who just gives up when kidnapped, complacent to remain with their captor, no questions asked?

Stepping from the shower, I dried my body before slipping on the shorts and T-shirt he'd given me earlier. Slowly opening the door, I stepped into his bedroom, but only once I deemed it safe... and abandoned. I crawled under the covers and pulled the material to my nose, strangely comforted by the scent which suddenly wrapped around me.

Drifting off to sleep, something I surely would have thought impossible, I envisioned a life where I wasn't a victim. Where I hadn't been snatched from my 'family.' Where I wasn't used as the most intricate part of a pawn played between two clubs who'd been at war for as long as I could remember.

My fantasies consisted of a life where I lived a simple existence, one which didn't involve constant fear and self-loathing.

At least you're away from your father and Vex, my inner voice screamed. The thing was I had no idea what kind of devil lurked in the darkened hallways of my new 'home.'

Fourteen

Marek

I had every intention of leaving her alone, allowing her the night to herself, certain she was overwhelmed and probably scared out of her mind. Although, depending on the answer she gave me about who'd desecrated her body, she might be thankful to be away from the Savage Reapers.

Her family.

As I opened the door to my room to check on her before I left for the evening, I heard faint whimpers drift through the air. Stepping inside, I moved closer to the bed and noticed her spread out, jerking in her sleep and pushing at the air as if she were shoving someone away from her.

Who haunts your dreams?

While I made sure to remain as quiet as I could so as not to scare her, my eyes drifted down her body. She'd thrown the covers off and was lying in the clothes I'd given her, the sight of her in my shorts and top stirring up a possessiveness I'd never felt before. The bottom of the shirt rode up enough that I saw her stomach, the scar prevalent enough to fuel my anger all over again. Her full breasts pressed against the fabric, and it was everything I could do not to rip it from her body. My shorts, the ones she was wearing, hung so low on her hipbones that if they were any lower, I would see all of her. Not that I hadn't already, of course, but the slight tease of her pussy made my dick push against my jeans.

The longer I invaded her personal space the more she seemed to fight her nightmare, a scream suddenly erupting from her perfect mouth. Before I realized what I was doing, I rushed forward to wake her. For some reason, her thrashing around pierced my heart, but I had no time to dissect why I even cared.

She was the prize.

She was the enemy.

She's a game changer.

"Sully," I called out, gently shaking her shoulders to wake her. When she continued to cry out, I shook her harder. "Sully, wake up, damn it," I whispered harshly.

Her eyes popped open and looked directly at me, but she didn't see me. She saw whoever was in her dreams. "No... no... no," she whimpered, cowering toward the edge of the bed. Then suddenly, gone was the fear. Instead, a rage I knew all too well consumed her, her body lurching forward and connecting with mine. She raked her nails down my neck and, when I didn't back up quick enough, she clenched her hand into a fist and punched me, hitting me directly on the chin.

"Sully!" I roared, the sting of her nails settling over me in the oddest comfort. "What the hell!" Roughly pushing her back down on the mattress, I straddled her waist and held her flailing hands above her head, pinning her so she couldn't attack me again.

"Get off me!" she yelled, the vacant look on her face telling me she still wasn't present. Not mentally, at least.

Tightening my hold on her wrists, I dared to lean close so she could hear me. Restraining the anger in my voice, I tried to calm her down. "I'm not gonna hurt you." She continued to fight me. "What the hell? Why are you acting like this?"

Her legs bucked underneath me, trying her best to throw me off. But her efforts were completely wasted. She was no match for me and we both knew it. Well, she didn't know it, lost to whoever was tormenting her in her nightmare.

"You did nothing," she sobbed. "You just stood there while that bastard took me... and raped me." She took a few quick breaths. "I know you hate me, but why didn't you try to help? I'm supposed to belong to you"—she hiccupped— "but you let another man take me in the next room." Tears streamed down her flushed cheeks, and I didn't know what to do. She was obviously lashing out, but I had no idea if what she was saying was the truth or just a nightmare.

Not knowing what else to do to soothe her, I leaned closer still until my warm breath danced near her earlobe. "Sully, I'm not gonna hurt you. That man isn't here now. He can't hurt you. I'll protect you." My soothing words calmed her, her tears slowing while her breathing evened out.

Her warm body beneath me threw me into another world, one where I imagined us together, her looking at me adoringly, hungry for my touch each and every time her eyes fell on me.

What the hell is wrong with you, Marek?

She started to whisper something but I couldn't hear her, and it was driving me nuts. Was she revealing yet another piece of her story?

"What's that?" I questioned, careful to keep my tone calm so I wouldn't incite another episode.

"I tried to love you, but you hated me as soon as you claimed me." Her arms fell lax under my hold. "You hurt me so much. Every time you could, even when I didn't do anything to deserve it." Quick, terrified pants racked her body, tears still cascading down her cheeks as she said her final peace.

"I hate you, Vex."

As soon as that vile piece of shit's name fell from her lips, she drifted back to sleep. Hopefully, she would find the peace she craved, deep in the recesses of her damaged mind.

"Time to get up, Sully," I called out, walking toward the bed and pulling the curtains open to allow the sun to shine through the room. "You slept half the day away." Still consumed with thoughts of the previous night, I refused to allow myself to go there while in her presence.

Groaning, she stretched her limbs and turned her attention to me. A shyness crept over her face, something I found oddly adorable.

I didn't think I'd ever used that word before, especially not when referring to a woman.

Pulling her shirt down so her skin was completely covered, she swung her legs over the edge of the bed and waited a few precious seconds before rising to her feet. She kept her head down as she moved past me and stumbled toward the bathroom. I waited impatiently while she finished her business.

When she finally emerged, I pointed toward the clothes I'd left for her. "One of the guys' wives brought those for you." She eyed the jeans and tank top, worry drifting off her in waves. Sighing loudly, I asked, "What's the matter?"

Her eyes found mine, and I swore she was about to break down right in front of me. "I don't think they'll fit," she mumbled.

"They'll be fine. Put 'em on." With that, I sauntered back toward the door. "And hurry up 'cause you're gonna help some of the women with the food." I left before she started spouting off questions which would only serve to irritate me.

I'd fallen under some kind of spell last night, sympathy drifting toward her because of her nightmare. But I had to snap out of that shit, had to remember she was the enemy, no matter how beautiful and enticing I may find her. She was brought here for one reason and one reason only—to become a permanent member of the Knights Corruption, essentially securing our advantage in the ongoing war with the Savage Reapers.

I hope she's up for what I have planned.

Fifteen

Sully

I'd spent five long minutes just staring at the clothing he'd left on the chair for me. I knew what my hesitation was, but there was no way out of it. It'd been drilled into my damaged mind that I was worthless, so it was pointless to try and tempt other men with my body. At least that's what Vex had always told me, punishing me if I ever tried to wear 'sexy' clothes—or, in other words, clothes that were sized to my shape.

A light knock on the door yanked me from my recollections, the handle turning before I even made a move.

"Sully?" a soft female voice called out. There was something soothing about her tone, and I instantly relaxed. Adelaide peeked her head into the room, her long blonde hair falling over her shoulders in long waves. "Are you okay, hon?" she asked, stepping closer. "Do you need help with anything?"

Was it all a setup? The clothes, her coming to check on me? Were they waiting for me to make a mistake so they could finally punish me like I knew they were itching to do?

"I... I don't have any clothes... that hide me," I confessed, waving my hand back and forth over my form.

Adelaide's brow furrowed, glancing back and forth between my apprehensive face and the clothes on the chair. Reaching forward, she snatched them up and walked them over to me. "Here. These will fit just fine." She smiled but eyed me cautiously, clearly baffled as to what the problem was. "Do you not like them?"

"No. I mean yes, I like them, but they'll reveal too much," I all but whispered. "I'll be punished."

"Oh, honey. No, you won't. No one here is going to hurt you." She reached for my hand and gave a gentle squeeze. "Trust me." And for some reason, I did. "Now, hurry up and get ready. We need more help preparing food for the party." She smiled quickly, turned around and left me standing there, a million questions poised for her.

Looking at myself one more time, I deemed I was surely going to be punished, no matter how hard she tried to convince me otherwise. The jeans were dark and fit like a glove. The tag said they were skinny jeans, whatever that meant. I was very self-conscious about the red tank top. While the only exposed flesh was my neck and arms, I was wearing it sans bra, since I hadn't been wearing one when I was taken. My breasts weren't ginormous, but they were certainly too big to wear the shirt without being noticed.

Blowing out a nervous breath, I walked from the bedroom and made my way toward the common area. As soon as I was within view, I heard a few whistles, and at first I had no idea they were directed at me. That was until I found the man who'd taken me. I believed some of the men had called him Marek. He was in mid-conversation when I appeared, whatever he'd been talking about coming to an abrupt halt as soon as his eyes found mine.

I couldn't hear what he said, but I saw the angry look on his face, saw him mouth a few choice words. He was fast approaching, causing all of my muscles to lock up tight, fear coursing through me like a tidal wave. I prepared for his backlash, closing my eyes the closer he came, but it did nothing to stop my lip from trembling.

My body sensed when he was near because the hairs on the back of my neck stood up, goose bumps breaking out all over my skin as his presence overwhelmed me. When I finally opened my eyes, I saw he was staring at me, anger still prevalent in his stance but he was also... *intrigued?*

"Damn, Sully. What the hell?" he asked, but I had a feeling he really didn't want me to respond. His eyes lowered, skating his gaze over my practically exposed chest before focusing his attention back on my face. "You look beautiful," he offered, the rasp in his voice causing my body to shudder.

Did he really just say that? What the hell is going on?

I couldn't respond. Instead, a fierce flush washed over my skin.

"Nothing to be embarrassed about," he teased, grabbing my hand and pulling me through the crowd, past people I hadn't initially noticed. But as their faces came into view, I recognized a few of the men from the night before, and Adelaide of course. The rest of them, however, were complete strangers.

The majority of the men were drinking, some of them well on their way to becoming quite drunk, and as far as I knew it was still early in the day. There were plenty of women gathered as well, milling about the wide open space, laughing and carrying on as if it were the happiest day of their lives.

I wonder what it would be like to feel that free. I was jealous of my enemies, and I hated myself even more because of it.

Children ran through the throngs of people, laughing and screaming as they chased after each other. A few of them even knocked into me in their wild abandonment. I would have smiled but I was too focused on where Marek was leading me, the warmth of his hand on mine enough of a distraction as it was.

He directed us toward the bar, tapping on the counter to get the older man's attention—Trigger, I believe he'd called him. "Gimme two shots, Trig," he said, turning his head to look back at me. I met his focus briefly before lowering my head and breaking the connection. "Here," he commanded. "Drink this. You're gonna need it." He threw his drink back before I could deny his offering. Noticing I hadn't moved, he placed the shot glass in my hand and tipped it toward my mouth. "Drink it," he urged, his tone dripping in seriousness.

I placed the tip of the glass to my lips, counted to three then chugged it. I immediately started coughing, the amber liquid burning the back of my throat. Shit! I could feel the alcohol warming my chest the longer I stood there.

"Good, huh?" Trigger asked, strands of his graying hair falling from his ponytail as a wide smile spread across his face.

Again, I was at a loss for words, more so because I had no idea what to do. I shouldn't be engaging with the likes of the KC, let alone pretend as if I'd been with them for years. They didn't treat me badly, all things considered, but I was still waiting for the other shoe to drop.

"Come on," Marek urged, pulling me further into the room. People parted down the middle, flanking us on both sides. Curious eyes watched my every move. I heard them whispering as I passed. "Reapers' daughter" was the one comment I caught over and over. Feeling lightheaded all of a sudden, I reached for Marek's arm, the commotion of the room becoming too much for me to handle. All I wanted was to return to his bedroom and lock myself away from everyone. Especially him. He was making me think and feel things I shouldn't, and that wasn't sitting well with me.

"You okay?" he asked, turning around to catch me as I staggered forward. "You hungry? 'Cause we can get you somethin' to eat."

Tugging me forward a few short feet, he pushed open a door leading into their kitchen. Stepping inside, I noticed there were even more people back there, most of them women. They were laughing and telling stories, amusingly berating one of the men for stealing a piece of food from one of the trays.

Adelaide stepped around an older, dark-haired woman, and walked toward the both of us with a big smile on her face. "Sully," she greeted. "Don't you look pretty." Pulling me in for a momentary hug, she retreated, but not before eyeing Marek with a curious look. I was too concerned with not fainting to read too much into her glance, though.

"I was gonna have her help you all, but now it doesn't seem right," he pondered, tapping his finger on his lips and bringing all of my attention there. *Damn him.*

"Marek," Adelaide warned. "You better not. Not today of all days," she said, retying her apron behind her back, looking like she was ready to get back to it.

Curiosity got the better of me and before I could stop myself, I blurted out, "Why? What's so special about today?"

Marek turned around fully to face me, taking my other hand so both were encased in his strong, warm hold. Leaning in close, his breath licked across my suddenly dry lips. His eyes held mine, and I swore my heart skipped a damn beat. "Today is special, Sully," he promised. "Because today is the day you officially become a permanent member of the Knights Corruption." My heart skidded to a halt altogether. I tried to pull out of his grip, but it only tightened.

Arching a dangerous brow, he proclaimed, "Today's our wedding day."

Sixteen

Sully

Trigger must have surely put something in the shot Marek practically forced me to drink. Something so powerful it caused me to hallucinate. A thin bead of sweat broke out on my hairline, my face and body suddenly feeling very overheated. The voices around me dimmed to an almost inaudible level, the women's movements distorted and blurred.

There was no way in hell he had just said what I thought he did.

Today is our wedding day?

Trying again to pry my hands from his, he tightened his hold once again and pulled me to him. His clenched jaw and steeled posture loomed over me with a power I'd never known before.

"Don't fight it, Sully. There's no way out of this, and it's useless to try and think of one." His scent tortured me, flicking on a light inside me I never even knew existed. Yet, he enraged me to the point that all I wanted to do was shield myself by lashing out at him. Hurt him like he was hurting me. Surely, he knew such a union was the same as signing my death warrant. He'd grown up in the same type of life I had, so he knew exactly what he was doing.

He was using me as a ploy to get back at the Savage Reapers for God knows what. But whatever it was, it must have been life-altering to be pulling a stunt like this.

Struggling with every ounce of energy I possessed, I wore myself out. And quickly. When he started walking forward, I dragged my feet and made it harder on him to move me. Or so I thought. My resistance was a mere annoyance, seeing as how he towered over me, no match for his sheer strength and will.

"No," I cried, but Marek trudged toward someone standing in the far corner of the room. The man's hands were clasped in front of him, an amused look on his face while he watched us approach.

"Yes," my captor sneered, whipping his head in my direction to show me how pissed he was. "Let's go." He jerked me forward so harshly I swear he almost ripped my arm out of its goddamn socket. There were fleeting moments when he showed me an ounce of compassion, and I'd been a fool to think he was being nice during those times. But he wasn't. He was playing me, just like everyone else in my life did, although he was the nicest man I'd ever encountered, which evidently wasn't saying much.

"I can't marry you!" I yelled, kicking my feet at the backs of his legs, struggling to dislodge his hold on me. But he was fierce, dragging me forward until we came to stand in front of the man with long gray hair, another club member who was obviously going to officiate the *marriage*.

Jerking his chin in the man's direction, he bit out, "Git on with it." Besides the fact that the bride-to-be was trying desperately to flee, everyone had a big fat smile plastered on their stupid faces. They all acted like what was transpiring was the most normal thing in the world. Then again, for all I knew, it was. Maybe they made a habit out of kidnapping other clubs' women and marrying them the following day.

What the hell did I know, anyway?

The man before us started speaking, but stopped briefly when someone entered the room, yelling and carrying on enough to disrupt the forced arrangement.

"Shit! Did I miss it?" the VP to the club yelled. He walked toward us, his brows arched and waiting for an answer.

"Sit down, Stone," Marek demanded. "We're just gettin' to it." I saw Marek wink at his second in command, and it pissed me off even more than I already was.

The one thing I was thankful for, however, was that Stone's unannounced interruption was the one thing which drew Marek's attention away for a split second. Enough time to loosen his hold on me. As soon as I felt the tension leave his hands, I yanked mine free, turned around and fled.

But I didn't get very far. Blinded by paranoia and fury, I wasn't paying attention to where I was going and instead of running toward safety, I ran right into the strong hold of the one man who'd just allowed me the opportunity to hightail it out of there.

Smacking right into his large frame, Stone's hands came up to hold me captive. "Whoa, sweetheart," he mocked. "Where do you think you're going? Don't you know what an honor it is to marry the president of the Knights Corruption? Fuck! I don't even think he's ever had a girlfriend before now," he said, looking directly over my head and straight at Marek, I was sure. Turning me around, he shoved me toward his friend, laughing at my back while I tried to find another way free.

But it was useless.

There were too many people present, blocking any plan of escape I could think of. I guessed there really was no way out of my new predicament. With drooped shoulders, I shuffled the few feet necessary to stand next to Marek, keeping my head down and away from his piercing eyes.

"Well, can we continue now?" the man presiding over our entanglement asked.

"Yes," Marek said curtly.

I tuned out most of what he said, until he came to the part about taking each other as husband and wife. Marek's simple answer when asked was, "Yeah." Not 'I do,' or even a standard 'Yes,' but what did I expect? That the man was in love with me? He was simply doing it to seal my fate, as well as his club's standing in the war between our two worlds. He didn't give a shit about me or what I wanted or needed; I was just a piece of property to him, just like I'd been to Vex and my father.

When it was my turn to respond, I picked my head up, looked Marek square in the eyes and said very loudly, "Hell no." I was hoping it was the loophole to get out of it, my blatant refusal a definite deal-breaker. Didn't he need my verbal consent?

Maybe outside of club life it would be enough, but not here.

"Don't need your agreement, darlin'," Marek condescended. "This is happening either way."

And it did.

He forcefully slid a ring onto my finger, and the president of our biggest enemy had just made me his wife.

Seventeen

Marek

The plan to marry Psych Brooks's daughter had come to me *after* we'd taken her from them. Hell, I hadn't even planned on taking her when we breached their shitty compound, nothing but a few drunken assholes guarding the gate.

At first, we thought it was too easy, thinking it was a setup and they were gonna surprise us as soon as we stepped foot onto their grounds. But there were no Reapers hiding around the corner ready to attack.

It'd been quite easy, until we knocked down the door to their clubhouse. It was there we came face to face with the soulless men of our enemy. The ones who weren't drunk or high were extremely skilled in defending their territory, but in the end they were simply no match for me and my men.

Stone had shouted something about snatching Psych's daughter for the ultimate payback, and I'd readily agreed. When we came to the barricaded room, we knew instinctually she was hiding in there. Over the years, we heard stories of the woman who was kept hidden from the world, her beauty unmatched to any around her. Her hype was built up so much I half-expected to see a used, life-beaten-down woman when we broke down the door.

But as soon as I laid eyes on her, crouching in the corner of the dark room, I knew instantly the rumors were true. Not being able to fully take her all in until we arrived home was torture, but I'd seen enough to sate my curiosity. She was beyond beautiful, even with all the scars and marks, the sunken look of despair in her eyes. Hell, even with the mixture of awe and disgust she threw my way whenever she saw me.

We stood in silence in front of everyone after I shoved the ring on her finger, her defiance coming full force even though it was guarded. She still wasn't completely sure how I was gonna react to her outbursts. She'd flinch when I moved too quickly, surely from years of abuse at the hands of that psychopath, Vex. Shit, probably from her father as well.

Psych Brooks was the Devil incarnate.

Her fingers twirled the band, and I knew she was gonna try to remove it. I stopped her before she made the attempt. "Don't even think of taking that off." I gestured toward her ring. "You won't like my reaction if you do." I had to threaten her to do as I commanded, otherwise, things were gonna get out of hand.

Her hand dropped to her side, and she glared at me swiftly before lowering her head. I didn't blame her for not wanting to look at me, but there was no going back now.

We were married.

And no one was gonna change it, not even her.

A silence fell over the gathering, everyone curious as to what was gonna happen next. No one had found out about the impromptu wedding until a few hours prior. There were no questions asked. They all knew better.

My word was law, and it was never to be challenged.

"Kiss her!" someone shouted a few feet away. Sully's head

jerked up and looked at me with wide eyes. *Fuck! She's beautiful.* I had no idea when I gave her those clothes how alluring she would look. Her tits were flawless, and don't get me started on that round, perfect ass of hers. It was a real shame our marriage was one of necessity, otherwise, I would have dragged her back to my room and fucked her long and hard. And each time she looked at me like she was now, I'd slam her against the wall, wrap her legs around my waist and sink inside her so fast she'd give up the breath in her lungs just to keep the connection.

I hadn't intended on kissing her, but I didn't let her in on the secret. I was bored, so I decided to play with her instead. Gripping her arms, I tugged her closer, licking my lips and throwing her a quick wink.

"Whatcha think, wife? Wanna give our guests a show?" She tried to pull away, her head shaking back and forth like she was having a goddamn convulsion. Her repulsion bothered me, even though I tried not to show it. My fingers dug into her soft skin and she winced. I hadn't meant to be so rough, but I couldn't help it. Yes, my face didn't show my annoyance, but my body had taken another directive. My jaw ticked and the mocking look on my face quickly disappeared, replaced by something I had yet to identify.

Every woman I knew would jump at the chance to have my mouth on them. But not her. No, she was freaking out, and it was all due to the thought of being kissed by me. My plan to tease her had just turned into the ultimate goal of planting one on her right there, in front of everyone to see.

I leaned in.

She pulled back.

I leaned in again, pulling her close so she had nowhere to go. She whimpered in my hold, but I didn't care; she was my wife now, and I would do whatever I wanted to her—within reason, of course.

I hadn't kissed a woman in years, but my need to make her comply drove me forward.

Slowly inching my hands upward, I rested them on the sides of her face, her body going still when she realized I was gonna go in for the kill. The closer our mouths came together, the more her body relaxed, which was quite odd. I would have thought it'd be the opposite.

Her demeanor softened slightly and I actually thought I might enjoy tasting her. I was but a breath away from her delectable lips when I heard someone close by whisper, "He's really gonna kiss her."

Women talked. I knew they did. Although club whores weren't allowed into the clubhouse unless a ruckus was going on, I knew their chatter spread to all the women of the club, old ladies alike. Everyone knew it was a steadfast rule of mine not to kiss. Again, no psychological reason why, I just didn't, not with the wannabes I fucked.

"You ready?" I whispered, my lips hovering over hers. I asked the question more to myself than to her, but it didn't really matter. As I was about to close the deal, Hawke barreled right into me, spilling his drink on the floor at my feet. He was half-drunk and already acting a fool.

Breaking the built-up tension between Sully and me, I backed up immediately and scowled at Hawke, his eyes glazed over as he mumbled an apology. He staggered away, bumping into people while he walked toward the bar to get another drink.

"Trigger!" I shouted. "Cut him off." I glared at Hawke, the priceless look of shock on his face almost worth me not tasting Sully's plump lips.

"Come on, Prez," he pleaded, slumping forward because he realized he wasn't gonna get another drop of liquor. Edana sidled up next to him, whispering something in his ear which made him smile. Taking her hand, he led her back toward his room, disappearing from sight before I could impose another punishment.

Movement in my periphery caused me to turn my head back toward Sully. She was shifting from one foot to the other, her obvious nervousness becoming quite annoying. She wouldn't say anything, however, choosing instead to just fidget next to me.

"What's the problem, Sully?" I growled, my patience evaporating into the air around me. The drawn look on her face almost made me correct my tone, but the fierce look in her eyes when she leered at me pushed that idiotic thought to the side.

"I want to go back to the room now." When I didn't answer, she added, "Please." I realized how hard it was for her to utter the word, but it did nothing to stop me from continuing to be difficult.

Strictly because I wanted to.

Nothing more.

"No. Everyone here came to celebrate our wedding. And, as my wife, you will entertain them." Flicking my wrist toward the crowd, I demanded, "Go mingle."

"Mingle?" She sounded shocked. "I'm not your wife. I'm your prisoner," she angrily huffed.

"You *are* my wife. Everyone here is a witness. Now, go and play nice," I said, patting her ass and ushering her forward into the throngs of people gathered together. Catching Ryder's attention, I motioned for him to come over. Once he'd gotten close enough, I inspected whether or not he'd been drinking. Beer was fine, but if he'd been drinking hard liquor? Forget about it. I had enough shit to worry about; I didn't need to wrangle up a few of the brothers to watch his volatile ass.

"What's up?" he asked.

"You been drinking?"

"It's a celebration, isn't it?" He smirked. "Of course I'm drinking."

"What?"

"What... What?"

Frustration shot out of me. "What the hell are you drinking? Beer?"

"Yup. In fact, I'm about to get me another. Want one?" he asked, already preparing to retreat to the bar.

Grabbing hold of his arm to stop him, I laid a very important task on him. "Listen, Stone and I have to talk. I need you to watch Sully while we're in Chambers."

Knowing damn well he wouldn't refuse, he rolled his eyes before agreeing. "Where did she get off to?" he huffed, peering around the room to try and locate her.

"She's talking to Adelaide. Near the kitchen." As I walked past, I warned him, "Don't lose sight of her, Ryder. If anything happens to her, or if she takes off, I'm holding you personally responsible."

"I know, I know," he grumbled before snatching a beer from the bar and heading toward the two women engaged in conversation. Well, Adelaide was doing most of the talking, while Sully was propped against the wall with her arms folded tight across her chest.

I'm married.

I'm fucking married, and I have no idea who my wife is.

What the hell was I thinking taking it this far?

Eighteen

Sully

I was beyond exhausted. The day's surprise debacle took its toll on me, and I wanted nothing more than to crawl into bed and drift off into the darkness. But I would be sleeping in *his* bed. Again. *I don't have any other choice unless I want to sleep on the floor, which I just might consider depending on what happens when he retires for the evening.*

Did he expect me to have sex with him now that we were married?

Refusing to give in to my paranoia, I focused on what Adelaide was saying. We'd been talking the majority of the day. Thankfully, she'd saved me from having to talk to everyone else. Well, besides Ryder. The man had become my shadow and butted into our conversation every now and again, especially when Adelaide complained about men. I had a feeling she was talking about one man in particular, but she kept her comments generalized so as not to give anything away.

I was still very much a stranger to these people. Actually, 'prisoner' was more accurate. It was as if I were living in a parallel universe. I'd been taken from my home, forced to wed my enemy, yet no one hurt me. Besides the guy who tried to kiss me in Marek's room, no one had bothered with me. Adelaide was very sweet. Hell, Ryder was even pleasant, growing more so the more alcohol he consumed. Stone was a little rough around the edges, but even he was complacent around me. Granted, I'd only been there for a day, but a lot had transpired during that time.

A lifetime seemingly passed me by in a mere twenty-four hours.

Finding a brief reprieve in our conversation, I grabbed hold of the opportunity and ran with it. "Adelaide, do you think it would be all right if I went back to my room?" My hopeful eyes pinned hers while she contemplated my question.

"Don't you mean Marek's room?" Ryder chuckled. He was drunk and feeling no pain. At least he was a pleasant drunk, laughing and fully engaged, regaling us with stories of pranks he'd been a part of over the years. Leaning against the wall with one arm, his eyes took me in but he wasn't lecherous about it. It almost seemed like he was assessing the newest member to his club, friendliness and caution meshed together to form a whole new emotion.

"Well... Yes. I suppose so," I retorted, not sure if I should react defensively, coyly or shyly. I was completely out of my element but the two of them made me relax a little, the fear I'd held on to since I was abducted taking a step into the shadows. Not too far, though, because I would need to be on guard once out of their company.

I had a feeling I wasn't out of the woods. Not by the longest stretch of the imagination. And the majority of my fear had to do with the man who ruled the KC. The man who'd succeeded in snatching me right from under my father's nose. The man who'd forced me to join into a union with not only him but his club. The man who made me feel things I'd never experienced before, no matter how briefly they rattled my emotions.

My husband.

Saying my goodbyes, I moved past them and headed toward the back of the building, toward the one room where I could escape. The spray of the hot water beckoned me, and I found I couldn't move fast enough. Ryder was right on my heels, never once leaving me by myself. I guessed he was instructed to do so, and there was no way he was going to disobey Marek.

"I think I can handle it from here, Ryder." I shooed at him, but he kept on following.

"Not a chance. I'm not letting you out of my sight until Prez comes back."

Back? Where did he go?

Noticing the puzzled look, he answered before I uttered a single word. "He's in Chambers talkin' to Stone about club business. Should be around shortly," he explained, taking a long swig of his near empty beer.

I had no idea what he was talking about. Chambers? Was that the same thing my father and Vex referred to as Church?

Deciding not to inquire about the whereabouts of my new husband, I walked into the bedroom, turning around to close the door behind me. But Ryder stepped inside before I could shut him out.

"What are you doing?" I asked, backing up a few steps. He closed the door and sauntered forward.

"I told ya already. I'm not goin' anywhere." He swayed slightly on his feet. "I was told to babysit you, and that's what I'm doin'." Plopping on the small couch against the wall, he leaned back and rested his hands behind his head, looking at me as if he were seeing me for the very first time.

From what I gathered about Ryder, he was friendly, but he also seemed a bit reserved, if that made any sense. His dark eyes hid secrets—I knew because I saw those same shielded pupils when I looked in the mirror. Short, dark hair adorned his head, a faint shadow of hair prickling his jawline. He wore dark jeans and a white long-sleeved shirt under his cut.

He was attractive... for the enemy.

Actually, quite a few of the KC men were handsome, their ruggedness hiding any vulnerability they may have possessed. Their looks were disarming, their ability to blend into society a most definite attribute. I hadn't witnessed it thus far, but I was sure they had charm in spades whenever they felt it necessary.

His eyes glided over my body, a hint of appreciation for what I was wearing most definitely shining bright. "You're quite beautiful," he offered, finishing off his drink and tossing it aside.

The tone he used was sedate, but the longer I remained in his presence the more I feared he was going to *show* me how beautiful he thought me to be. Would he do such a thing? Did the men share each other's property? Their wives? If it was anything like my club, they didn't, although that was the only rule I knew of. A man didn't go after another man's old lady, not unless he wanted to die.

But the rules for the Knights Corruption might be different. I had no idea, and I didn't want to find out. It was enough that I was forced to become one of them; I didn't want to be passed around between brothers. Fending off his advances before he even offered them, I took a few steps back.

"I'm going to take a shower, then go to bed." I kept eye contact with him the entire time, preparing myself for any unexpected moves. "Are you going to be out here when I get done in there?" I asked, flicking my thumb toward the bathroom.

"Yup."

"Oh...." In my uneasiness, I was instantly reminded that the only thing I had to wear to bed was the T-shirt and shorts Marek had given me the night before. At least the clothing was large enough to hide the majority of my body. With the simple realization, I turned my back on Ryder and hid away inside the comforts of the simple bathroom.

Once finished, I reentered the bedroom only to find a passed-out Ryder slumped back on the couch, his head lolled to the side. He was snoring, not too loud to be extremely distracting but loud enough to assure me he wasn't a threat.

Crawling into bed, I pulled the covers under my chin and prayed I would remain safe until morning. Being as defenseless as I was, I knew I would be no match for the likes of any of these men, and although my mind drifted off into imaginary scenarios, logically I had no cause for concern.

Not yet, at least.

Marek

We'd been at it for three hours, and I was fucking exhausted. I tried to keep my brain focused on the task at hand, but I found it easily wandered to my new wife. It was useless. I couldn't get her out of my head and Stone knew I was distracted, repeating himself a few times throughout the meeting.

Hidden away in Chambers, we'd told everyone we weren't to be disturbed. We had some heavy shit to figure out for the club before it was too late. We had to make a move and do it quick, or our retaliation on the Savage Reapers would have been in vain. Well... sort of. I still had Psych's daughter.

And I'd be damned if I was ever giving her back.

No, she was mine now. No matter the consequences.

"Fuck, Marek!" Stone shouted, pounding his fist on the table. "Pay attention, man." Normally, if any other member had talked to me like that, they would have been facedown on the ground right then, but my VP was different. We'd grown up together. We were more like brothers than anything, and he knew he could get away with it. At least he only did it in private, making sure not to test my patience in front of everyone else. Otherwise, I would be forced to react in some way.

"What?" I feigned nonchalance. "I am. We have to set up a meeting with Los Zappas cartel—Rafael Carrillo, to be more specific. I'll call in my one favor, essentially cutting the Reapers off from the cartel's supply and crushing the entire club into the ground. They'll have nothing. Their supply will be dried up, and with it their money and livelihood as well. Yeah, they may be able to secure product from somewhere else, but it'll be shit, and their customers will eventually move on." I leaned in close to Stone. "Paying enough attention for you?"

"Fuck you." He smiled. "I'll set it up. Just be ready to ride in the next few days." He leaned back in his chair, his fingers tapping against the wood of the table while he studied me.

"The hell you lookin' at?" I grumbled, hating that he was inspecting me rather suspiciously.

"You're thinkin' about her, aren't you?" He rested his mouth on the lip of his bottle, waiting for my answer before allowing the cold liquid to fill his mouth.

I knew damn well who he was referring to, so I didn't bother to ask. Instead, I chose to lie. "No."

"Uh-huh," he replied unconvinced. Swallowing his beer, he gave me a cocky grin before rising from his seat. "You gonna fuck her tonight? She *is* your wife now, you know."

"I'm fully aware she's my wife. I was there, wasn't I?" Frustration laced my voice and there was no point in hiding it. I had no idea what the evening held once I entered my room and found her lying on my bed. My body certainly wanted to sink inside her but property, captive, wife or not, I wasn't going to force myself on her. I wasn't built that way, and neither were any of my men. I made sure of it. What was the point of forcing yourself on a woman when there was plenty of pussy available around the clock? All it took was a simple phone call, and we all knew it.

"Well, if you *do* fuck her, you have to tell me how she was. She's quite stunning. And that body of hers... Fuck, Marek." His words slurred the more he spoke, and it was only then that I realized he'd had quite a bit to drink. The more he talked the more he pissed me off, though, so I decided to return the favor. Finish him off so I wouldn't have to listen to him anymore.

"Actually, Adelaide is still here, so I think I'll see if she wants to have some fun. Trigger left for the night, so I won't have to deal with his cock-blockin' ass." Licking my lips I added, "Think she'll wanna fuck the prez?"

Stone's reaction was priceless... and expected. Kicking his chair behind him, it skidded across the floor, knocking against the wall before it finally stopped. His hands clenched into tight fists while his chest rose and fell with heavy rage. Sweat beaded on his brow and his face turned red. "Don't you dare go near her," he seethed, his warning telling me more than I wanted to be privy to. He'd given everything away with his response.

"Why do you care if I take her to bed, Stone?" I taunted, knowing damn well he was losing his mind.

"Because..."—he faltered—"you're married now... and off-limits." *Lame excuse.*

"What does me being married have to do with it? I'll continue to get pussy wherever I want. Sully won't put a stop to that." My pokes had begun for pure amusement, but the further we took it, the more I realized I was telling him how things would be for me going forward. Just because I had taken a wife, her of all people, didn't mean my life would change.

He took a step toward me, fury dancing in his eyes as he silently challenged me. "Just don't go near her, Marek," he gritted.

"Tell me why," I taunted. "If you don't give me a good

reason, she's as good as riding my cock." My smirk challenged him right back.

All sense of protectiveness poured forth, the need to claim what was his too strong to back away from. "Because, mother-fucker... She's mine!" he roared. "Don't you dare touch her or I'll kill you."

Wow!

Stone had never threatened me before. He was drunk, but that did nothing to excuse his outburst, and it was my job to remind him of that.

Snatching his throat, I slammed him against the wall, my grip tightening to show him how serious I was. "Don't you ever threaten me again, *friend*," I bit out. "I was just fucking with you. I know there's something going on with you two but didn't know how serious it was until right now." Pulling back my arm, I released him and he stumbled forward. Stone was trained to kill, more so than me, but it was my surprise attack which worked to my advantage.

His blond hair fell over his eyes and with a heavy hand, he pushed it back, flicking his stare in my direction before punching the wall, ripping the door open and staggering from the room. Most likely to search for Adelaide.

I didn't know the extent of their relationship, but I'd never seen Stone react like he just had toward any other woman before. Jealousy and possessiveness barreled from him like an unstoppable train.

I didn't blame him, though. Adelaide was quite beautiful, but no one was supposed to mess with a member of one of the men's family. It was an unwritten—or, in Trigger's case, a stead-fast, written, spoken and threatened-about—rule. Never mind that she wasn't a part of our lifestyle. Sure, her uncle was, and she helped out from time to time when we needed her, but she wasn't involved with the way we lived.

She was a good girl. She was educated and had a good career. Her life was promising, but getting involved with Stone threatened all that. Everyone in the club knew the dangers of our business. The dangers of our mere existence.

It was one of the main reasons I chose never to get involved with anyone, even someone 'in the life.' Sure, I was married now, but I didn't love Sully. Hell, I didn't even know her, and I planned to keep it that way. For everyone's sake.

Letting Stone cool off a bit, I stayed in Chambers a few extra minutes before making my way back out to the common room. There were still plenty of people milling around, laughing and having a good ol' time. All of the kids had been sent home, as well as most of the old ladies, but some remained behind, helping clean up from the day's impromptu festivities.

Seeing Breck lounging on one of the sofas, a woman perched on each leg, I motioned him over. I didn't care that I interrupted his fun, and he knew it. Pushing the women off him, he streamlined straight for me, his pants already half-undone.

Adjusting himself, he jerked his chin and asked, "What's up, Prez?"

"You seen Ryder?" *That fucker better still be watching over Sully or so help me....*

"Nope, not for some time. Last time I saw him, he was following your wife to your bedroom." He grinned when he said 'your wife,' not caring to hide his amusement about the whole thing.

I grunted because I simply had no words left for him. Turning around, I snatched a fresh beer from the bar, taking a moment before walking back to my room. The longer the seconds ticked by, the more heat shot through my body at the thought of the two of them alone, and in my room of all places. She looked at me like she hated me and to a point, I didn't blame her, but I saw the exchange she engaged in with Ryder when they'd all been talking earlier. She smiled at what he said, even going so far as to accept a drink from him, her fingers lingering on his hand a little too long for my liking. Maybe I was imagining the touching, but I sure as shit didn't imagine the way she'd talked to him. Her long black hair flowing freely around her, covering her tits until she flicked it behind her shoulders.

Why the hell didn't I take a closer look at the damn shirt before I gave it to her, or remembered she didn't even have a bra to wear? I saw the way the men leered after her, and who could blame them? She was gorgeous, but nonetheless I didn't like it.

"Then I'm leaving, you ass!" I heard someone shout from the back hallway. Adelaide stormed forward, looking like she was ready to kill someone. And, of course, Stone wasn't too far behind. They'd been arguing, but it ceased as soon as they were around everyone else.

She searched the room until her eyes fell on me. Breaching the tiny distance between us, she came to stand before me, her eyes glassy and looking like she was ready to let loose at any minute.

Steeling her resolve, she straightened and abruptly said good-bye. She'd always been polite, more so than was necessary, but it was how she was raised.

"I want to thank you for inviting me today, Marek." She touched my arm in a genuine gesture of appreciation, nothing more, but you wouldn't know it from the way Stone watched us. Then I'd remembered what I'd teased him about earlier and it made me smile, but Adelaide probably thought I was returning her politeness. "I really like Sully," she confessed. "If there is anything you need me to do for her—you know, to help her get adjusted to being with you crazy men—just let me know. Okay?"

Finding the perfect opportunity, I blurted out, "You could buy her a bra."

She looked stunned, apparently taken back from such an odd request.

"Okay...." She stalled, not quite knowing why I'd said what I did.

"Well, she came with us so abruptly that she didn't have much with her. Actually, I would really appreciate it if you could pick up a few more things for her as well. Stop by tomorrow after work and I'll give you a list."

"Sounds like a plan." She smiled then leaned in to give me a quick hug, her innocent affection nothing new. When I glanced across the room, Stone looked like he was ready to go nuclear.

Adelaide walked right past him on her way out, completely ignoring him, even when he called after her time and time again. Disappearing from the clubhouse, I continued to hear him call her name, their voices swallowed up by the growing distance.

He was shit at hiding his feelings for Adelaide when she was around. Sooner or later, Trigger would find out for sure, and shit was gonna hit the fan in a big way.

He'd already threatened to put a bullet in my VP, and that was only when he'd *suspected* something was going on with Stone and Adelaide.

What would he do when he found out it was for real?

Twenty

Sully

The soft click of the door woke me. At first, I was confused as to where I was, but I quickly heard the soft snore coming from the couch across the room. Ryder was still there with me. Turned out he wasn't much of a watch dog after all.

The noise from the club filtered into the room, along with the light from the hallway. A tall, broad form filled the doorway, frightening me enough to cower. Until I realized who it was.

Marek.

"Christ!" he growled, advancing toward a sleeping Ryder. "Good use you were, ya bastard." He nudged Ryder's leg with his foot but nothing happened, so he tried shoving at his arm. Still nothing. "What the fuck, Ryder," he grumbled, before smacking the man in the head. "Get. Up," Marek ordered.

That time, Ryder shifted awake, assuming a fighting stance because he had no idea where he was. I couldn't help it; I laughed, the sound so soft I didn't think either of them heard me. But Marek did, because he turned toward me.

The room was still bathed in darkness so I couldn't make out his expression, but I knew he was staring intently at me. My body just sensed it. Ryder rose off the couch and clumsily walked from the room, mumbling under his breath the entire time.

After closing the door, Marek flicked on a side light and instantly blinded me. I brought my hands up to my face to shield my eyes, allowing myself time to adjust to the brightness.

"I'm gonna take a shower," he announced, throwing his cut on the chair before grabbing the hem of his shirt and pulling it over his head. Spreading my fingers over my eyes so I could see what he was doing, I inhaled a quick breath at the sight of his naked chest. Intricate designs wrapped around both arms, drifting over his shoulders and disappearing behind his back. A skull was inked in the center of his chest, flames shooting out from both sides, a large sword slicing through the middle of it. I'd seen that same design on the back of his cut, leading me to believe it was his club's emblem. Images of dark and light traced down his sides, the designs foreign to me because I was too far away to inspect them in any detail.

He was a walking work of art, and I'd never seen anything so beautiful before in my entire life. I'd seen men with tattoos before, but none that exuded such raw beauty like his.

His sun-kissed skin brought the artwork to life. Every twitch of his hard muscles moved the images, entrancing me the longer I watched him flit around the room. Before he said another word, he disappeared into the bathroom. I heard the running water and counted the minutes before he was standing before me again.

Is he going to sleep in here? Will he take the couch, or does he expect to sleep in the bed with me? My worry kept me occupied while the clock mocked me, time moving slow but fast all at the same time.

The bathroom door flung open and the steam from the shower billowed into the room, looking more like smog it was so heavy.

Marek sauntered into the room, and what I saw made me gasp out loud.

He was completely naked.

He busied himself running a towel through his wet hair, the fabric covering part of his face so he couldn't see me gawking at him. Maybe he forgot for a brief moment he wasn't alone. Or maybe he didn't. Maybe it was his way of telling me I didn't affect him, or his actions. He would continue to live his life just like he had, not caring at all that I was now involved.

Tossing the towel on the floor, an action which immediately irritated me since I liked the bedroom to be a place which was nice and neat, he stalked toward the bed.

Oh, my God! Is he going to get into bed with me naked? Does he expect to have sex? Is he going to force me?

I hadn't even realized my expression had changed, but it apparently had because he stopped walking and stood still. I couldn't help myself; even in my frightened state, I blatantly admired his body. He was extremely fit, not an ounce of fat anywhere on him. His hardened muscles enticed me to touch, but I didn't dare. Running my eyes slowly down the length of him, I eventually came to the most intimate part of his body. Defined lower abdominal muscles in the form of a V encouraged my gaze to sink lower. It was then I saw all of him. His cock was flaccid... and very large. But the more my gaze tickled him, the more his body reacted, his thickness hardening right in front of me.

I licked my lips, both fear and desire dueling inside. When my eyes finally made their way back up to his face, my skin prickled at the way he watched me. A curl of his lip told me he liked the way I appreciated him.

My face flushed a bright red, my embarrassment at being caught ogling him beyond devastating.

"Are you done now, or do you wanna keep lookin'?"

I had no idea what to do or even say, so the only thing that came out of my mouth was a barely audible apology. "I'm sorry."

It was as if he was waiting to banter with me, his response so quick his deep voice actually startled me. "Don't apologize, sweetheart. Look all you want. I'm your husband now, so it's your right." Pulling the covers back, he added, "Just like it's now my right to look at you."

Scrambling toward the head of the bed, I gripped the covers tighter and watched him carefully while he situated himself on top of the mattress. He never made a move to grab me or to cover his nakedness, too busy basking in my uncertainty.

The longest minute passed between us before I finally broke the silence. "Are... Are you going to...?" My ragged breaths stopped my voice altogether.

"Am I going to what?" he asked, raking his teeth over his bottom lip.

I swallowed hard, the sound piercing my ears and accelerating my panic. "Are you going to rape me?"

"Well, considering you're now my wife, isn't it your duty to give it up?" He chuckled, the sound both enticing and disarming.

"I-I... can't..." I stuttered.

Hopping off the bed, he grabbed a hunter-green T-shirt and some dark, loose-fitted jeans from his chest of drawers and quickly put them on. Pulling on his cut, he moved to the side of the bed I was lying on and leaned down so close his lips hovered above mine.

"Don't worry your pretty little head, Sully. When we finally do have sex, *you'll* be the one begging *me* for it." I balked at his audacity and the sheer madness of his statement. But I never said anything, too stunned to come back with a retort.

Walking across the room, he turned the handle on the door and pulled it open. Turning his head to the side, he gave me his parting words. "I'm gonna lock the door from the outside, but just in case you get creative in trying to escape, I always have a few men on duty walking around the compound." His voice became deeper all of a sudden. "Keeping out those we want *out*... and holding on to those we want *in*."

The last thing I saw was his back as he disappeared from the room, indeed locking me in with my own thoughts and fears.

Twenty-One

Sully

Hot breath kissed my cheek.

Fingers trailed over my collarbone, latching around my neck before I could even open my eyes.

"You little cunt! Did you not think I'd find you?" the enraged voice seethed. "And here you are, in *his* bed." His grip tightened, cutting off any chance I had of taking breath into my starved lungs. "Did you let him fuck you?" Stars flashed behind my lids. "I bet you liked it too, you whore."

He straddled the bed, his thighs pinning my arms in place so I couldn't move. Opening my eyes, I saw Vex sitting on top of me, a large, sharp blade held in his free hand. His green eyes were darker than I'd ever seen them before, his square jaw ticking in an uncontrollable rage.

I tried to shake my head, but his grip was so tight I couldn't move. I tried to struggle underneath him, but he was no match for me.

I was completely immobilized.

I couldn't breathe to scream.

I couldn't move to escape.

I was going to die without the chance to defend myself—not that it would do much good anyway.

Just when I was falling into blackness from lack of air, he took his hand away from my throat, and sat back as if he was fascinated with what he'd done. I instantly started sucking in air and coughing uncontrollably. But I didn't scream. I couldn't. My throat burned from the pressure, bile threatening to spew forth if I wasn't able to control my response soon.

While I struggled with the scene unfolding in front of me, I dared to look up at his face, and what I saw had me closing my lids a few times just to refocus.

After the third time of opening and closing my eyes, I came to rest on the image of the man above me.

It was Marek, but he spoke with Vex's voice, his tone not as deep as my captor's.

"You're going to die now, Sully," he threatened, the blade glinting off the single beam of moonlight filtering in the room.

I tried again to scream but my vocal cords were paralyzed, my own body betraying me in my desperate time of need.

It was mere seconds before the sharp tip of the blade ripped open my skin, tearing through my chest and puncturing my heart. He pushed all of his weight down on the weapon, practically slicing me in two.

When he retracted the knife, he licked my blood from the metal, smiling insanely while he prepared to stab me again.

It was then that I found my voice and I let loose like never before, wailing loud enough for anyone to hear me. I prayed someone would come and save me, but the only person who showed up was my mother. She was standing in the corner of the room, bathed in white light, her arms outstretched to welcome me. I knew in that moment that I would be taking my final breaths, my pierced heart taking its final beats. My mother had been dead for years, and she was there to usher me home.

But I wasn't ready.

I fought it. I screamed and cried and begged for him to let me go.

His arms came down on my shoulders and he started shaking me. "Sully," he called out, his voice hard and unyielding. "Sully," he said once more. "Wake up," I heard, warm breath tickling my lips while my brain tried to understand what was going on.

Flickering my eyes open, I saw Marek's face suspended above me, a look of fear and anger pouring off him in waves. Letting out one final cry, my cheek burned from the connection of his hand on my face.

He'd slapped me.

I was hysterical and wouldn't calm down, but the shock of his hit balanced me in some small way. Focusing my gaze on the man above me, realization calmed me enough to stop my screaming.

I glanced around the room to see if there was anyone else there with us, and there was. Ryder and Stone stood by the door, watching on in confusion.

"Sully... It was just a dream," Marek soothed. "You're okay now." Backing off me so I could breathe, I pulled myself up into a sitting position, tucking my knees under my chin and rocking back and forth.

"It was so real," I confessed. "You... It was... It was you trying to kill me," I said, looking at him, not even knowing what to feel right then. "But it was Vex's voice. Your face but his voice," I mumbled, trying to make sense of the dream in the dawn of realization. "My mother... She was there too. I was dying, and she was there for me." I babbled on and on about my nightmare for the next two minutes, continuing to rock back and forth until I'd finally calmed.

Marek had no idea what to say or do. He was at a loss, so he just sat on the edge of the bed. Ryder and Stone had disappeared, leaving the two of us alone to hash things out.

"I thought you left," I said, my heartbeat finally falling back into a normal rhythm.

"I was just down the hall, staying in someone else's room."

For a split second, I thought he was referring to a woman, and a pang of jealousy ripped through me. My heart momentarily picked up its pace and my fingernails dug into the skin of my palm. Having no justification for the strange emotion, I shoved it aside and focused on his face instead. The way he looked at me was strange. He seemed annoyed that I'd woken him with my screams, yet compassion danced in his eyes. Or was that pity? I was still too unfocused to tell.

He rose from the bed. "Are you all right now?" he asked, shoving his fingers through his tousled dark hair.

"Yeah. I think I just need to wash up." Looking at the clock on the bedside table, it was only then I noticed it was six in the morning. Had it not been for the bright red numbers blaring at me, I would have no idea what time of day, or night, it was.

"Good, 'cause when you're done, we're gonna eat then I'll take you to my house. You can't stay here anymore. No females camp here," was his simple explanation. He took off before I could ask him any questions. What was going to come out of my mouth, I had no idea, but he didn't even give me time to think of something. He was always disappearing after he'd had his say.

Another minute and I was calm enough to scramble to my feet and walk toward the bathroom. A thick layer of sweat glistened on my skin and my clothes stuck to me, making me uncomfortable. I knew the hot water would work miracles for not only my body but my mind as well. I longed for the calming arms of peace to rain down over me, washing away my nightmare and helping to soothe the predicament of my new life.

My fingers trailed over my skin, the smell of Marek's body wash invading my senses and making me think only of him. An ache kicked up inside me, starting in my chest and traveling lower until my clit pulsed with a need I'd never experienced before.

I was aroused.

I'd explored my own body in the past, but I'd never felt such an explosive desire toward a man before.

A stranger.

An enemy.

Marek's handsome face appeared in front of my closed eyes. I'd seen him angry. I'd seen him cocky and condescending. And I'd also seen him concerned. Worried about me.

No one had ever been worried about my well-being before.

Not my father.

Not Vex.

It was astounding that the man who'd kidnapped me from my home would be the one to show me an ounce of compassion.

I palmed between my legs, trying my best to sate the need growing inside me. As I rubbed my finger over my clit, I remembered his promise from just hours before.

When we finally do have sex, you'll *be the one begging* me *for it.*

He sounded so sure of himself, his arrogance surprisingly quite a turn-on, although I would never voice such a thought. I never knew if he was testing me, or waiting for me to mess up so he could punish me. Usually, I kept quiet, minus the few outbursts which seemed out of my control at the time.

I pictured the way he licked his lips then bit down on the

lower one while he'd stood naked in front of me. My own slickness allowed my finger to glide back and forth with ease, shooting bolts of desire through me, so pleasurable I never wanted to stop.

I recalled his large cock growing to life right before my eyes, how he seemed to love my appreciation for his glorious body, the way he remained still while I committed him to memory.

My back arched and I spread my legs, rubbing faster and faster until my body seized up. Balancing myself with one arm against the shower tile, I finished myself off, my orgasm tearing through me while I pictured the one man I shouldn't have.

My husband.

"Sully, Prez says to hurry the hell up." I was so involved with 'taking care of business' that I never even heard anyone enter the bathroom. *Oh, my God! Did he see me? Did he hear me? Was I even making any noises?* I was so wrapped up in my own head I had no idea if any sounds had escaped my lips.

I thought it was Ryder who'd scared the shit outta me, but I couldn't be sure. Shutting off the water, I slowly slid the shower door open to make sure no one was standing in the bathroom waiting for me.

The coast was clear.

I was almost done drying myself off when the door opened. I screamed out in surprise and quickly wrapped the towel around me. Marek stood in the doorway staring at me, his eyes narrowing the more he took me in.

"Why is your face all flushed?" He moved closer, the tension between us increasing with every step. "Were you playing with yourself in the shower?" His lips turned up in a sexy grin. "Were you thinkin' 'bout me?"

There was no way he could know, was there? Did he have cameras in there? My paranoia gave me away and he picked up on it. But I still tried to deny it.

"No," I whispered.

"No, you weren't playing with your pussy, or no, you weren't thinking about me?" He chuckled and moved even closer, the air suddenly extremely stifling.

"Uh... n-no... t-to both," I stammered. All I wanted was for him to leave, but then I knew once he did I'd miss his presence. He was nothing like I'd expected, and I found I craved his attention when he wasn't near me. But again, I would never let on to that because it was insane.

I should hate him.

I should cringe every time he came near me.

I should fear him.

But I didn't.

"Just say the word, Sully, and you could be riding my cock." He winked then walked from the room.

Again with the disappearing after he said shit like that.

Twenty-Two

Marek

We pulled up outside my place, a half hour away from the club, when a thought occurred to me. Pulling out my phone once Sully had slid off the back of my bike and was stretching her legs from the ride, I dialed Jagger's number.

"Hey, I need you at my place in an hour. And bring shit with you for a few days." Ending the call, I swung my leg over the bike and planted my feet on the ground, rifling through my bag to find the keys.

"Let's go," I said, ushering my wife toward the front door. *My wife. Shit!* That was still such a fucked-up concept. It'd only been a couple days, but I didn't think I would ever get used to saying it.

Out loud or in my head.

Since I'd pushed the limits already by allowing Sully to stay at the clubhouse for more than a few hours, I knew it was best to set her up in my own personal residence. My house wasn't anything fancy, but it wasn't a rundown shack either. It was a nice log cabin I had built six years back, the wraparound porch one of my favorite features. What I loved most about it was that it sat on ten acres of solidarity, not a soul in sight, which was exactly how I liked it. I hated neighbors, and the less people I had to deal with the better in my book. Outsiders were judgmental, and could be quite dangerous if their curiosity got the better of them.

Pushing open the door, I guided her inside and set my bag down on the floor, walking toward the kitchen to grab a drink. I was thirsty, and the hot summer day only exacerbated my need for cool liquid. Twisting off the cap to a bottled water, I took a few long gulps then walked back over and handed it to Sully.

She frowned and looked as if I'd just handed her a dead kitten.

"What?"

"That's gross," she huffed, pushing the bottle away from her.

"What the hell are you talking about? It's just water."

"I don't want to drink after you. Why can't I have my own?" she asked before taking a step back. My expression probably put her on alert, although I didn't know why. I wasn't upset, just merely confused.

"What's the problem?" Shoving the bottle back in front of her, I said, "Just take it."

"Germs, bodily fluids... Should I go on?" Shocked she was speaking so freely, I crossed my arms over my chest and settled in. *This should be fun.* I stared at her so intently that she blushed and stopped talking.

"No, please continue."

"That's all," she whispered before lowering her head.

"Sully. Look at me." She raised her head and looked me directly in the eyes, her tongue sneaking out and wetting her bottom lip. My dick pulsed and pushed against the seam of my pants. Her dark eyes roved over me, leaving my face briefly before lowering them to take in the rest of my body. I didn't even think she realized she was checking me out, lost in a faraway place in that beautiful head of hers.

I cleared my throat, loving the unexpected back and forth between us, visually as well as spoken.

I was going to put our little conversation to bed. "As far as bodily fluids go, my spit will be the least of your worries." Reaching out, I grabbed hold of her wrist and pulled her to me. She didn't fight, which was a good sign, but I wasn't sure if she was shocked or if she was easing up around me. Lowering my mouth to her ear, I promised, "When I fuck that sweet pussy of yours, I'm gonna leave behind a reminder that I was inside you. So much of a reminder that it's gonna be dripping down those sexy-ass thighs of yours."

I heard her gasp and it made me smile. I had no idea why, but I loved toying with her. Maybe it was the innocent way she looked at me, trying her best to hide her desire for me. Maybe it was the pleasure of having someone who was all mine. Maybe I was trying too hard to show her she was safe in my club. Well, physically safe. Not so much sexually or emotionally.

Whatever the reason, I enjoyed getting a rise out of her.

She placed her tiny hands on my chest and tried to push me away, but I held steady. When I wouldn't budge, she lowered her arms to her sides, waiting for what would happen next.

Countless seconds passed, the only sounds our ragged breaths circling around us. I inhaled her scent before releasing her, smelling her hair like some kind of animal. But it was what she made me feel like when I was this close to her. Like some kind of beast that needed to claim her, mark her with my own scent so the others would know who she belonged to.

In reality, everyone knew she was mine, so they knew to stay clear of her—that was unless they wanted to deal with the repercussions of crossing me.

"Where's the bathroom?" she asked, avoiding any and all eye contact.

"Why? Do you need to play with yourself again?" I smirked when I saw the blush creep up her neck and explode across her cheeks. I'd been teasing her back at the club about it, but now I knew I'd hit the nail on the head. Her blatant reaction told me so.

"I have to go to the bathroom. I've had to go since we left." She shuffled back and forth, and I realized she was telling the truth, or she was a pretty good liar. Pointing down the hallway, I directed her to the second door on the left.

After checking my messages and staring into the refrigerator for a whole minute, trying to decide what we could eat, a loud knock on the door pulled my attention. As I moved toward the front of the house, Sully came walking down the hallway and headed toward the couch, sitting down and clicking the TV on, but only after asking my permission

It was gonna take her some time to get adjusted to living with me, but I was patient. Well... sometimes.

Cocking the gun at my side, I slowly opened the door. Jagger was standing on the front porch, looking put-out for having to rush right over, but so be it. He was a prospect, which meant he was the lowest man on the totem pole. Therefore, he would do whatever was asked of him, whether it was doing a pick-up run, cleaning up someone else's puke or babysitting my new wife.

As soon as he saw me, he straightened and gave me a smile. "What's up, Prez?" he asked, picking up his bag and waiting for me to invite him inside.

Jagger was all of twenty-two and was the fighter in our group. He'd competed in a few low-level MMA-type fights over the past year and won every one of them. He had a mean roundhouse kick as well as a lethal right hook. He and Stone had even gone toe-to-toe a few times, my VP showing him a few moves to make him even more of a contender. With his fighting skills, I trusted him to keep Sully safe while I wasn't around.

"I need you to watch over her while I'm not here," I told him, opening the door wider so he could enter. "I have business to attend to and will be gone for a few days."

It was all the explanation he needed. He placed his bag in the corner and stood near me, waiting for instructions. He didn't want to assume he was allowed to make himself at home, but seeing as how he was going to be staying there for a bit, I instructed him to relax.

And he did.

I didn't need two people with sticks up their asses keeping each other company.

Looking at my watch, I cursed out loud after realizing I needed to take care of a few things at the club before Stone and I headed out in the morning.

I walked around the couch until I stood in front of Sully, making sure she was paying attention to me before I spoke. "I have to leave now, but Jagger is gonna watch over you and make sure you don't try anything." She looked a little dejected. "Plus, he'll keep you safe. Just don't do anything stupid and you'll be fine."

Turning toward the prospect, I jerked my head toward the front door. "Walk me out," I demanded. As soon as we were outside, I laid down my strict list of rules. "You are not to leave her side. Where she goes, you go. If she goes to the bathroom, you follow and wait outside. If she's in the living room, then so are you. You two are not to leave this house, and the only other person allowed inside, besides you two, is Adelaide. She'll be dropping off some clothes for her." Handing him a key, I continued, "I had a new lock installed on my bedroom door yesterday, one you can lock from the outside. That's where she's to sleep. Make sure to lock her in, that way you can get some rest and not have to worry about whether she's gonna escape in the middle of the night." I grabbed him by the neck and pulled him close. "Sully is now my wife, Jagger, which means she's off-limits. Keep your distance... but keep her close. You feel me?" I growled.

Quickly nodding, he knew exactly what I was saying without having to spell it out. Jagger was a good-looking kid and he pulled down a lot of tail. I just didn't want him thinkin' he could fuck with my property.

Twenty-Three

Sully

"So, how have you been getting along these past couple days?" Adelaide asked, cupping the hot mug of coffee between her hands, and blowing on the liquid before bringing it to her lips. She'd stopped by to bring me some underwear and clothes, the sizes she picked out being a perfect guess.

Eyeing me ever so precariously, I knew damn well she wasn't quite sure how I'd come to not only suddenly be part of the KC, but also ended up living in Marek's home.

I'd considered telling her the whole story about how he'd kidnapped me and taken me hostage, putting a guard on me every second of the day so there was no chance of escape, but for some reason I chose to keep my circumstances to myself. What good would it do? She was the niece to one of the club members. Even if she believed me, what was she going to do? Rat out her family for a complete stranger?

Plus, there was the tiny fact that I had nowhere to go. I was stuck and I knew it. Trying to escape and go back to the Savage

Reapers was a suicide mission. They would never take me back. In fact, they were probably ordered to shoot me on sight.

No, thank you.

I refused to suffer one more second of their hatred toward me, and I sure as shit wasn't going to allow myself to die at their hands. Not when I had a choice.

Sort of.

It was funny. I used to pray for death... before I was stolen from my life. I lived only to exist. My days were gloomy, the only bright spot when I'd gotten my hands on a secondhand romance novel one of the club whores had left behind. I think some of them felt bad for me, witnessing how downtrodden I was, watching the way Vex and my father treated me. To be pitied by women who lived to have sex with as many men as possible was utterly pathetic. But it was my life, and I envied those women. Not for being used as nothing more than a place for any man to stick his dick, but for the freedom their lives held.

I was trapped.

Suffocating and slowly dying on the inside.

Then I was rescued.

I didn't see it that way when I was forced to leave with the enemy, but since I'd been in their company, I'd come to realize just how messed up my life had been. Not once since I'd been in the Knights' compound had a single person raised a hand to hurt me. Not once did someone say something to degrade me. Not once did they look upon me with disgust or go to the total opposite end of the spectrum and ignore me.

Ignore my cries.

Ignore my broken bones and bruises.

Ignore my broken spirit.

A breath of promise had been pumped back inside me, the vigor for life slowly coming back to me.

Eyeing Adelaide cautiously, I contemplated how to answer. I wanted to be truthful with her. She'd been the closest thing to a friend I'd ever had and I didn't want to jeopardize our budding relationship, but the fact remained that she was still a stranger, and I didn't know if I could trust her.

Tempting fate, I took a deep breath and opened my mouth. "I'm okay." *So much for a big revelation or confession.* Her kind eyes prompted me to keep speaking, which I decided was necessary, needing the banter to make me feel like a human being again. "It's weird being here, tucked away in this house with someone watching over me every second." I left out the part about Jagger locking me in Marek's bedroom when I slept.

"Well, that's how these men are. From what I gather, at least. They're very protective of their women, their families," she offered, smiling before she took another sip of her coffee. Shuffling closer, she propped her chin up with her hand, tipping her lips in curiosity. "So... How long have you known Marek, and how the hell did you tame that man?" She wiggled her brows in jest, but I knew she really wanted answers.

"I've only known him for a few days." I stopped talking and bit my lip in nervousness. I dropped my head from her glance but could feel her eyes burning through me. Thankfully, she didn't push, reading my body language and realizing I didn't wish to expand on my statement. For the next hour, we conversed about clothes and movies, two topics I had limited knowledge about, so I was happy she took the lead and did most of the talking.

Looking down at her watch, she made a face of disapproval and rose from her chair, carrying her cup to the sink. "Sorry, Sully, but I have to leave. My shift at the hospital starts soon, and I don't want to be late. I can stop by tomorrow. Do you want me to bring you anything else?"

"No, thank you. You've done enough."

"Okay, well, give me your number and I'll call you before coming over, just in case you change your mind." She pulled her phone from her purse and swiped the screen, lifting her head and waiting on me to give her my information.

"I don't have a phone," I mumbled.

Jagger walked into the kitchen just then, glancing back and forth between the two of us before heading to the fridge and snagging a beer. Twisting off the top, he took a long pull, the muscles of his throat working feverishly to allow the liquid to pass. He drank half the bottle before pulling it away from his lips.

"What?" he asked, frowning at the look Adelaide gave him.

"Is there a phone here? A landline?"

"Not that I know of. Why?"

"Because I'll be coming back again tomorrow, and I wanted to call Sully to see if she needs anything." Adelaide advanced on Jagger and he backed up a step, not quite sure what her agenda was.

She was forceful when she wanted to be, and I liked her even more because of it. "Give me your cell," she demanded.

"What for?" He truly looked baffled.

"Just give it to me, Jagger. Or I'll tell my uncle you tried to kiss me," she threatened, a slight tilt to her lips as she watched his eyes widen in fright.

"Fuck that!" he shouted. Pulling his phone from his back pocket, he handed it to her, shaking his head in disbelief. "You better not tell Trigger that shit. I mean it. Or my death will be on your hands."

"Oh, calm down, pretty boy. I'm just messing with you." She punched in her information then handed him the phone back, but only after she used it to call hers first. "There, now we have each other's numbers. I'll call you tomorrow before I come over," she said, looking at me while she spoke. "You let me know if you need anything, Sully. Anything at all."

Rising from the table, I breached the short distance between us and stood in front of her, not quite sure what to do next. I was still very awkward with interactions of any sort, slowly fumbling through with each passing day.

"Thank you so much for the clothes... and for visiting with me." Tears welled in my eyes before I could lock them up. I hated appearing weak in front of people, but unlike every other time during my life when tears meant sadness and pain, my emotion was a happy one. No one had ever taken the time to ask me how I was doing, let alone bring me a gift and purposely engage me in conversation.

"Don't think twice about it," she said, suddenly pulling me in for a quick hug. Awkwardly hugging her back, her sudden gesture of affection throwing me off, I stepped back and watched her move to the door.

Turning her head, she playfully threatened Jagger. "If you don't answer your phone when I call, you'll be gettin' a visit from Trigger." She laughed as she walked out the door.

Jagger didn't find it too amusing.

Twenty-Four

Marek

Two days.

I'd left her alone for two days with one of our prospects. Jagger. A young, good-lookin' guy. A guy who looked like the boy next door, but with an edge. A guy who was probably jerking himself off every night just to the image of her.

Fuck! What the hell was I thinkin'? I should have made someone else watch over her, but my resources were limited. The other men in the club had better, more important things to take care of and couldn't be saddled with such a shit assignment. Though, they might have thought differently simply because they would have gotten the opportunity to be around her. All alone.

No matter who I picked to babysit her until I returned, I would have driven myself half-insane, so I guessed it didn't really matter.

Hitting the button on my phone, I frustratingly waited for the call to connect. *At least this will ease my mind for the time being*. "Hello," Jagger answered on the third ring, seemingly out of breath for someone who had the easiest job in the world.

"What are you doing?" My tone was downright accusatory and he knew it as soon as he heard the growl in my voice.

"Nothing, Prez. Just helping Adelaide with some of the groceries."

"What? Why is Adelaide there with food? I left the fridge and cupboards fully stocked." Running my hands through my hair, I flicked a glare at Stone, but he was too busy focusing on the name I'd mentioned. He was practically hovering over me and trying to listen to my conversation simply because he heard *his* woman's name.

Well, according to his prior reactions, Adelaide was his woman. But if Trigger ever found out something was going on between them, I'd be looking for a new VP.

"She's stopped by a few times, telling me she wanted to cook dinner for Sully, seeing as how she's still adjusting to being here." I heard the hesitation in his voice and instant jealousy raged deep within me, tearing through my throat and out of my mouth before I could filter my words.

"If I find out you touched one hair on her goddamn head, prospect, I'm going to tear you apart," I seethed. "Do you understand me?" Stone backed away as soon as he saw the volatile look on my face. *Smart move.*

"No! I haven't done any-anything," he stammered, but his quivering voice told another story. I wasn't sure what, but something was going on, and I couldn't wait until I was back home and could keep an eye on her myself.

Why I cared at all was probably the thing which was pissing me off the most. Never before had any woman affected me, twisting me up inside until I questioned my motives, thoughts and... dare I say feelings?

"Let me talk to her," I commanded. "Now!"

Hearing my heartbeat in my ears, I tried to take a few calming breaths, realizing I was more than likely blowing things out of proportion. But my mind only sped up my body's reactions, a small bead of sweat breaking out on my forehead, my heart beating even quicker inside my chest.

"H-hello." A soft voice sounded over the phone, and I'd instantly regretted leaving her. *What the hell is happening to me?*

Instead of asking her how she was, making sure she was settling in okay, what did I do? I freaked out on her and accused her of something I was almost positive was false.

"What the hell are you doing with Jagger? You lettin' him fuck you, Sully? Don't think for one second that I won't punish you both for going behind my motherfucking back! You think just because I'm not there I wouldn't find out? Huh?" I couldn't help myself. I kept going and going and when I was finally done, silence screamed in my ear. Tiny pants of breath came through the phone and made me even more infuriated.

Did her silence mean I'd hit the nail on the head? Or had I just scared the shit out of her for no reason?

Before I could start in on her again, another voice ripped through the line, her voice hysterical while her words crashed together as she spoke.

"What did you just say to her?" she cried, unease nestling deep in the timbre of her voice.

"None of your business, Adelaide. Now, put Sully back on the phone," I grated. I looked to my right and Stone was already headed my way, no doubt hearing her name fall from my lips again. I glared at him and he stopped mid-stride. "Don't even think about it," I threw at him.

"Then don't talk to her like that," he said, bracing himself for a fight.

"Mind your own goddamn business, Stone. I mean it," I

warned, moving the phone away from my mouth while I continued to speak to him. "Just because I'm talking to your woman doesn't mean it has anything to do with you. Back off. I mean it."

Placing my cell back into position, I was ready to start arguing again when Adelaide's shrill voice barreled into my ear. "I'm not his woman, Marek! Don't start that rumor or else something bad is going to happen!"

"What's she sayin'?" Stone asked, forgetting himself and walking toward me again.

She was screaming in my ear while Stone continued to talk to me, the back-and-forth noise sending me off the deep end.

To hell with this!

"Give me your phone," I told my VP. When he looked confused, I hurried him along. "Give. Me. Your. Phone." Tossing me his cell, I made an even exchange, giving him the one with Adelaide ranting and raving on the other end.

Scrolling through his contact list, I found Adelaide's number, hitting the Call button while I shook my head. There was no reason whatsoever for him to have her number saved in his phone, unless they were fuckin' around. Her digits were another nail in his coffin if her uncle found out. But that was between the three of them. I had other shit I had to deal with.

I heard a brief silence from the other room, Stone's voice quieting long enough for Adelaide to answer her own phone.

"Hello?" she greeted, confusion evident in her voice.

"Where is she?" I grated. I swore if I were there in the room with her, I would have seen the disapproval written all over her face.

Another bout of silence passed before I heard her shift her phone to Sully.

"Hello?" I knew she had the cell pressed to her ear because I could hear her breathing. I hadn't meant to go off on her like that before, but my building jealousy had gotten the better of me, hurling unfounded accusations at her before I could reason with myself enough to calm down.

"I'm not doing anything wrong," she squeaked. I heard the tears in her voice and they instantly tore me apart. "I promise. He barely talks to me."

I believed her. It took me exploding, her fear, and then the sincerity in her voice to calm me down and realize I'd overreacted. I would never admit it, though. Not to anyone.

I never apologized.

Ever.

Choosing to ignore her words, I switched topics. "I'll be longer than I thought." I sighed, running my fingers over my face in utter frustration. "I'll call you in a couple more days and let you know." Stone came strolling out from the other room, a pissed-off look on his face, one I knew wasn't because of me, but instead because of the person he'd been talking to. Or the one who'd been shouting at him, to be more accurate.

"Okay. Did... Did you want to talk to Jagger again?"

"Yes." *Short and sweet.*

"I swear, Prez, I'm not doing nuthin' to her. I'm just watchin' over her like you told me to do," he started in, his words coming so fast I almost didn't understand him.

"Calm down. We'll be gone longer than anticipated. I'll call you soon when I know exactly when. And Jagger?" I waited for his acknowledgment. "Don't make me regret my decision to leave you at the house."

"You won't. I promise."

I hung up before he could say anything else.

I'd been staring down at the phone and hadn't realized Stone was scowling at me from across the room. I was too consumed with all the new feelings eating at me to pay much attention to anything else. Wrapped up in not only the image of

Sully, but in what I'd just done to her, I clenched my jaw and fisted my hands. I was pissed at myself, but what was done was done.

"What was all that, Marek? Have you gone off the deep end?" My VP's voice startled me, and when I finally picked my head up to look at him, I saw true concern etched deep into every line of his face.

I was normally a pretty laid-back guy. Well... as laid-back as I could be running an entire MC. I wasn't known for blowing up at the drop of a hat, or acting irrational for no reason at all.

I wasn't sure if it was that Sully distracted me from my main goal, which was to remain unattached and focused solely on the club. Or if it was because she now belonged to me and another man being in her company, all alone, wasn't sitting right with me. Even if they weren't doing anything wrong.

But I'd been the one to make the decision to have Jagger watch over her in my absence, so I had to deal with the consequences. Like it or not.

"Nothin'," I promised. "All good." I thought if I tried to smile right then, he might've had me committed. Instead, I switched the subject. "Where we at with meeting with Carrillo?"

"I was gonna tell you before you went nuclear a few minutes ago, but he isn't coming. Some shit about too much heat and not being able to get away. Instead, he's sending his second in command, Yanez. He said we could finish things through him."

Rico Yanez was a lecherous man. No morals of any kind. Almost worse than the Reapers. Almost. I didn't like or trust him, but if he was who we had to deal with then so be it. The quicker we came to an agreement, the better.

Shrugging, Stone leaned against the wall opposite me. Tired and weary, the past couple days' events looked to have taken a toll on my dear friend. He had something going on with Adelaide, no matter how much he denied it. Then there was the added dangerous element of finalizing our end with Los Zappas cartel. Even though the head honcho, Rafael Carrillo, had given me his word he would release the KC from smuggling in and selling their product, there was always the chance he would go back on it, although I seriously doubted it.

He was a man who hated to be indebted to another, and it was exactly what he was to me. Not that I held it over him or anything, but I would use the opportunity to get what I needed, exploit the fact that I'd saved his life.

On a drug run last year, we were intercepted by a rival cartel. Gunfire thickened the air around us and we scarcely made it out alive. Rafael's men ran for cover, and he found himself without shelter. The look in his eyes reflected that he was prepared to die, although there was still hope underneath he would make it home to his wife and three kids that night.

I knew if I wanted to extract my club entirely from their grips, I had to make my move.

Save him from meeting his maker too soon.

If I knew anything about the man who hovered between life and death, it was his undying need to not owe anyone anything, and my saving his life would prompt him to do something in return.

My gesture paid off. In exchange for saving him, he agreed to let my club walk away, but only after they'd found another one to take our place. He'd also agreed to cut all ties with the Savage Reapers, crippling them and cutting their legs out from beneath them.

But still, nothing was guaranteed until I heard the head of Los Zappas cartel tell me we were no longer in business with them.

"Well, when are we meetin' him then?"

"Tomorrow," he answered, walking toward the door and circling the handle with his fingers. "But tonight, we relax and have a good time. Right?" he shouted over his shoulder, pulling the door open and heading toward the common room.

We were staying at our Laredo charter. The guys there were most accommodating, pulling together a last-minute ruckus. Not that it was a problem by any means—any chance to overindulge in alcohol and pussy was certainly a most welcome event.

Later that evening, when I'd buried myself inside some woman whose name I never asked, I tried my best to push aside all thoughts of the woman waiting for me back home.

But it was useless.

With every thrust and moan, I imagined it was *her* I had pushed against the wall, my hand wrapped around *her* throat while I fucked *her* from behind. I envisioned it was *her* pussy clenching down on my cock as she rode out her orgasm.

Sully was the woman I pictured writhing in front of me, and it was the only thought in the past few days which helped soothe the rising inferno inside me.

Twenty-Five

Sully

Still trembling from Marek's accusations, I excused myself from the room, quietly disappearing inside the bedroom I'd been staying in.

His bedroom.

Everywhere I looked, I was reminded of the man who'd forced me to marry him. His clothes hung in the closet, no order to the wardrobe whatsoever. His shoes littered the floor of the small space, strewn about as if he'd literally kicked them off his feet and left them wherever they fell. Crumpled receipts, along with a few watches and old Harley magazines covered the top of his dresser. Dirty laundry was piled up in the corner of his bathroom, even though an actual hamper stood right next to them. His beard trimmer, razors, and brushes littered the top of the small sink, and it was all I could do to take a deep breath and breathe through my anxiety.

Because of the way I preferred things, I began to tidy his room. All the clutter and mess didn't sit well with me. I tried to ignore it my first two nights, but since he'd told me he wouldn't be back anytime soon, there was no way I could continue to stay in a room so out of sorts.

A tidy room made me feel as if I had control over some aspect of my life. It gave me a sense of solace, no matter how false it may have been.

I didn't want to, but I couldn't help remembering our phone conversation, word for word. Every accusation he'd flung at me tore away a little bit more of my soul. I didn't trust the man, but he'd given me a sense of safety I'd never had before, only to rip it away with every word he spewed down the line. *What the hell are you doing with Jagger? You lettin' him fuck you, Sully? Don't think for one second that I won't punish you both for going behind my motherfucking back! You think just because I'm not there I wouldn't find out? Huh?*

I should have expected he was going to show his true colors sooner or later—apparently, it had been sooner. I was a fool to think he was any better than Vex or my father, but the way he'd looked at me, the way he'd tried to comfort me when I'd woken up screaming from my nightmares... It was all a façade.

Actually, he was worse than the men in my life because at least with them, I knew what I was in for. I knew exactly what they would do and say. But with Marek, I simply had no idea.

Finishing up the mess in the closet, I closed the door to the small space and headed toward the bathroom, but a soft rap on the bedroom door stopped me in my tracks.

"Sully," Adelaide called out. "Are you okay? Can I come in?"

I never answered, instead pulling the door open and giving her a faltering smile. I couldn't hide the hurt from my face or from my voice, even though I tried. The last thing I wanted to do was bring her into the mix of what was going on. I had no idea if she would be punished simply for interfering.

Crossing the room to sit on the edge of the bed, she leaned

back on her hands and gazed at me, waiting to see if I would speak first. But I let her take the lead, as I did with most people.

"I'm so sorry for what he said to you, Sully." Her eyes pitied me, and I hated that she felt that way toward me. "Marek is usually pretty easygoing, all things considered. I'm not sure what's up his ass, but please don't take it personally," she pleaded.

"How do you know what he said to me?" I wasn't used to people interfering on my behalf or conversing with me about things which happened to me. My tone was more curt than I'd intended, but I didn't think she took any offense to it.

"I got the gist of it when I threatened Jagger."

"With your uncle again?" A small smile curved my mouth, mimicking her reaction.

"You know it. I can use that man as a threat any time I want to get my way." She laughed, pushing her hair behind her shoulder, continuing to hold my gaze until she knew I was okay.

"Don't pay him any mind. Seriously. Don't worry about it." Situating herself so she was sitting with her legs tucked underneath her, she continued to try and persuade me to talk. "What did he say when he called you on my phone?"

Playing with my hands in nervousness, I stood in front of her, not quite sure what I was allowed to reveal about my conversations with him, no matter how insignificant. I'd never had anyone to confide in before, and although it was an amazing feeling, it was also a bit frightening. I still wasn't quite sure who I could trust yet.

Patting the bed beside her, she widened her smile and put me at ease. Climbing next to her, I mirrored her and tucked my own legs under me, resting my hands on my thighs while I spoke. "He just told me he was going to be longer than expected and would call me in a couple days."

"Yeah, Stone told me that too."

Before I could filter myself, I blurted, "Are you and Stone together?"

Her eyes widened, her words suddenly caught in her throat. She appeared to be hiding something and wasn't sure if she should tell me the truth, probably not trusting me completely, much like I acted toward her.

But something inside her forced her to give me tidbits of information. "Can you keep a secret? And I mean from everyone, even Marek?" She looked pensive, but because I so wanted to know a private detail of someone else's life, I readily agreed. And meant every nod.

"Yes, I promise."

"We're not *together* together, but we've fooled around before. And, even though I really like him, we can't be together." Her expression turned, her sudden unhappiness pressing her lips into a frown while casting its veil over her eyes.

My intrigue forced me closer, all while continuing to give her the personal space she needed. "Why not?"

"It's complicated really." She hesitated for a brief moment before continuing. "I'm not part of your... their lifestyle, nor do I want to be. I love my uncle dearly, but I never wanted to grow up around what they do, how they ultimately handle themselves and their lives. And he didn't want that for me either. I'm more than happy to come by and help out when I can, like with Tripp, but other than that, I don't really want to be associated with the club. And Stone knows that." She looked dejected, as if she was reminded of a specific conversation she'd had with him.

"Would he ever leave the club? For you?" I knew I sounded like a twit, fantasizing and romanticizing her and Stone's complicated relationship, but I couldn't help myself. I'd read my share of romance novels and in those books, the main characters always found a way to work it out, their love conquering everything and all that happy stuff.

Looking at me as if I'd lost my mind, she shook her head and crushed my idiotic thoughts. "He grew up in this club, just like most of the men. He loves the KC, the men are his family. He'll never leave them for me, and I don't think I even want him to. He'd resent me if I made him make that choice." Throwing her head back so she was looking at the ceiling, she continued telling me her innermost secrets as she relaxed in my presence. "He keeps calling me, showing up at the hospital and begging me to be with him. Some days, I think I can be with him fully, give him what he wants... what *I* want, but then shit happens, like with Tripp, and I put that wall back up to protect myself. It kills me when I look at him, knowing he'll never truly be mine."

I was surprised when a lone tear streaked down her cheek, her thumb quickly brushing it away before her emotions became too much for her. She smiled lazily and straightened up on the bed. "Don't mind me, Sully. I think I'm getting my period." She laughed, the air of seriousness suddenly disappearing.

"Well, I think if you really want to be together, you'll find a way which will suit both of you. But from what I hear, your uncle won't be too pleased." I'd witnessed an encounter between Trigger and Stone, and even I was scared of the older man.

"Yeah, there's that too," she grimaced.

We finished our conversation and were about to move off the bed when Jagger came crashing into the room, stumbling over his feet and instantly putting us on alert. His dark golden hair stuck up in a few spots, his amber eyes wide in fright while he gave us time to collect ourselves.

"What the hell, Jagger? Where's the fire?" Adelaide threw at him.

"Funny you should ask," he rushed. "It's downstairs." If what had come out of his mouth hadn't been so serious, I would have laughed at the frenzied look on his face.

"Oh, shit!" she exclaimed. "My food." Scrambling off the bed, we all ran downstairs to assess the damage. Luckily, it was only smoke, but whatever Adelaide had been making was burnt to a crisp.

"Looks like pizza it is," Jagger announced, the two of them busting out into laughter while I stifled my amusement as best I could, a tiny sound escaping my lips to add to the surprise of the free-falling emotions.

Twenty-Six

Marek

"Are you sure this will be our last shipment," Stone asked, nervously shoving his messy hair off his face. The guy was pacing, mumbling to himself and making me tense just watching him.

"Yeah, Rafael gave me his word that after this next pickup, he's shifting his supply to the club in Vegas he's slowly been using, testing them for the past year to ensure they're the right fit." I was as nervous as my VP, but I played my concerns off as mere agitation, trying like hell to calm the air around us.

Stopping mid-stride, he hit me with yet another question. "Why do you really think he sent that asshole to meet with us then, instead of coming himself?"

"Not sure. I guess we'll find out soon enough." Rico Yanez called five minutes ago to let us know he would be arriving shortly. Normally, we didn't have meetings with anyone from Los Zappas cartel on club grounds, but there was too much heat on them nowadays to be seen out in public places meeting with the likes of two bikers. The three of us together would look way too suspicious. After making sure he wasn't being tailed, he'd arrive at the compound and disappear between the concealing metal gates.

Leaning forward with my arms resting on my thighs, a small bead of sweat gathered on my brow. The meeting Stone and I were about to have was of the utmost importance, our futures being decided in the next half hour.

Were we still gonna be in bed with the cartel, unwillingly going along with constantly risking not only prison, but death as well?

Or were we finally gonna be able to breathe the fresh air of legitimacy for the first time in over six decades? Having been on the wrong side of the law for at least that long.

We realized that, if we were indeed free after this last run, there would be initial blowback from our enemy. But once some time had passed and they were no longer strong enough to be a threat, we could start to really enjoy our lives.

Shit, I didn't even know what that would feel like.

A loud rapping on the Chambers door tore both Stone and me from our anxiousness. "He's here, Marek!" Salzer yelled from the hallway. He was one of the original members of the Laredo charter, old as hell with a mean streak to boot. If someone found themselves on his shit list, look out. His physical appearance was deceiving. A full head of white hair, a clean-shaven face and a dimple in his left cheek made him seem like someone's sweet old grandpa, though he was anything but. Most overlooked his temper because he was loyal as hell, willing to take a bullet for any one of his fellow brothers, home and charters alike. It didn't matter. And no one could ask for better than that.

My VP and I walked out toward the front entrance of the clubhouse just as Yanez and another man were ushered inside. It didn't surprise me one bit that he'd brought someone along with him, since I probably would have done the same thing had the roles been reversed. In our world, you couldn't trust a lot of people, especially virtual strangers.

A quick jerk of my head and the two men from Los Zappas followed us to a back room. The only people allowed to enter Chambers were actual club members, and although what we were going to discuss was technically club business, there was no way in Hell the likes of the cartel were going to be allowed inside those doors. Sacred shit and all that.

After we were all seated, I wasted no time in getting down to business. "So," I started. "I was hoping to meet with Carrillo face to face, but he assured me I could finalize through you." I eyed Yanez cautiously, his dark, beady eyes assessing me right back. His gaze flicked from me to Stone, and back to me again. I had no idea what he was expecting to happen, other than confirming the last run the Knights Corruption would make for Los Zappas.

"Pretend I'm him," he grumbled, obvious jealousy in his voice. The man was shit at hiding emotions, and I was sure right then that it was going to prove fatal for him in some future circumstance. I prided myself on reading people, and the man sitting across from me was a dangerous, soulless scum of the earth. Thankfully, it was probably the last time I'd ever have to lay eyes on him.

"Anyway," Stone interrupted, pulling Yanez's focus. "The final shipment for us is coming through in five days. We'll have guys there to pick it up and transport it across state lines, with the final payment meeting to be arranged in the next week."

The man who accompanied Yanez finally spoke up, his accent quite thick. While I had a hard time making out what he said, I understood three key components. Carrillo. Meet. Money. What the hell else was there to know?

Seeing we both struggled with his words, Yanez felt

inclined to clarify what his man had just said. His thin lips parted, his lizard-like tongue sneaking out and wetting his bottom lip.

"Carrillo will get in touch with you to set up the final meet." No more words were exchanged as both Los Zappas men rose from their seats and headed toward the door.

Well, I guess that's the end of our meeting.

Twenty-Seven

Sully

"No, no... NO!" he yelled. "Don't go in there!" The noise from the movie did nothing to drown out the worry in Jagger's voice. He was all caught up in the film, and while I'd been scared throughout the majority of it, witnessing his reaction did something to calm me. Seeing another respond so fiercely almost lightened the darkness of the movie for me. Almost.

It'd been five days since Marek had dropped me off at his house, and with a babysitter no less. And since there wasn't much to do, we'd taken to watching DVDs to help pass the time.

While I remained quiet around the prospect, he'd opened up rather quickly, although something nudged at me that it was simply his personality. He'd become borderline jovial over the passing days, and I soon realized people could discover a lot about one another in less than a week if they spent every waking moment of their time with them.

Now I, on the other hand, was a tightly sealed box of secrets. I gave him short and simple answers when he tried to politely interrogate me. Anyone trying to extract personal information was someone to be wary of. It was how I was raised, what was ingrained in my head over the years. But Jagger was slowly tearing away that notion, his simple curiosity making me start to rethink everything I'd ever been told. To a certain degree, of course.

A loud, crackling noise burst forth from the speakers of the television, so loud I literally jumped in my seat and practically ended up wrapping myself around Jagger. His body instantly tensed, the muscles of his arms rigid against my touch. I hadn't meant to react in such a way, but the damn movie he'd picked out was the newest horror movie. And it scared the hell out of me.

I'd quickly come to discover scary movies were not my thing. My life was enough of a fear-fest; I didn't need to watch that shit for entertainment. With my fingers splayed over my face, I was able to block out at least one of the senses, allowing me to continue with the movie.

"Is this too much for you, Sully?" Jagger asked, genuine concern in his voice. He had no idea what my life was like before Marek swooped into our clubhouse and kidnapped me.

Saved me.

The only information he knew was probably what he'd heard about the Savage Reapers, but why would any reasonable human being believe they would treat one of their own so badly? They wouldn't, so I kept it a secret. Only my new husband knew of such things, the evidence splayed all over my fragile stature.

"I'm okay," I answered. No sooner had I spoken than the sound of a chainsaw erupted on the screen, throwing me into yet another spasm of fear. He knew I'd obviously lied, and being the kind person I was learning he was, he reached across me and searched for the remote.

The warmth of his toned body helped to relax me, but stir me up as well, in a different way. A way I refused to acknowledge. While Jagger was extremely good-looking, and had a body to drool over—which I'd encountered when he'd walked into the kitchen in nothing but a towel—he didn't affect me like Marek did.

It just wasn't the same.

Any girl with a pair of eyes would be drawn to the prospect. His dark golden hair was a little longer on top than the sides, a style he kept pushed off his face at all times. Amber eyes looked back at me with growing friendship, his pupils dilating whenever he became excited about a specific topic, movies and music being the main two.

While I could admit I was attracted to the guy who'd become my shadow, he wasn't the man who consumed my thoughts day in and day out. I'd become somewhat comfortable enough with Jagger to actually enjoy his company with each passing day, and while I remained closed off about my life, my dreams were certainly up for discussion. Never having anyone to banter back and forth with before—besides the few interactions with Adelaide, of course—was something I never even knew I missed.

"That's okay," he reassured, clicking off the movie and choosing a home renovation show instead. "I can see horror movies aren't your favorite. How about a romantic comedy? Chicks love that shit, right?" He chuckled, staring at me as if he'd hit the nail on the head.

"I guess so, although I haven't seen many of them myself." I'd since moved back over to my side of the couch, embarrassed I'd basically ended up in his lap to begin with.

I watched intently as he rose from the couch and rummaged through the box of movies Adelaide had dropped off the other day, searching for something he thought I might like.

To anyone else, it was a simple gesture, nothing to even think twice about. A normal everyday occurrence. But to me, it was huge. His actions spoke volumes, and my lips turned up at the thought that we were quickly becoming friends. His concern for me was touching.

Shaking a movie in front of me, he smiled wide as he opened the case. A strand of his hair fell forward and covered his left eye, and in the moment he reminded me of someone younger, someone innocent and not a part of the evil ways of the world yet. He was only two years older than me, all of twenty-two, but I knew he'd seen things most people would never witness their entire lives. Much like me.

When his eyes reconnected with mine, I saw something new, an emotion I couldn't quite pinpoint. Gone was the playfulness he'd displayed seconds before. His beautiful eyes quickly assessed me in a way he'd never done previously. Not while I'd been looking at him, at least. How he gazed at me when I wasn't paying attention, I couldn't say.

My breath lodged in my throat while I wondered what he was going to do or say next, the moment freezing us both in time, promising to shatter the second either one of us found our opportunity.

During my short life, I'd only been looked at as a means to an end, for some man to use and abuse as he saw fit. Never before had anyone stared at me in utter fascination. It was quite overwhelming and while I preferred it to being stared at like a piece of meat, my inner voice warned me to be careful. Of Jagger and of myself.

As if realizing he was staring a little too intently, he brushed his hair off his forehead, gave me a nervous laugh and turned around so his back was to me. I didn't want to do it, but I couldn't help but stare at his backside. His dark-washed jeans were baggy and hung low on his hips, but they did nothing to detract from the firm muscles of his ass I knew existed just beneath the fabric.

While I was learning to trust Jagger not to hurt me, I was now aware he desired me. And if I knew anything, I knew it was a very bad thing. For both of us. Even though I didn't return his affections, if Marek ever suspected his prospect harbored such feelings for his new wife, he'd probably kill him before confirming his suspicions.

Jagger sat down on the couch next to me, exactly where he was before getting up to change the movie, but for some reason it suddenly made me nervous. He wasn't doing anything differently, but because the air between us had changed, his close proximity shifted things between us.

Everything was unspoken, yet it lingered in the air just the same.

"Ready?" he asked, looking at me expectedly. His sharp jawline was clean-shaven, unlike most of his brothers. Beards were a common theme among the members, although each one varied in length.

"How did you get your road name, Jagger?" I asked, the question coming out of nowhere. I'd meant to simply nod when he asked if I was ready to watch the movie he'd picked out, but apparently my brain wanted to know more about the man who'd been put in charge of watching me in my husband's absence. Plus, I wanted to erase the tension-filled moment we'd just shared.

His expression shifted back to casual, his features softening while he leaned back on the couch.

"Well," he started. "Ryder and me got to talkin' about music one day and I mentioned how I loved the Stones. Long story short, he ended up nicknaming me Jagger." I had no idea who he was talking about. It was written all over my face, so he graciously elaborated. "Mick Jagger. He's the lead singer of the

Rolling Stones. Only the best band in the world." He chuckled, turning his body fully toward me, his arm resting on the back of the couch. His fingertips accidentally brushed over my shoulder, and when I jerked involuntarily, he apologized with his eyes and righted himself so he was facing forward again. "I'll play you some of their music someday, if you want," he offered.

"I'd like that," I said truthfully. My life had been so sheltered I jumped at the opportunity to learn something new.

"Great. Now, what do you say we watch this movie?" He never waited for me to respond before he hit the Play button.

Twenty-Eight

Marek

I loved my bike and reveled in the feel of the open road, but two days of continuous riding took its toll on me. Stone and I should have taken one of our trucks to Laredo, but like the dumbasses we were, we decided to ride instead, figuring the weather was nice enough to enjoy the trip. While the temperature had been favorable for the journey, my legs and arms were sore and my fucking balls ached. All I wanted to do was get home and take a long, hot shower. Preferably with some company.

I'd been successful in not thinking about Sully for the past hour, but there she was again, popping up in my head, knowing I'd missed her image. What could I say? My new wife was stunning, and the simple fact that she was now all mine made her even more enticing. I was fully aware of the way she watched me, especially when she thought I wasn't paying attention, her beautiful brown eyes roving all over my body. The funny part was she thought she was being inconspicuous. There were a few times when I'd been tempted to drag her to my bedroom so

I could return the favor. But I never did, fearing if I pushed her too fast, she would shut down completely.

And the simple fact that I even cared about such things was quite irritating.

Stone and I waved to each other as we parted ways at the intersection, which was twenty minutes from the clubhouse. I went right and he went left. We were both headed home after a very long trip, which couldn't end soon enough.

When I'd finally made the turn toward my house, my tires kicking up the gravel of my driveway, I exhaled a long breath and smiled at the sight of my simple and welcoming home.

It was late, too late for anyone to still be awake, so I made sure to be as quiet as I could while unlocking the door and stepping inside. I soon came to realize there was no need for my thoughtful consideration when I saw the prospect and my wife cuddled together on my couch. Sleeping.

Slamming the door so hard I thought I broke a window, I cursed out loud in case the sudden noise hadn't been enough of a disturbance to wake them up.

Jagger was the first to stir, his eyes fluttering open before he realized who was standing ten feet away from him. At first, he looked calm, but as soon as he glanced to his left and noticed Sully's head resting on his shoulder, her legs tucked underneath her, his expression turned from serene to pure panic.

He jumped up so fast his sudden absence from Sully made her fall onto the cushion, her shoulder hitting the couch before she woke up. The nightshirt she wore barely covered her, riding up her thighs while she scrambled around on the couch.

"Jagger, what's the matter?" she groaned. The way she said his name made my blood boil, and it took everything in me not to shove my gun in his goddamn mouth.

Turning all of my focus back on the guy I wasn't sure if I was gonna kill yet, I clenched my jaw hard enough to keep me from freaking out. I opened my mouth to speak, but before a single word slipped out, he spoke so quickly he tripped over his words.

"Prez, w-we weren't doing n-nuthin'. I swear," he stammered. "We ju-just fell asleep watchin' a m-movie." All the color drained from his face, so much so it made me think he was actually guilty of something. Something that would get his life snatched from him. In other words, something that would cause me to put a bullet between his eyes. Before tonight, I'd actually liked Jagger.

Not anymore.

Sully had finally come around, her eyes wide and round as she sleepily rose to her feet. Taking a few precious steps toward me, she stopped suddenly when she saw the look of rage on my face. My nostrils flared from the sharp intake of air, my pulse kicking up a notch while I glared at the both of them. I was sure I probably looked like the Devil himself in the soft glow of the corner light.

"Marek," she whispered. "Jagger's tellin' the truth. We must have fallen asleep watching a movie." Her worried eyes pinned me. "I'm sorry. It won't happen again."

"Did you fuck him?" I seethed.

"No!" she gasped. "We're just friends." Her head tilted down, her eyes staring at the ground as her long black hair covered half her face from me.

"Friends?" I sarcastically laughed, a sound that drew her attention immediately. Her eyes locked on mine again while I continued to mock her comment. "You think Jagger's your friend, sweetheart? No," I said, stepping away from the prospect and toward the one woman I couldn't stop thinking about. "He's not your fucking friend. He just wants to get into your pants. Don't let him fool you."

"No, he doesn't," she countered, fear and worry still dancing behind her dark brown eyes.

"Shut the hell up, Sully!" I yelled, running my hand through my hair in utter frustration. Too much shit was swimming around inside my head, and it was taking everything in me not to beat both their asses.

"Prez," he pleaded. "That's not true. I swear, we—"

I cut him off before he could finish his lame-ass argument. "Get outta here, Jagger, before you end up eatin' my gun."

Instead of hightailing it out of my house, however, he made a move which proved my goddamn point. He walked past me and stood in front of my wife, his stance protective, instantly giving everything away. *This fucker has feelings for her.*

"You're not gonna' do anything to her, are you?" His tone quivered, although he tried his hardest to appear strong and calculating. For some reason, I had the urge to assure him no harm would befall Sully, but as soon as I saw her hand touch his shoulder, I lost it. Gone was any shred of control I'd been holding on to. Gone was any sense of logic I had when first walking through the front door. Gone was the rationale to not overreact to a situation which was most likely innocent. Just like they both claimed.

Before I knew what was happening, I rushed forward and snatched Jagger by the throat, squeezing tightly before throwing him to the ground. His body hit the floor with a loud thud, his head smacking off the side of the table on his way down. His fingers rubbed at the side of his skull, covered in blood when he pulled them away. A grimace covered his face and in that moment, I knew I'd lost all control.

Not from realizing I'd hurt him, but for what I was about to do next.

Twenty-Nine

Sully

My breath stuck in my throat while I waited to see what Marek was going to do next. Jagger and I hadn't been doing anything wrong, except for falling asleep after a very long day. I didn't even know Marek was due back that night, otherwise, I would have made sure not to be so comfortable around the prospect.

He and I were quickly becoming friends, something which was still a very new concept to me. Especially with a man. I found I was still reserved around him, but I allowed myself to laugh when he did or said something funny. I craved the genuineness he offered me, and now everything was being destroyed because I'd gone and fallen asleep next to him, laying my head on his shoulder while I rested. It was all my fault, and Jagger was going to pay the price for it.

And I would probably be next.

Marek reached down and grabbed him by the throat again, picking him up in one fluid motion and slamming him against the wall. The picture hanging above them fell to the ground, the frame splintering in two at their feet.

"Don't you ever question me again about my wife, *prospect*," Marek yelled. "You hear me?" He pulled Jagger toward his body before slamming him against the wall once again. "The only reason I don't kill you right now is because I don't feel like cleanin' up the mess. If you so much as look at Sully again, I won't think twice about snatching your life, though." He pulled him close. "Do you understand me?"

"Yes," Jagger croaked, his president's hand still wrapped tightly around his throat. When Marek finally released him, Jagger quickly walked toward the door, grabbing his keys from the side table. He disappeared from the house and true to his word, his eyes never once fell on me before he left.

My heartbeat picked up pace inside my chest. Fear shrouded me. I had no idea what Marek was capable of, especially in a state of rage, never mind that I was the only one left to deal with his rantings.

On top of being genuinely afraid, I was also sad because one of the few people I would have liked to call a friend was no longer allowed near me. Would he prohibit Adelaide from speaking to me as well?

It seemed as if he was going to make me revert back to the introvert I'd been my entire life. The small taste of freedom and budding friendships were glorious, but I guessed it was too good to be true.

Marek's back was to me, but I could tell by his posture he was struggling with not freaking out on me right then. He kept running his hands through his disheveled dark hair, his broad shoulders rising and falling in quick succession. Appearing as if he were trying to calm down, I relaxed a fraction.

Until he turned around.

And strode forward, every step toward me completely frightening.

Before I could step back, he reached forward and pulled

me to him, his warm breath hitting my lips he was so damn close. When I dared to look up at him, his eyes held mine for a brief moment, something passing between us that neither of us understood.

Then he broke the connection.

"Did you fuck him, Sully?" he grated, his hold on my arms intensifying while he waited for my answer.

"No, we didn't do anything wrong. I swear it." I all but mumbled the last few words, the closeness we shared very confusing. I was scared of him, yet I hadn't realized I missed his hands on me until I'd felt them again. Even in his anger.

His silence threw me into another inner struggle. *Does he believe me? Is he going to punish me even if he realizes I'm telling him the truth?*

Without another word, he reached for my wrist and dragged me toward his bedroom. The only resistance I gave him was a slight tug of my arm, a gesture he completely ignored. Once inside his room, I glanced around the area where I'd laid my head since he'd left, suddenly missing the solace I'd been able to create for myself.

Releasing my arm, he looked around his room, incredulous eyes giving away what he was seeing. "Did you clean my room?" he barked, walking away to look in his closet, then in his bathroom. When he came back inside the bedroom, he shrugged off his cut and threw it over the back of the chair in the corner.

Why I would clean the area I spent the majority of my time in was surprising, I had no idea. But then again, he was a man, and in my short twenty years of life, I'd never known a man to clean up after himself.

"Yes," I answered, unsure if touching his things was going to push him over the edge or not. I stood near the door while he continued to look around, watching his every move and preparing myself for anything. While my body remained still, my eyes followed him everywhere, focusing on the stretch of his black T-shirt when he bent over to inspect underneath the bed. Although I wasn't quite sure why he was looking under there, I didn't ask; I remained silent, waiting to take my direction from him. His muscles strained against the fitted material, his multiple tattoos twirling around the thickness of his arms, beckoning me to... what? Feel them? Long for them to wrap around me and hold me close? The notion was ridiculous and I knew it, shaking my head to try and rid myself of the crazy thoughts.

"You didn't have to do that," he calmly said, advancing on me now that his curiosity was sated. I braced myself. When he saw the rigidness in my posture, he slowed, but never stopped. Standing incredibly close to me, he hooked his finger under my chin and raised my head to him.

"I didn't mean to scare you, Sully, but you have to understand you belong to me now. And if any other man puts his hands on you or looks at you like they want to fuck you, I will deal with them in the only way I know how."

"Violence?" I squeaked. I knew I was pushing my luck, but I had to make sure there was no misunderstanding him.

"Yes, violence. You know as well as I do that it's how things are done in our way of life. You can never show weakness or else you die." The intensity in his blue eyes frightened yet drew me in at the same time. Differing emotions pinged through me, and I had no idea which one to latch on to and ride out.

Maybe he'll make the decision for me.

"But Jagger and I were just watching a movie. Then we fell asleep. He didn't touch me," I promised.

"He may not have touched you, but he certainly wants you. There's no denying that." I opened my mouth to argue with him, but he wasn't having any of it. "I know what I saw when he looked at you, never mind that the little bastard tried to shield you from me, protecting you as if you were his."

"He's my friend," I whispered, our continued closeness making me shift from one foot to the other while he silently demanded my eyes remain on him.

He backed away before shouting, "He's not your fucking *friend*, Sully! The sooner you get that through your head, the better. I mistakenly sent him to babysit you, to keep you safe and out of harm's way until I got back. That's it. No more, no less. But he went and caught feelings for you. That much I'm sure." Redness stole over his face, and I knew he was becoming more enraged the longer he stood there ranting about Jagger. I chose to agree and let the topic die before he lost control and did something I feared.

"Okay," I mumbled, retreating a step to ensure there was a big enough space between us. Tears welled in my eyes and before I could stop them, they drifted down my cheeks and revealed my sadness.

"Goddammit!" he cursed, turning his back on me and walking into the bathroom. Slamming his fist against the countertop, he cursed some more before regaining some sort of calm.

Choking on my sobs, I tried to gather my wits and soothe myself before he reentered the bedroom, but he was too quick. I needed more time alone, but he stole those precious moments from me. Rushing toward me, he snatched me up and dragged me toward the bed, pushing me down on top of the mattress until I was completely vulnerable to him.

The long nightshirt I wore rode up my thighs the further I retreated. His gaze drifted to my exposed legs, and a sudden heat washed over me. Lust danced behind his beautiful blue eyes, but not in a way which scared me. I loved the way he watched me, even though I knew I should be on guard to any move he may decide to make.

Thankfully, I'd been wearing a bra, hoping and praying he couldn't see my body's reaction. My nipples pebbled and brushed against the soft material, their ache blossoming and making me fidget even more. My hopes were dashed that he hadn't noticed when his eyes landed on my breasts, his tongue snaking out and wetting his full bottom lip.

I wonder what his kiss tastes like.

What the hell was wrong with me? The man before me, my husband, could possibly decide to force himself on me, and I was enthralled with how his lips would taste against mine?

"You're so beautiful. You know that, right?" He reached for my legs and pulled me to the edge of the bed, prying my thighs apart with his large hands. "I didn't mean to make you cry, but what I told you was the truth. I don't want to talk about it again, though. Understand?" he asked, while continuing to open my legs to him.

What the hell is he doing?

I tried to move away again, but his hold was strong. "What are you doing?" I whimpered, not sure how I felt about being this defenseless.

"I never apologize," he affirmed, "but I want to make you feel better." Those were the only words he chose to speak before he ran his hands up the full length of my thighs, hooked his fingers in the band of my panties and removed the material from my body. His expression softened while he watched me, trying to calm me without words.

Was I ready to have sex with him?

Would he ultimately force me, taking the decision away from me?

Before another wayward thought barreled through me, I felt his warm breath between my legs.

Thirty

Marek

The sight of Sully spread bare before me was too much. I needed to taste her, make up for scaring her a few moments ago. I wasn't apologizing for anything I did, but I meant what I'd said. I wanted to make her feel better, to chase away all her fearful thoughts with the simple swipe of my tongue.

The entire ride home, I pictured exactly the position we found ourselves in, but I never really thought it would happen. I knew she was scared of me, even though it was obvious she also desired me. Then, when I'd walked in and saw her and Jagger on the couch, my rage bloomed to heights I'd never experienced before. I'd never been jealous over a woman, but I was quickly realizing things were much different with my new wife.

She was mine, and no other man was ever gonna have the opportunity to touch her.

But there was much I still had to learn about her. Like why she looked at me with lust in her eyes, her body reacting to the mere sight of me with hardened nipples and quick pants of breath, yet she denied herself my touch.

All other women would have readily thrown themselves at me, promising me the world if they could just get a taste. But the woman lying before me broke all those molds. She was different, and it intrigued the hell out of me. While there was no way I would ever force myself on her, I didn't think she realized that.

I guessed it was time for me to assure her.

Gently nipping at the insides of her creamy, toned thighs, her breath hitched as she waited for my next move. Her arousal was prevalent, her need for me wafting through the air and calling for me to act soon.

She rested on her elbows and waited, her eyes pleading with me to do something. Only problem was, I had no idea if she was too frightened to say anything or if she was waiting for me to dive right in.

Licking her inner thigh, dangerously close to her pussy, I uttered four words I'd never spoken before in my entire life.

"Can I taste you?" I asked, prepared for her to say no, but praying to God she'd say yes. I continued to lavish her with my tongue until she gave me the words I quickly became desperate to hear.

"I... I don't know. I've n-never had someone do th-that before," she stuttered. It wasn't a no, so I was halfway to tasting her on my tongue. The notion that no other man had eaten her pussy before was incredible, the best thing I thought I'd ever heard. Knowing my cock wouldn't be the first to enter her body was disappointing, but at least I could own this act.

I tried not to react to her statement, fueling the paranoia which was undoubtedly engulfing her right then. Instead, I chose to simply wait until she finally gave in. She watched me with careful eyes, silently pleading with me to do something, or stop altogether.

I chose to do something.

Lowering my head until the scent of her filled my nose, I opened my mouth and licked her slowly. One swipe of my tongue was all it took for her to moan out a throaty breath, collapsing back onto the bed in satisfaction. And reserve. She tried to close her legs again, unsure of what she was experiencing, but a simple growl from me told her to stop.

"Is that okay?" I asked, stunned I was even asking for permission. But I didn't wish to push her too hard, especially after frightening her with my outburst earlier. "Do you want me to stop?" I waited at least ten seconds and still she remained quiet. "Sully, do you want me to stop?"

"No," was her quick response, spreading her legs wider for me. I smiled big and tasted her again, this time with more urgency. I kissed and licked her as if I were eating my last meal, the scent and taste of her pushing me over the edge. Eating her out was different from fucking her, an act I wasn't sure she was quite ready for. But my cock didn't care, painfully pushing against the seam of my jeans, bouncing between pleasure and pain.

When my lips closed over the bud of her clit, she moaned loudly, fisting her hands in my hair and driving herself further into my mouth. "Marek...." She writhed against me, trying to find a rhythm which would ensure her release.

"Cole," I corrected, continuing to push her toward the edge.

She stopped moving and pulled at my hair. "What?" she asked, breathless and needy for my next touch.

"My first name is Cole. That's the name I want you to scream when you come," I demanded.

She never responded, instead pushing my face back down so I could continue. I smiled wide. She was close to diving off the cliff, so it wouldn't take much to push her over. Thrusting two fingers inside her tight heat, I sucked on her clit until she almost shot off the bed.

"That's it," I encouraged. "Give me your pleasure. I want all of it," I commanded while driving her crazy. Crooking my fingers and hitting against the sensitive spot nestled deep inside her, she cried out my name and pumped faster against my face.

"Cole!" she screamed, her body locking up tight as her pussy clamped down on my fingers. Her panting drove me to milk every last bit of pleasure from her delectable body, my cock pushing even harder against its restraint, begging to take her and finally consummate our forced marriage.

No more words were needed from either of us as she rode out her high. As soon as she'd come back down, though, embarrassment stole over her, her entire body covered in a light pink tinge. I found it rather satisfying that she could let go completely during the act, yet be shy enough afterward for her body to betray her, revealing her true feelings to me without her consent.

When I crawled over her, I took notice of the scars I'd tried to ignore when my head was buried between her legs just seconds before. The mere sight of them fueled my simmering rage, this time for a different reason. The fact that someone had done such things to her was incomprehensible, but then again she'd belonged to one of the worst clubs I knew, which obviously meant nothing to those bastards.

Lightly tracing my fingertip over the harsh, jagged scar on her lower belly, she stiffened, trying to push away from me while not being too obvious about it. But I knew. I knew she was embarrassed or ashamed or whatever crazy emotion she was trying not to show me right then.

"You have yet to tell me who did this to you."

"Why does it matter?" she retorted, rising up on her elbows again so she could see my face. It was a brave move on her part, one I didn't expect at all. The fierceness in her chocolate eyes bore into mine, her black hair fanning around her like a cloak.

"It matters because I'll end whoever dared to mark your body."

"I know I'm disgusting to look at, but it's hardly a reason to go start a war on my club." Her eyes widened with the realization that she'd given something away. She struggled to pull her body free from underneath me, but she wasn't going anywhere. Not until I'd finally gotten some answers.

Pinning her to the bed beneath me, every part of me covered every part of her. Her mouth was close, so close I longed to see if her kiss was as sweet as her pussy. But I didn't move, instead choosing to focus on the effect I had on her. Resting on my forearms to try and keep some of my weight off, I stared down at her, keeping my eyes on her face even when she looked away. A single tear escaped and trickled down her cheek, hitting the bed below.

"Look at me," I commanded. When she finally did, I tried to ease her worry. Somewhat. "You're far from disgusting to look at, Sully. In fact, even with all your marks, you're rather stunning." I spoke the truth, and I hoped she believed me. Why it was so important she trusted what I was telling her was confusing, but I didn't have time to delve into it if I wanted her to tell me what I'd been asking since I'd taken her. "Who put those marks on you? Tell me now." My voice was calm but my body was tense, the slow tick of my jaw probably giving away everything.

She tried to turn away from me again, but I directed her face back to mine with a simple touch. Since she had no other choice, she finally gave me what I wanted, although hearing the words fall from her lips didn't prepare me for the onslaught of rage I was soon to feel.

"Vex and my father marked me." Just when I thought she

was going to clam up again, she continued speaking, her tongue wetting her lips before her next words. I berated myself for wanting to kiss her again, all while she was exposing her soul to me, but I couldn't help myself. She was too enticing. Luckily, I was able to focus again before she caught the distracted look on my face.

"They are both responsible for the bruises—new and old. The burn marks on my lower back are from when my father thought I was providing information to the cops during a raid two years ago. They approached me and asked if I was okay. When I told them I was, pleading with them not to talk to me too long... Well, that piqued their curiosity. They took me into a back room and questioned me for a half hour, twenty-nine and a half minutes too long for my father not to automatically jump to conclusions. Immediately after they left, he dragged me into his office, ordered me to take off my shirt and bend over his desk. He then proceeded to burn me twice, my screams doing nothing but making him laugh." She spewed out word after word, as if she'd been dying inside by keeping the cause of her abuse secret. I saw a calmness drift behind her eyes when she finished the first part of her story, a weight lifted from her soul that she didn't even realize had bound her to agony.

There were so many things I wanted to say and ask her, but I knew if I did she would shut down again. So, with controlled breaths, I allowed her to continue without my barrage of thoughts on the subject.

"Vex claimed me from my father when I was fourteen. He was eighteen. My father had been raping me before Vex took me as his own, but stopped as soon as I belonged to another club member. He told Vex I was a lousy lay, but if he wanted to find out for himself, that was his choice. He's the one who stabbed me. Twice. Once when he thought I was flirting with one of the other members, and once just because he wanted to hear me scream. He was coked out of his mind and told me he needed some amusement." Another tear danced down her cheek. Mortification and shame stole her next breath, and I decided right then that I couldn't restrain my temper any longer.

Pushing myself off the bed, I paced in front of her, cursing before swiping everything off my dresser. The crash soothed me. A little. But it wasn't enough. I needed to hurt someone, and it would preferably be Vex and that fucker of an old man of hers. The president of the Savage Reapers. Hell would rain down on that club, the likes of which they'd never seen before.

All in due time.

Sully crawled up the bed, pulling her nightshirt down so she was completely covered. Her eyes glanced from me to the mess I'd made. I frowned at her sudden anxiousness, her switch in mood puzzling me. Looking for a distraction was probably her way of coping, but I still found it odd.

"What?" I questioned, keeping my eyes trained on her.

"I... I just feel out of sorts... when there's a mess. Especially in my bedroom." Her words weren't lost on me. She'd said 'my bedroom,' and like a giddy asshole it made me smile for some reason.

Feeling bad for her, especially after finally giving me answers, I tried my best to put her mind at ease. "I'll clean it up. Don't worry about it." I strode toward her, reached for her hand and pulled her to stand in front of me. Placing my hands on the sides of her beautiful face, I promised something I knew right then I would die to hold true.

"No one will ever hurt you again. Do you hear me?"

She nodded and relaxed in my hold, averting her eyes to the mess behind me. With a soft chuckle, I released her and began the task of cleaning up the scattered and broken items.

Thirty-One

Sully

Never before had I imagined what it would feel like to trust someone, to believe the words they told me and instinctually know they weren't a lie. I thought it was all fantasy. Those feelings of security only happened to other people. Not me.

Cole's promise to never allow anyone to hurt me again relieved a harrowing burden I hadn't realized I carried. Deep down, maybe I was waiting for my club to barge in and reclaim me, or maybe I thought Cole would change his mind, decide he made a mistake and return me himself. Either way, I was waiting to return to a life of pain and torment, thoughts of extinguishing my own existence a constant desire.

Every moment living in my new life brought me closer to allowing fate to right the wrong I'd lived so far. And although it was hard for me to have faith in anyone, I was beginning to open myself up and believe there were good people in the world.

Shoving aside that Cole had just brought me to the brink of bliss, pushed me over and brought me back all within mere seconds, I focused on what he was doing now. Cleaning up the mess he'd caused. He knew it was a source of anxiety for me, and it said a lot that he cared enough about my unease to want to help me.

While I watched him gather the broken pieces of clutter into his hands, I noticed how his hair kept falling into his face, the strands in much need of a simple cut.

Walking up behind his crouching form, I offered to help him out. "I can cut your hair if you'd like." Vex had always expected me to perform the simple act, never giving me a thank you or showing any kind of appreciation when I'd finished. One time, because he'd moved, I'd cut his hair crookedly, and even though I was able to fix it easily enough, I'd earned the wrath of his displeasure. My finger still throbbed when rain approached, even though the once broken appendage had been healed for years. I wasn't about to disclose any more war stories to Cole, though, fearing he would certainly go off the deep end and do something very dangerous. All in order to seek justice for me. While I found the thought comforting, I didn't wish to be the cause of something popping off and harming the club that was essentially protecting me.

When he managed to pick up the last piece of disarray, he rose to his feet and turned in my direction. "You don't like my hair?" he asked, tilting his head to the side, a gesture which caused more of his hair to fall over his eye. Blowing the intrusion off his forehead, he curved his lips up at my expression. I thought I'd insulted him and was instantly regretful, but his grin succeeded at putting me at ease.

"I like your hair just fine. It seems like the length is bothering you, though." I patiently waited to see if he was going to accept my offer or not.

"Sure, why not?" he said, ushering me toward the bathroom. Once inside, he took a seat on the edge of the bathtub,

196 / S. NELSON

pointing toward the drawer of the vanity when I asked if he had a pair of scissors and hair clippers. I hadn't seen them when I was cleaning off the countertop in my urgency for order but sure enough, there they were hiding toward the back.

Pulling them free, I checked the quality and decided I could definitely work with what he had. Now all I had to do was keep my hand steady enough not to mess up his lovely thick hair. Stepping closer, I straddled his leg to gain better access. I worked quickly but efficiently, making sure not to cut it too short. He told me he liked a little bit of length on top. Running my fingers through the thickness of it, making sure to shake any loose strands free, excited me, for some reason. I'd had my hands tangled in his hair when he was pleasuring me, but the simple act of cutting it and checking my work almost made me feel normal for a brief moment.

A feeling I grasped onto and held tightly.

"How's it lookin'?"

"Good. Almost finished," I answered, twisting my body to check out the back. My foot slipped on the tile and I stumbled forward. Luckily for the both of us, the scissors were nowhere near his head.

His large hands steadied me, resting on my waist and gripping me firmly. "You okay?" His fingers continued to dig into my flesh, but he wasn't hurting me. In fact, his touch was exciting.

Cole Marek certainly had a way of disarming me, and since I knew I wasn't quite ready to take it there, I knew I had to keep my wits about me. What happened before was wonderful, but I wasn't prepared to have sex with him yet. Yes, he'd had his face buried between my legs and brought me untold pleasure, but joining with him was something else altogether. Maybe I was holding off because I wanted it to be special and not because I felt obligated. I had no idea because I had no frame of reference, every other time the act had been forced on me. All I knew was I wanted our first time to be different.

Plus, there was the small fact that I still battled with being kidnapped and forced to marry the president of our greatest enemy, even though I was coming around to the idea that fate had sent him to save me.

When I tried to back away, his grip held me in position, stable until he deemed it time to let me go. When he decided enough time had passed, he spread his legs and pulled me in front of him, leaning forward and resting his head on my belly. No words slipped from his lips as he found some sort of solace with being so close to me.

My heart thudded inside me, pushing against my ribs so hard I felt like it was going to explode. Every move he made was new, the gentleness of his touch foreign to me, although I was learning to expect such things from him.

Would he wait for me to decide when the time was right? Or would that be pushing things too far?

Thirty-Two

Marek

Her smell drove me insane, a break with reality I most surely embraced. I had no idea why I chose to rest my head on her stomach. It simply felt right.

The woman standing before me was unraveling my carefully orchestrated existence. I was the leader of the Knights Corruption. I wasn't supposed to fall for a woman. A woman who was going to make me weak. A woman who was going to have the power to crush me if I let her.

A woman who was going to be my destruction.

I prided myself on my ability to detach myself from certain feelings, affections toward the opposite sex being number one. I used them just like they used me, for pleasure and nothing else. Then Sully came into my life—or I should say I barged into hers—and ever since then, I'd been questioning my choices.

Even though I'd basically just met her, I hated being away from her for the time it took Stone and me to deal with Yanez. I hated that I ended up leaving her alone with Jagger. I hated that I'd found out he'd developed feelings for her in their short time together, and that she seemed more comfortable around him than she was with me.

I hadn't spent much time with her since I'd brought her here, but all that was gonna change. If I wasn't involved in club business, then I would be with her, getting to know her. We *were* married, after all. Might as well get to know the old ball and chain.

Cringing at my callous thoughts, I focused back on Sully. I continued to lean my head against her body. When she didn't make a move to dislodge me, I took it as a sign to see how far I could take things. Running my hands up the backs of her thighs, over her plump ass and up her back toward her bra, I stopped only when I'd reached the clasp. Unhooking it before she said anything, I felt the breath leave her body in a rushed gasp. Slowly trailing my fingers along her soft skin, I stopped when I reached the bottom of her heavy tits, feeling the goose bumps which broke out all over her skin.

"Sully," I groaned, my cock thick and ready to come out and play. When she still hadn't made a move, I reached up and palmed her glorious mounds, pinching the already hardened nipples between my greedy fingers.

A moan fell from her lips as she took one step closer. Her hands wrapped around my wrists and held tightly. *I need more of her.* Raising her nightshirt over her head, and disposing of the thin material that had covered her breasts, I sat in front of her, admiring her glorious body. I'd seen her a few times before, but never like this. She allowed my hands to roam freely, and the experience was like none other I'd ever had before with any other female.

My tongue connected with her skin and she moaned once again. Taking a pert nipple into my mouth, I swirled my tongue around the aching bud while sucking it deep into my mouth.

She tasted like Heaven.

Everywhere.

"Cole..." she cried out. "Yes," she panted shamelessly. I switched to teasing her other one, groping her while sucking reverently. My free hand dropped to her pussy, gently stroking her while I tuned up her body as best I could. She'd never put her panties back on from before, and I'd never been so thankful to have such easy access.

"You're so wet. Do you want me to stop?"

Hesitation emanated off her. "Yes... No... I don't know," she mewled. Her confusion not only came from her mouth, but it was in her body language as well. She pushed her tits into my mouth but struggled when I tried to fuck her with my hand. She was at war with herself, and I had to do something about it.

Standing quickly, I picked her up by her waist and placed her on top of the vanity, nudging her thighs apart with my leg. Yanking down the zipper of my jeans, I pulled myself out and rubbed the tip of my cock through her swollen, wet folds. "Tell me to stop, Sully. Otherwise, I'm gonna take you so hard, you'll forget your own fuckin' name." I was ready to explode any second if she didn't give me an answer.

Placing her hands on my chest, she pushed me back, looking into my eyes before telling me something I didn't want to hear. "I don't think I can. Please don't be mad. I'm just... I'm not ready yet."

My control shattered. "But you were ready to have my face buried between your legs before?" I grabbed her chin when she tried to turn her face away from me. "What? Now that I want some relief, you're gonna deny me? Is that how this is goin' down right now?" I hadn't meant to say something so harsh, but it just came out. I berated myself for every single word, but for some reason I couldn't stop myself. The hurtful words flowed easily and it upset not only her, but me as well.

"I'm sorry," she whispered, her head jerking from my hold before she looked down at her own naked body.

"Yeah, I'm sure you are," I snarled, putting my cock away and zipping up my jeans. Backing away, I took one final look at her before retreating from the bathroom.

What I did was a prick move, but I didn't see it turning out any other way. I was pissed that she made me feel as if I was on guard around her, asking for permission to take what essentially belonged to me. I could have demanded she fulfilled her wifely duties and fuck me as many times as I saw fit, but I wasn't that much of a bastard. Although the way I reacted told a different story.

At least she seemed to crave my touch. Maybe, given a little more time, she'd come around and give me what I wanted.

But what to do until then, I had no idea. Not wanting to stick my dick inside the same old club whores, I was fucked and I knew it.

Soon, my club would know it too, my mood already cresting toward miserable.

After calling Ryder to come watch Sully while I made a trip to the clubhouse, threatening his life if he acted inappropriately with her, I hopped on my bike and rode to the one place I could escape from the woman twisting me up inside.

There was already a commotion as I stepped through the front door. A few of the brothers were gathered around, laughing and poking fun at whomever was in the middle of their crowd. Shoving my way through, I saw Hawke sitting in the center with a pissed-off look on his face. It took me all of a millisecond to figure out what he was so upset about.

His head was shaved.

And from the look on his face, and those of his brothers, he hadn't done that shit to himself. One guess who did it, however.

"What the hell happened to you?" I asked, coming to stand directly in front of him, slapping the back of his bare head before he could answer.

"That bitch happened," he groaned, rubbing his hand back and forth over his shaved head.

"I don't know why you keep her around, man," Breck said, shaking his head while continuing to laugh.

"'Cause I love the crazy cunt." He half-chuckled, his semi-laughter quieting as he continued to rub his dome.

Kicking his leg, I drew his attention back to me. "What. The. Fuck. Happened?"

He leaned back in his chair and prepared to tell me his story, one he'd obviously shared with the other guys, seeing as how they were already grinning.

"I must have gotten drunk last night, somehow made it home, and passed out in bed. When I got up this morning, Edana had shaved my fucking head."

There was certainly more to the story than that. "Why?" I asked, already losing interest in their crazy-ass relationship.

Actually looking embarrassed for once, he winced before revealing, "I guess I forgot to take the condom off before goin' to bed." Feeling the need to elaborate based on my confused expression, he blurted out, "We don't use condoms." Not something I ever wanted to know. "The one time she decides to wake me up with a blow job and that's when this shit happens," he grunts, rocking his chair back and forth until he'd had enough and jumped to his feet. Expletives flew from his mouth as he walked toward the bar, motioning for Trigger to hit him up with a drink.

Walking past him, I decided to hit him with a few words of condolence. "At least she didn't cut your dick off, Hawke. Be thankful for that shit." I smirked, slapping him hard on the back before walking toward the room I kept in the back of the clubhouse.

A loud noise woke me from sleep, jolting me upright and ready to fuck someone up for disturbing me. A loud crash followed by men hootin' and hollerin', music playing way too loud and women's laughter emanated through the hallway.

Dropping my feet to the ground, I took a few seconds to tamp down my rage, but the extra time didn't help, not at all. I couldn't go back to my house, the shitty way I'd treated Sully still weighing heavily on my heart and mind, but it seemed as if I couldn't stay here either.

Jerking open my door, I thudded down the long hallway until I came to the common room, and the scene in front of me was astonishing. Well, maybe not astonishing, since I knew my men liked to throw a good ruckus, but I had no idea one was planned for tonight.

I glanced around the room, looking for my VP, but he was nowhere to be seen. *Who the hell's in charge here? Oh, yeah, that would be me.* Sleep still cocooned me in her cloak, the fogginess dissipating slower than I wanted, leaving me hazy and not too alert.

That was until I heard another loud crash and Hawke yelled, "Let's get fucked up!" at the top of his lungs, shattering any remnants of rest I had left. I moved toward the bar, my steps slow and steady until I found a seat in the corner. Luckily, Trigger was still there, passing out drinks to the willing and able.

"Hey, Prez, how ya feelin'?" he asked, sliding a beer my

204 / S. NELSON

way. I guessed by the look of me, he wanted to start me off with something light and forgiving.

I chose to ignore his questions, instead asking one of my own. "What the hell is goin' on? Who planned a ruckus for tonight?" Swallowing a large gulp of the frosty beverage, my eyes connected with his once I'd placed the mug back down on the bar.

"Cutter suggested we should have one, you know, in honor of you and Stone making it back alive." Trigger laughed at his own joke, one I didn't find all too funny. "What's wrong with you, Marek? You always laugh at my jokes." His faux offensive stare almost had me smirking. Almost.

I felt a presence sneak up behind me. Before I turned around, someone threw their arm over my shoulder and leaned in to me. Fumes from too much bourbon hit my cheek and instantly made me tense up. *I'm in no mood for this shit tonight.* "He's just pissed his old lady isn't givin' it up yet," Tripp yelled into my ear. Swiveling around in my chair, I gripped him by his cut and slammed him against the bar.

How did he know she'd refused me?

Wincing in pain, then laughing it off simply because he was drunk, Tripp patted my hands which were still wrapped around his vest. What the hell was he even doing out of bed?

"Why would you say that?" I seethed, the look on my face sobering him up a little.

"Because you need to get laid, man. You're miserable, and everyone knows it." I released him, but luckily caught him before he toppled over, injuring himself so bad it would prob-ably take him weeks to recover. Hell, he still wasn't anywhere near healed from being shot four times.

"What the hell are you even doing out here, Tripp? Adelaide would kill you if she knew you were out of bed, and drunk of all things."

"She's not the boss of me." He chuckled. "Although, I'd certainly let her boss me around in the bedroom, if ya know what I mean." I didn't know if he realized what he'd just said, but the way he was feelin' right about then I doubted he cared either way.

A quick turn of my head and I saw it coming, but I was powerless to stop it.

Trigger's fist flew through the air and connected with the side of Tripp's jaw, knocking him to the left. Again, I was able to react before he hit the ground, splitting open his many stitches.

"What the fuck, Trig! You can't go around punching him, even if he *did* say something about your niece. He's still recovering, or did you forget that?" I shouted, glaring at him and daring him to argue. Thankfully, he held up his hands in surrender, but not before leering at Tripp one last time. I knew he wasn't sorry, but at least he didn't continue his beat-down on our nomad brother. Pulling his graying messy hair back into a neat ponytail, Trigger went about his business as if nothing happened.

A little while later, while I was nursing my second drink, I saw Jagger approach from the side and my body instantly went into fight mode. My muscles tensed, preparing to beat the shit out of him if he said the wrong thing.

When he finally stood next to me, he opened his mouth and spoke. Quickly and quietly. "Prez, uh... Do you think I can talk to you?" he pleaded.

"No," I gritted, never turning my head to look at him. Thankfully, he got the hint. He walked away with his head down, brushing past a few of the wannabes who tried to talk to him.

I'd deal with him when I didn't have to fight the urge to kill him.

The rest of the night passed by without incident, the men having a great time, overindulging in pussy and alcohol. Even Hawke, with his newly shaved head, was back to his old antics, fuckin' around with some of the club whores. *He'll never learn.*

But then again, what fun would it be around here if he ever did?

Thirty-Three

Sully

"Come on. Just come with me to the clubhouse and then we can go shopping," Adelaide pleaded with me. She told me she was in desperate need of some retail therapy, and I had to admit I thought it would be fun. Besides, it'd been three days since Cole had been home, no doubt still pissed because I wouldn't have sex with him. But at least he didn't force himself on me like I feared he might do. And even though he'd been cruel, he kept to his word and didn't hurt me. Well... not physically.

"I'm not sure if I'll get in trouble or not," I answered. Adelaide still didn't know the whole story surrounding me being there, but she never pried. The only thing she was aware of was that I always had someone watching over me, but she'd eventually admitted it was a normal occurrence with how protective some of the men could be.

Speaking of shadows, Ryder had been the newest chosen one since Jagger had been thrown out a few nights back. I didn't mind him hanging around, although, unless he was drinking, Ryder was a pretty quiet guy. His company was nothing like Jagger's, and I feared it was because Cole had threatened his life if he stepped out of line, which might be something as simple as engaging me in conversation.

"How are we going to convince Ryder? He won't let me out of his sight."

"Then we tell him he has to go with us." She smiled, and I knew exactly how she was going to 'convince' him to accompany us.

"Your uncle?"

"You know it." She laughed, tugging on my arm and pulling me toward the living room where Ryder was watching some show about Harleys.

A little while later, we were pulling into the compound, the heavy metal gates closing behind us while Adelaide found a parking space. My nerves took hold and shook me senseless. I had no idea if this one move would be the thing to send Cole over the edge. I'd believed him when he said no one would hurt me again, but was I pushing my luck by showing up unannounced? Did the man have his limits?

A single bead of sweat beaded on my brow. My hands became clammy and my breathing had stifled into short pants. I guess I was preparing myself for the worst, in case today proved to be the day I pushed the envelope one too many times.

A soft rapping made my head turn to the right. I hadn't realized Adelaide had left the car, but there she was, knocking on my window to get my attention.

"Come on, silly." She laughed. "You can't sit out here. You'll roast in the sun." The genuine smile on her face made me extremely happy I'd met her, but her warning didn't deter me from staying within the confines of her car.

"I'll roll down the window," I offered, fidgeting in my seat.

Opening the door, she reached for my hand and after a small amount of resistance, I allowed her to extract me. We walked through the courtyard of the compound, the sun blaring down on both of us and immediately heating us up to an uncomfortable level. Thankfully, we'd both been smart enough to wear light and airy sundresses. Adelaide's was a pretty pale blue color, hitting her just above the knee. It was strapless, and since she was smaller-chested than I was, it looked perfect on her. I, on the other hand, could never wear a dress without straps—too much up top to be comfortable. The dress I chose to wear was a beautiful multi-colored pattern, one Adelaide thought would look great. And, much like hers, my dress also hit just above the knee. A simple pair of flip-flops completed the outfit, although I probably should have worn more comfortable shoes after hearing about all the stores she wanted to visit. I'd chosen to wear my hair back in a stylish ponytail. It was practical and easy, plus it was off my neck, a smart decision given the sweltering heat.

When I gazed at my reflection in the mirror, I deemed it to be a lie. A stylish, vibrant young woman stared back at me, but I was anything but. Young, yes, but the other shit was a mirage.

My heartbeat picked up its pace the closer we came to entering the clubhouse, bikes lined up outside telling me there were a decent amount of members there today. We were walking too quickly for me to take the time to scan the area for Cole's bike, to determine if he was indeed inside those walls.

Opening the door, Adelaide reached for my hand once again and pulled me behind her, ensuring I wasn't going to take off running and abandon her. Although, something told me she would be just fine. All of the men in this club would protect her, or they'd have to answer to that uncle of hers. I wished I had someone in my life who had looked out for my well-being just a fraction of how he did for his niece.

Maybe in a different life.

The brightness of the shining sun was cut out once we

entered inside. A few of the men milled around the open space and true to form, Trigger was behind the bar serving drinks to anyone who wanted them. It was only a little after two in the afternoon, but a few of the brothers were already well on their way to becoming drunk. I wondered if they were trying to mask a darkness in their own lives.

"Addy," her uncle called out, a genuine smile tipping the corners of his lips. "Tripp's in the back resting off last night." His expression faltered for a split second and I had no idea why. Until he squealed on himself. "Look, honey, Tripp's probably in a bad way." The look of confusion on his niece's face made him elaborate. "He was drinking with the rest of us last night, made some comment about you bossing him around... and...."

"And what, Uncle Trig?" She leaned in closer. "Oh, my God! What did you do?" she exclaimed.

"Oh, calm down. I only punched him." When he saw she was starting to get upset, he tried to placate her. "I just punched him once. He's fine, but the amount of booze he shoved down his throat is enough to have him feelin' like shit today. You've been warned," he offered before talking to someone wanting a beer.

Adelaide turned her attention on me, asking if I wanted to wait out there or come with her to check on Tripp. I smartly chose to follow her toward the back of the building, not wanting to be a sitting duck in case Cole showed up.

Pushing open a small door toward the back, we both walked in on a naked man sprawled across a bed hardly big enough to fit the likes of his size. He looked to be at least a few inches over six feet, although lying down I couldn't exactly be sure.

I should have averted my eyes, but I couldn't help it; I stared at him like some kind of hussy, horny to get her next fix.

The man's body, even with all the scars, was pretty impressive. Well-defined muscles, broad shoulders and thick thighs held my fascination, but they didn't elicit a need to touch him like when I gazed upon Cole's body.

Oddly, I could identify with Tripp in some small way because my body was also punctured and scarred. It was an odd connection but one I would accept.

Thankfully, Adelaide stalked forward and threw a sheet over his manhood, shoving at his shoulder with her small hand to try and wake him. "Tripp," she called out. "Get up." When he made no move to awaken, she tapped his cheek lightly, trying to rouse him that way. Still nothing. With one knee on the side of the bed, she leaned in closer to make sure he was breathing before tapping his cheek once more.

All of a sudden, strong hands gripped her shoulders and tossed her across him, landing on the other side of the mattress. At first, I thought he was having some sort of nightmare, like I had from time to time where I was lost between reality and a haze of fright. But when I heard his laughter, I knew he was playing with her, and the sight, although scary at first, had me smiling and wishing I had those types of relationships with people.

Adelaide was quickly becoming one of those people for me, which I would forever be grateful for.

Tripp's voice was deep and rough, no doubt the effects of high amounts of alcohol from the night before. "My guardian angel." He laughed, kissing her cheek before releasing her.

"You're incorrigible," she scolded, slapping his arm before rising from the bed. "By the way, we walked in on you naked, sprawled out for anyone to see." I thought she was trying to embarrass him, but the man had nothing to be ashamed of. Not in my opinion, at least.

"Did you like what you saw?" he asked, a cocky grin on his knowing face.

"I've seen better," she teased, making my own laughter erupt into the friendly atmosphere.

Gently shoving Adelaide to the side when she'd risen to stand next to him again, his piercing green eyes came to rest on me, noticing me for the first time since he'd woken up.

"Well, well, well. Who do we have here?" he asked, that same self-assured grin spread wide on his handsome face. Unlike many of his brothers, the only signs of facial hair were from a two-day-old growth. Scratching the side of his face, he managed to call my attention to his mouth when he licked his lips. Although I had no desire to kiss anyone but my husband, I could see how women would want to latch on to that full mouth of his.

Making sure to keep himself covered with the sheet Adelaide threw over him moments before, he leaned against the bed frame and watched me, waiting for introductions.

Taking a step forward, I said, "I'm Sully." I had no idea what else to add to that, but my friend did.

"She's Marek's wife," she added.

"Holy shit!" he shouted. "I heard about the infamous woman who'd trapped and tamed the president of the Knights Corruption." Arching a brow, he finished with, "You're even more beautiful than they say, sweetheart."

His compliment instantly made me uncomfortable, although I tried to hide it. I wasn't used to people telling me I was attractive, so I immediately thought they were only saying such things to make fun of me in some way. But just like when Cole had told me so, Tripp's assessment seemed genuine.

"Thank you," I whispered.

"You better behave yourself, Tripp," Adelaide warned, slapping his hand when he tried to reach for her. "You mess with

Sully and Marek is going to bury you himself." I wasn't sure if she was teasing him or if she was serious.

Something told me it was the latter.

"Oh, I'm just having some fun. Keep your panties on... Or don't, it's up to you," he joked, looking at Adelaide with adoration. Turning his gaze back on me, he tried to comfort me, seeing the nervousness pouring off me in waves. "I'm harmless, sweetheart. Don't mind me. I love getting a reaction out of people." Glancing back to Adelaide, he confessed what happened the night before. "By the way, you need to tell your dear uncle to calm the hell down. Anytime anyone talks about you, he flips out." He instinctually rubbed his jaw. "He punched me last night when I made an innocent comment." Groaning when he touched a sore spot, he looked up at the woman at his side. "It hurts," he admitted, playing it up more than he needed to.

Stroking his face over the affected area, she lightly tapped him when he least expected it. "Ow!" he yelled. "What the hell, Adelaide?"

"Oh, I didn't hurt you. Stop being such a baby." She laughed then went about inspecting his numerous healing wounds. Tripp sat up straight so she could check his back as well. When she deemed everything looked good, she warned him about pushing himself too hard, like with the night before. "You shouldn't be drinking so much... and pissing my uncle off. You need to allow your body enough time to heal properly, Tripp. I mean it."

"Yes, ma'am." He saluted, reclining back on the bed. "Now, if you lovely ladies don't mind, I need some more beauty rest. Plus, my head's killing me." His groans sounded behind us as we left his room.

I liked Tripp. He had an aura about him which instantly

214 / S. NELSON

relaxed me. He was funny, and humor was certainly something I needed more of in my life.

Stepping into the hallway, I continued to smile from the encounter when we ran into Jagger. His hands came up and landed on my arms, steadying me before I tripped over my own two feet.

"Sully, how are you?" he asked before retracting his hands. A black eye and split lip greeted me when I fully looked at him. His blond hair was disheveled, as if he'd just rolled out of bed, and his amber eyes were bloodshot. Honestly, he looked like hell.

"What happened to you?" I made a move to touch his face, but he backed up. "Did Cole do that to you?" I asked, suddenly furious with the man I hadn't seen in days.

Moving back another step, he looked reserved before answering. "No, it was from a fight I had two nights ago. A legit fight," he confirmed, his eyes roaming all over me in concern. "Are you all right? He didn't hurt you, did he?"

I knew exactly what he was talking about, and I put his mind at ease immediately. "No, he didn't hurt me." I tried to smile but I faltered. I watched him while he stood in front of me, shifting nervously from foot to foot. He wanted to talk to me, as I did to him, but the tension in the air prohibited us from continuing.

"Well, it was nice to see you. Take care," he said before walking past me down the hall and disappearing into a room a few doors down.

I didn't have feelings for Jagger other than as a friend, but the fact that we were forbidden to talk to each other really hurt me. Nothing inappropriate had gone on between us the entire time he watched over me, but Cole had freaked out just the same. My husband hardly spent any time with me, yet he didn't want anyone else to either. Of the male persuasion, at least.

Forgetting Adelaide was standing near me, her voice brought me back from my depressing thoughts. "What was that all about?" Her sincere concern for my situation was touching.

"Cole freaked out on Jagger because he thought we'd been doing something in his absence." Reaching to touch her shoulder, I confessed, "But we weren't, Adelaide. I swear." What the woman standing before me thought of me had suddenly become very important. Tears swam in my eyes as I tried to hold it together.

"I believe you, honey," she assured me, pulling me in for a quick hug. She knew I needed the comfort, and I was grateful she could read me so well. "I'm sure everything will blow over soon enough. Marek is a good man. Usually, he's pretty laid-back, but I think you might have him all twisted up inside. Let him get used to the idea of... well... you, and life will get back to normal." She smiled, linking her arm through mine and continuing down the length of the hallway.

Thirty-Four

Marek

Standing close by, I heard a woman's voice say, "Now, let's go find Ryder so we can get our shopping on." Right then, I knew it was Adelaide and the hairs on the back of my neck bristled, but not because it was Trigger's niece. No, it was because I knew exactly who she was talking to.

Sully.

My wife.

But how could that be? Why was she here at the clubhouse when she should've been back at my house with Ryder? Quickly glancing around, I spotted Ryder in the corner, already locking his lips around a bottle of beer.

Both women entered the common room, instantly drawing the attention of all the men milling around. Most gave them a quick nod in acknowledgement, while one or two of the already-drunken bastards stared a little too long. Trigger was on alert as soon as his niece re-entered the room, and I was acutely aware of every movement Sully made... and of everyone who gazed at her longer than necessary.

It seemed Jagger wasn't the only one I had to worry about. Maybe I was being paranoid, but I would rather instill fear into them than let it go. "Zip!" I shouted over to one of our youngest members. "If you don't turn your fucking eyes away, I'm gonna pluck them outta your head. Feel me?"

"Sorry, Prez." He was halfway to passing out already and it was barely after two. But at least he had enough sense not to argue and did as he was instructed, gulping down the rest of his drink and turning his attention to whatever show was on TV.

My eyes found Sully's and like always, something passed between us. I was no longer upset with her for refusing me. Hell, I wasn't really angry with her for that reason to begin with. I battled between fighting the feelings she created inside me and giving in to them altogether. I'd lashed out and hurt her. Never mind that I hadn't been home in days because I was too much of a coward to face her.

Pushing all my errant internal ramblings aside, I approached them rather quickly. Blocking the pair from going any further, I reached out for Sully's hand. I had no idea what I was going to do or say but in that moment, I needed to touch her. As my fingers were about to skim hers, she pulled away, taking a half-step behind her new friend.

I wasn't gonna lie, it hurt. Was she still afraid of me? Or was she still upset that I'd yelled at her the way I had? Did she hate me now?

Part of me didn't blame her, not one bit, but another part, the Neanderthal part, didn't give a shit. She was mine, and there was no way I would allow her to embarrass me in front of my club. I felt everyone's eyes on the interaction, and I wasn't gonna be made a fool of.

"What are you two doing here?" I asked none too nicely.

Adelaide was the one who spoke, all while Sully kept her eyes on the ground. "I asked Sully to accompany me here to check on Tripp before we headed out to do some shopping." My eyes never landed on Trigger's niece, the whole time focused on my wife instead. Not until Adelaide mumbled something stupid, that was. "Well, I guess we'll be going now."

Two steps and I was standing directly next to my wife. Her body warred between leaning into me and pulling back. I saw it in her posture, and in her expression, even though her beautiful eyes were still avoiding me.

"No way are you two going anywhere without one of my men." A short and simple demand. Or so I thought.

"Look, Marek," Adelaide started, "I'm not involved with this club like that, so I can come and go as I see fit. No one will tell me what to do. Ever." Her voice raised an octave toward the end of her little speech. I had an idea that Stone had a little something to do with the unspoken reason for her 'I'm woman, hear me roar' rant.

"You're right, you're not. But she is," I said, pointing toward Sully. "She's my wife, and as such she's not allowed to go anywhere without me or one of my men." I didn't elaborate on my fear of her club coming to look for her, stealing her back right out from under my nose. No, Adelaide didn't need to know all that. Speaking of, I had yet to receive an updated report on their whereabouts. I found it odd that they hadn't tried to storm my club to reclaim her from us.

"Then *you* can come with us," she offered. What a ludicrous statement. I had better shit to do besides watching the two of them shop for clothes, or whatever the hell they were going out to buy. Although the thought of watching Sully try on different clothing was rather appealing. I wondered if they were going to one of those lingerie shops during their outing. What did that matter, though, when she wasn't ready to hop into bed with me? Then again, I *was* able to get her naked.

Yeah, that's where my head went, random thoughts

bouncing back and forth inside my brain. I was beyond frustrated, and if I didn't sink inside her tight little body soon, I was gonna explode.

I noticed Sully had raised her head, turning her face toward me, waiting to see if I would agree to come with them or not. Would she be upset or relieved if I said yes? I figured I wouldn't know unless I answered.

After a few seconds of internal deliberation, I decided it was best for me not to go, so I declined her offer. However, I was pleased to see Sully's face fall, letting me know she was indeed upset that I'd refused. It gave me hope that she was on her way to forgiving me for acting like such an ass. Any normal man would apologize, and while the thought had crossed my mind, it wasn't how I operated. *Apologize for nothing, but make amends to right the wrong.* Although, the beauty in front of me was changing me in ways I didn't want to acknowledge.

A fierceness to protect her, even from myself at times, swirled powerfully through me, making me question everything. I'd already made the move to take my club legit, which was one less thing I had to worry about, even though I had to make sure it came to fruition. Anything which would put me in better light in her eyes was quickly proving to be a driving force for how I conducted my day.

Then stop yelling at her, Marek.

Suddenly wanting to be alone with her, I snatched her hand and pulled her behind me toward my room. "We'll be right back, Adelaide." The warmth of her palm had my cock stirring to life. Man, I was easy. All it took was her simple touch and I couldn't keep myself from picturing how she would look beneath me, driving her heels into the backs of my thighs as I drove myself inside her.

Closing and locking the door for added privacy, I spun her around until she was facing me. "Let me see your eyes," I demanded, a softness in my tone I meant for her to hear. Once I had her attention, I started in with my ramblings. "Listen, Sully," I said, my thoughts so twisted together it was hard for me to find the right thing to say. "I won't pressure you again to fuck me." *Yeah, that's the sentence my brain-to-mouth filter released. Real smooth.* "You just let me know when you're ready, okay?"

"Okay," she answered, her dark orbs focused on me. Before she looked away again, I needed to let her know she wouldn't be going on any shopping outing. Something which was surely going to upset her, but it was the best choice. I wasn't going to risk her safety because she wanted to flit about town with her new friend.

"I don't want you going anywhere with Adelaide without one of the guys. And since she's gonna give me a hard time about it, it looks like you two will have to do it another time."

Wrinkling her brow at something running through her head, she nodded and averted her gaze.

"What?" I asked, wondering what in the hell she was thinking.

"Can't Ryder go with us?"

"No." I decided to elaborate when I saw the desperate look on her face. "Ryder already started drinking. He won't be of any use if something happens."

"What's going to happen? We're going to be out in public with people all around us." The one thing I noticed about Sully was that she was becoming more comfortable when talking to me, which was a good thing, in most cases. In instances where I didn't want to hear another word about something I'd said, though, it was a pain in the ass. I was used to people taking my word as law, so to have someone push the envelope was quite the challenge.

"Your father and Vex haven't made a move to come and

collect you. And, quite frankly, I find it odd, which tells me they're planning something. So, I'm not taking any risks." Turning my back on her to search for a clean shirt, I had a sneaking suspicion that the next thing out of her lovely lips was going to send me over the edge.

Call it a hunch, or intuition or whatever the hell.

Completely ignoring my statement about her family, she chose to bring up a topic she knew I would overreact to, yet she did it anyway.

"What about Jagger? He can come and watch out for us to make sure nothing happens."

Every muscle in my body locked up. My blood pressure rose and while I tried to convince myself to calm down, I couldn't help but grind my teeth together to snuff out the volcano erupting inside me.

Whipping around to face her, I moved closer. So close she backed up until she hit the wall, preventing her from escaping my temper. Before I started yelling, she placed her hand on my chest and pled her case. "I know you think there was something going on between us, but you have to believe me, there wasn't. He was a perfect gentleman with me. I swear. I don't have any feelings for him whatsoever. You can trust me." Her eyes stayed glued to mine, a gesture which helped to soothe me. Somewhat.

Gritting my teeth, I ground out my response. "You may not want to fuck Jagger, but trust me when I tell you this, Sully, he wants you. Badly. I saw it in his eyes, and I saw it in his body language when he thought he was protecting you from me. He won't admit it out loud, because he knows I'll snatch his life, but he does," I repeated.

Her hand continued to rest over my heart and I was doing my best not to explode right then, but it was becoming harder the more she pushed me about the prospect.

"But I don't want him, so what does it matter? He doesn't

make me feel the way you do." She mumbled her last few words, but I heard them loud and clear. Taking another step closer, my chest brushing against hers, she inhaled a quick breath before leaning her head back against the same wall which held her prisoner to me.

"And how do I make you feel?" I couldn't help myself; she'd opened up the topic, and I was gonna explore it.

"Breathless. Scared. Excited." Her eyes glossed over as if she was going to break down, but I had no idea why. *Am I scaring her right now? Or is she excited?*

"You know I'd never hurt you, right? I may say things from time to time which will hurt your feelings, but I would never do anything to tear you apart." Lifting her chin higher so her lips rested a whisper away from mine, I inhaled her sweet breath. I wanted so badly to claim her mouth, but I hadn't been intimate with a woman like that in what seemed like forever. Although, before our encounter a few days back, I hadn't gone done on a woman in as much time, either.

Her full pink lips trembled, her tongue parting her mouth to wet the very same things I wanted to nibble and taste. Goddamn it! Every reserve I held tight started to weaken and crumble.

Her eyes suddenly closed, and it was then I decided to make my move. "Do you want me to kiss you?" I asked, hoping like hell she said yes. I'd never wanted to taste a woman as much as I did her right then. The suspense tore me apart and just before I was going to make the decision for her, she said the one word I was praying for.

"Yes."

Short and sweet and to the muthafuckin' point.

Without further delay, I crashed my lips to hers. The feeling was incredible, my increasing attraction toward her fueling the blaze of longing inside me. There wasn't an area on her luscious body I didn't wish to devour. And her mouth was the perfect place to start.

She obediently opened up for me, and the first time I felt her gentle tongue caress mine, I almost exploded in my pants I was so worked up. Her fingers grabbed at the fabric of my cut, desperately trying to pull me closer, but if I moved forward any more I was going to crush her to me. But maybe it was exactly what she was looking for, to be melded as one. Or maybe that was what I wanted, to be so lost to her that we became the same person.

"Sully," I groaned, breaking our kiss for the briefest of moments. "You taste unbelievable. Even better than your pussy," I added, with a tilt of my lips I knew she could feel when I kissed her again. Doing my best to dominate her with my kiss, she suddenly flipped the script and was the one who ended up controlling me. I forced my tongue inside her mouth but it was Sully who set the pace, sucking on my intrusion before playfully biting the tip. The woman was driving me mad, and I kicked myself for waiting so long to connect with her like this.

While I wasn't going to push her to let me inside her, I needed to relieve some of the pressure of my cock. Placing my hands under her ass, I lifted her up my body and wrapped her legs around my waist, the wall behind her an added anchor. I would tell her later on how much I preferred her in dresses. Easy access and all that happy shit.

Rubbing myself against her core only made me want her more, but I would stay true to my word and wait until she was ready.

Thirty-Five

Sully

I was lost.

Ripped away was everything I'd ever known, and in its place was a man who both conflicted and excited me.

He made me feel bad for my decision not to have sex with him in his bathroom, although I pretty much led him on by allowing him to go down on me, then again by exciting me with his lips wrapped around my breasts. But when he pulled himself free from his jeans, and started rubbing himself against my core, something told me to wait. I wasn't sure why because I'd wanted him then, but I knew enough to listen to my inner voice, something which had been missing for some time.

And yes, he yelled at me for denying him, but he'd never made a move to take what was rightfully his. By law I was his wife, so I had to give it up whenever my husband wanted it. Right?

Then he'd gone and backed me against the wall in his room at the club. Asking me if I wanted him to kiss me. Of course I did, and I voiced as much, because my inner self told me to go for it.

The hairs of his beard tickled my chin, but that wasn't what I focused on. It was his lips and the way they were making love to my mouth. It was his tongue and the passion he poured forth, letting me know how much he was enjoying me. That I could give him something which he craved was a heady feeling. It was the way his thickness pressed against my core, the slight sting of his rough zipper against my barely clothed body sublime, the slightest friction against my clit mind-numbingly erotic. And it was the way his fingers dug into my soft skin, possessing and claiming me as his.

"I want you so bad," he groaned against my lips. His kiss was amazing, making me feel truly wanted for the first time in my life. Whenever Vex had kissed me, even in the beginning, it was rough and demanding.

Never gentle.

Never passionate.

Never like this.

It was true I didn't know much about Cole Marek, but I knew enough from the way he tried to protect me that he was a good man. I knew enough from his kiss that he desired me, and I knew enough from the way he talked to me to realize he was conflicted about his feelings for me.

But in a good way.

My instinct told me it was certainly in a good way.

A loud pounding on the door interrupted our little tryst, and it was me who complained by cursing into the air around us. We tried to continue devouring each other with a rawness I'd never experienced before, but whoever was in the hallway wasn't going away anytime soon. So it was best he address the intruder.

"What?" he yelled, before running his tongue along the

side of my neck, only to stop to suck on my earlobe, tickling me with his breath when he whispered into my ear, "I wish we were back at my house right now."

"Me too," I confessed, telling him the truth, and in turn basically letting him know I would have given into whatever he wanted to do to me. He looked surprised by my admission, but the look quickly faded into growing agitation toward the person outside his door.

"Marek, open the fuckin' door, man!" Stone yelled through the thick wood. "Looks like I'll be taking these two shopping." He rapped on the door again. "Come on before I change my mind." I heard Adelaide say something to him but I couldn't really focus, not with Cole's mouth still so close to mine again.

"I'm gonna kill him. For real this time." He said the words, but I knew he didn't mean them. I saw the way he was with his VP, and it was like they were true brothers. They shared a special bond, a connection only death's grip could break. So, he could threaten him all he wanted, I knew they were just words said in sexual frustration. It actually made me smile.

"What are you smirking at, woman?" he asked, setting me down to rest on my feet before walking toward the door.

"Nothing," I lied. Watching him move would never get old for me. He possessed a certain swagger when he walked, a dominance which couldn't be taught.

Swinging open the door, he stared at Stone while waiting for him to say something else. A silent message passed between them, and it wasn't until Stone looked at me then back to Cole that I understood what they had communicated. He knew he'd interrupted something big, and his eyes were apologetic, as was his posture.

A couple tense seconds ticked by before anyone spoke. "I'll take them, Marek. You don't have to worry about a thing."

Looking back at me, Cole extended his hand and I readily

accepted. He walked me out toward the front door, Adelaide and Stone following close by. Once outside and standing next to Adelaide's blue Honda, she gave up her keys, but not without a few choice words first.

"I'm fully capable of driving, Stone. Don't be so pig-head-ed." She huffed and puffed, but the look in her eyes while she verbally dueled with the man was very telling. I'd never told anyone what my new friend confessed to me about their 'rela-tionship,' and I never would. Not that I had much choice, seeing as how I only talked to a few people, but I would still never betray her confidence.

"I'm not riding in the passenger seat like some kind of pussy, Addy. Now, stop giving me a hard time about this."

"Well, you could ride in the backseat if you want," she said, smiling because she knew how much her arguing bothered him.

"That's even worse." Opening the passenger door for her, he grumbled, "The man is supposed to drive. Always." As soon as she was completely seated inside the car, she tried to retort, but he closed the door right when she started talking. Chuck-ling to himself all the way around to the driver's side, he glanced up at us still standing there and said, "Come on, Marek. Say good-bye. I don't want to be gone all goddamn day."

"Fuck you," Cole answered, smiling as he opened the back door for me. Before I stepped a foot inside, he grabbed my waist and pulled me to him. "I'll bring something home for dinner. Then maybe we can watch a movie, if you're up for one." Such a simple plan for tonight, but it meant more to me than I could ever express. It seemed he was trying to turn over a new leaf, and the gesture went a long way in my book. When he placed a lingering kiss on my lips, all I wanted to do was wrap myself up in his arms again, but I knew it had to wait.

We were on the road for a full two minutes before Adelaide or Stone finally spoke. "What the hell was that back there,

Sully?" Stone asked, staring at me through the rearview mirror. The confusion on his face was rather comical, and if he hadn't been so serious, I would have laughed.

"What do you mean?" I asked, fidgeting with the hem of my sundress.

"What do you mean, what do I mean? The goddamn kiss. Marek doesn't kiss anyone. Ever," he practically shouted.

"Calm down or you're gonna scare her," Adelaide scolded, hitting him on the arm for good measure. "Jeez, Stone. What the hell's gotten into you?"

"I'll tell you *who* I'd like to get into," he retorted, and had I not known about the two of them his reply would have completely gone over my head.

My friend huffed in the front seat, but when she turned around to check on me, she winked and smiled, masking her expression as soon as she faced front once again.

Thirty-Six

Sully

My day with Adelaide was so much fun, more than I think I'd ever had. Her ease, confidence and humor soothed me, bringing out sides of my personality I hadn't even realized existed. Our banter back and forth wasn't forced but simply flowed, although Stone was the one who received the brunt of it when he started complaining we were taking too long.

I'd never had a girlfriend before, and while the dynamics of the relationship were new to me, Adelaide made it very easy.

My father chose to homeschool me my entire life, so I was never surrounded by girls my own age. Yes, our club had gatherings from time to time, and while there were other kids present, I often chose to keep to myself. Either the other kids made fun of me for how black my hair was, calling me a witch, or they'd call me a slut because my body decided to develop early.

When Stone and Adelaide dropped me off back at Cole's, it wasn't until I was standing on the front porch that it even dawned on me that I didn't have a key to his house. I was in mid freak-out, prepared to walk back toward the car to tell them I had no way inside, when the front door opened.

Cole stood on the threshold in nothing but a pair of black sweatpants, holding a white towel and running it back and forth over his wet hair. His bare torso was glorious, every muscle twitching with the exertion to dry himself. The beautiful artwork on his skin danced, and if it wasn't for the sharp burst of the horn behind me, I would have certainly lost time watching his every movement. Daring a glance below his waistline, I noticed the outline of his thickness through his sweats. And while I was utterly turned on, I was also a little wary that Adelaide had seen him as well. It was hard to miss, and I wondered how many other women had the pleasure of sneaking a peak at Cole Marek's goods.

A sudden feeling of jealousy wrapped its ugly arms around me and almost suffocated me. The emotion was foreign, and I had no idea where it had come from. *Is this how he feels when Jagger's around me? Is this why he almost killed him that night? Because if this is the same thing, I don't want any part of it.*

Realizing I was being irrational, I beamed a smile at him as he ushered me inside.

"Did you ladies have fun? I hope Stone behaved himself," he said, walking toward the kitchen to grab a bottled water. After taking a swig, he made a move to pass it to me, but then decided against it at the last minute. "I forgot you don't like to share my germs," he taunted, a smirk resting nicely on his lips.

I'd had the man's tongue in my mouth. What was so bad about sharing a drink with him?

"That's okay. I think I've changed my mind," I responded, reaching out to take the drink. After a satisfying gulp, I handed it back, waiting for his next move.

I wasn't gonna lie; the sight of him half-naked was doing wicked things to my body, and if there was any reservation before today about finally joining with my husband, all fears and concerns were washed clear away. First by his soul-crushing kiss earlier, and then by the feelings firing off inside me from the mere look of him.

"Did you just get out of the shower?"

"Yeah. I just had a quick workout and wanted to wash up before you got home." *Home.* What a weird concept. But he was right. His home was now my home as well, and the sooner I accepted it, the easier things would fall into place.

Leaning against the kitchen counter, Cole kept his eyes on me. His hair was sticking up in a few spots, but he'd never looked sexier. A few beads of water ran down his torso between his strong pecs, disappearing into the waistband of his pants. I watched the liquid vanish, and it wasn't until he coughed that I realized I was blatantly checking him out. Again. A light blush crept over my face, instantly giving away my embarrassment at being caught.

"Like I said before, it's your right to stare at me as much as you want." He grinned and turned around to grab a large white box. "I didn't know what you'd prefer, but everyone loves pizza. Right?"

"I know I do."

"Good." Gesturing toward the small table in the corner of the kitchen, we both sat down and he dished out a slice for me. We ate in silence, our gazes connecting every now and then. Neither one of us knew what to say, plus I was too famished to think about anything other than downing the yummy food in front of me.

Once I'd had my fill, I leaned back in my seat and reached for my drink. He'd finished off his initial water and ended up handing me a fresh one. This one I didn't share, drinking the majority of it after my meal.

"So," he said, startling me from the silence of the room.

"What have you heard about my club?" With arms folded across his chest, his biceps popped even more. I itched to feel them wrapped around me again, but all in due time I supposed. He'd started a real conversation, and I would be an idiot not to snag the invitation.

Trying to hide my smile, because I now knew it was bullshit, I revealed the worst thing I'd heard about the Knights Corruption growing up. "Well, I heard that, twice a year, the members of your club were involved in a huge orgy, and at the end, one person was chosen to be sacrificed. The blood of the chosen a gift to ensure the club's prosperity, or some stuff like that." My lips curved up, but quickly fell when Cole leaned forward with a surprised look on his face. At first, I thought I'd said something which was in fact true, but seconds later he frowned before smacking the top of the table, laughter pouring from him in complete hysterics.

"Are you fuckin' shittin' me, woman? That's the kind of crap they told people we did?" His rumble of happiness was music to my ears, never mind that the sight of him smiling was mesmerizing. He was gorgeous. His ice-blue eyes lit up from the inside out, his lips provoking me to jump across the table and bite them, they were so alluring. I'd gotten so lost in the sight of him that I almost missed what he said next. "We only have the orgy once a year, and we sacrifice two people. Tell 'em to get their facts straight," he teased, winking at me while he continued to find amusement in what I'd told him.

A short time later, we found ourselves sitting on the couch. For as intimate as the space was, it was very homey. A single couch, recliner, and end table were the only furniture in the room. A big-screen TV was mounted over a huge fireplace, the beams of the log cabin becoming the second focal point of the home. There were no pictures hung, or any personal effects throughout his house, something I took notice of the first night I stayed there. The color scheme was brown and cream, the lighter color coming from a fleece blanket thrown over the back of the couch, as well as from the few pillows littering the sparse furniture.

"You really need some pictures or something in here," I offered, watching him move about in front of me while he decided which movie to pick.

"Okay. Why don't you pick something out then? Maybe on your next excursion with Adelaide, you can bring something home that you like." His back was turned toward me as he spoke, and while I wanted to look at his face, I wasn't too upset about having to look at the back of him either. He'd thrown on a white T-shirt after dinner, the fabric molding to his body in perfection. If I didn't watch myself, I would literally start drooling.

"How about a scary movie? What do ya think?" he asked, turning around to display a few of the horror movies Adelaide had initially dropped off.

I didn't want to disappoint him, but I knew from experience they weren't my cup of tea. I should have just said no, and asked for a comedy or action film. But instead, without thinking, I blurted out something I should have kept to myself.

"I tried to watch a scary movie with Jagger and I practically ended up in his lap, I was so scared." Initially, I chuckled at the recollection, but my choice of words hit a very tense nerve of his.

Gone was the laid-back look on his face, replaced with a controlled anger. The mere mention of the prospect had his jaw clenching and nostrils flaring, his large hands fisted so tight I thought he was going to lose all feeling in them. "Is that right?" he asked, the clench of his teeth, shouting at me how upset he was, even if he did try to hide it.

The only thing I could do was apologize, so that's exactly

what I did. He may not say 'I'm sorry' for anything, but I grew up tasting those words every damn day.

"I'm sorry. I didn't mean anything by it. Honestly. I... I just don't like scary movies," I mumbled, hoping like hell he was going to let my slipup go. Turning his back to me once more, he rooted through the box and picked out a different movie, one he didn't show me before sliding it into the DVD player.

Just Friends was the title. One I'd seen with Jagger, but I sure as hell wasn't going to mention his name again.

A half hour into the film and my eyes started to drift close. It'd been a long day, one filled with warring emotions. I'd been scared, confused, aroused, happy, and conflicted, all within the span of twelve hours, and it seemed my body had had enough. Without even realizing, I cuddled closer to Cole's large frame, my hands tucked into my lap while I rested my head on his shoulder. I knew he watched me. I could feel his eyes on me, but I was too exhausted to read into it.

Wanting nothing more than to rest, I closed my eyes for good and gave into the dark slumber beckoning me.

Thirty-Seven

Marek

I figured out my new favorite pastime was watching Sully, whether she was awake or off somewhere in dreamland. She'd fallen asleep barely past the beginning of the movie, and I knew it was because she'd had quite the day.

Carrying her sleeping form to our room, I removed her dress and bra and laid her on the bed. Since there was no place I'd rather be, I locked up the house and decided to join her, crawling under the covers and pulling her close to me.

She stirred slightly in her sleep, her lips parting in the softest moans I'd ever heard, but it wasn't clear if she was having a nightmare or dreaming of something naughty. I had my answer when she reached for me and whispered my name, the sound floating in the air above us, waiting to be snatched and held close.

"I'm here," I whispered, pulling her closer. My cock was at full attention, nestled against her plump ass, and it didn't help any when she started moving her hips and grinding her backside into me. Whatever restraint I still had control over was quickly fleeing. I didn't want to take advantage of her, but if she kept that shit up, I was gonna flip her over, spread her luscious thighs wide and take her once and for all.

"Cole... please," she cried out, that time louder than before. What was I doing in her dreams? Was I angry with her and she was pleading with me? Or was I teasing her and she wanted more? I couldn't wait to find out, so I shifted our bodies until she was lying flat on her back with me hovering over her, resting on my forearms so as not to crush her delicate form.

Leaning down, I ran my lips over the smooth expanse of her neck, licking, biting and kissing my way up toward her earlobe. "Tell me what you want me to do to you, Sully," I growled, low enough to not scare her, but firm enough to make her comply. When she didn't answer me, I nudged her legs further apart and settled myself in between, the rigidness of my cock brushing over her barely clothed pussy. I thought leaving her panties on would be a deterrent, a barrier to leave her alone while she slept, but everything changed when she called out my name.

Asleep or not, I had to act on that shit.

Softly kissing her jaw, making my way toward those delectable lips, I continued to demand she tell me what she wanted from me. Finally, once I laid my mouth over hers, our breaths melding together as one, she gave me something to work with.

"Cole," she cried out again. "Please take me, make me yours." Instinctually, she wrapped her legs around mine, digging her heels into the backs of my thighs just like I'd imagined she'd do. I could have easily freed myself and taken her, but I needed her to be fully awake for this, give me her permission before I finally claimed what was mine.

I wouldn't steal her passion like some thief in the night.

"Sully... Wake up." I kissed her lips once more, grinding myself into her to try and rouse her from sleep. "Sully," I said more harshly. "Wake up, baby."

Her eyelids fluttered open and it took her a few seconds to focus on me, to realize she wasn't still dreaming but was instead staring into the face of the man she'd just been fantasizing about. "Cole?" Confusion painted her lovely face. A beam of moonlight filtered into the otherwise dark room, illuminating her jet-black hair, which was fanned out over her pillow, the starkness of it against her creamy skin a fascinating contrast. Her dark chocolate eyes pinned me, and I was unable to move or speak. I wanted to drown in her gaze, and if she wanted we could stay like this for all eternity.

I was losing my reality with her, and I knew it.

Whatever hold she had over me grew, and I didn't foresee it ever stopping.

"What are you doing?" she asked, licking her lips while her eyes focused on my mouth.

"You were calling my name in your sleep, so I thought I'd wake you," I answered half-truthfully.

"By lying on top of me?" She smiled, the slight tilt of her pink lips entrancing me. Before I could answer, she tightened her legs and ground herself against me, my cock jerking from the pressure. I'd never wanted someone so badly before, and if she didn't give in to me this time, I thought I was literally going to go off the deep end. Dive over the cliff into insanity.

"Do you want me to kiss you again?" I wanted to start small then work my way toward my ultimate goal.

"Yes," she panted, raising her head to take the step before I could. Her soft tongue dueled with mine, the kiss even better than the first time. Although we were new to each other, our passion was an age-old dance, our rhythm falling into place rather quickly.

We teased and enticed.

We demanded and submitted.

We stole each other's hunger and returned it with a fervent desire, the likes of which I'd never felt before.

When I couldn't take it any longer, I dared to ask her the question I hoped she was ready for. "Do you want me to take you? To claim you as mine once and for all?"

An exhale of breath was all it took for her to respond.

No hesitation.

No waiting.

"Yes."

Changing positions so I was on my knees, I reached for the thin material around her hips and drew the fabric down over her legs, discarding them once they reached her ankles. Needing to savor the moment, I teased her skin with my mouth, working my way from her feet up to her knees, then finally resting just below the one place I wanted to bury myself. Raining light kisses all over her heated flesh, I brought my hand up to play with her, stretching her apart with two of my fingers, pumping in and out of her sweet pussy, my vision blurring with lust.

"Oh, God, Cole... Yes," she gasped, writhing under me and gripping the sheets in ecstasy.

Wanting to taste her desire for me once again, I licked her slowly, reveling in the way my touch made her feel. She cried out, calling my name over and over again until she finally clenched on my fingers and rode out her orgasm, my lips wrapped around her clit to draw out every last drop of pleasure.

Her satisfaction painted my face when I finally crawled up her body, pushed my sweats the rest of the way off, gripped myself and teased her opening with my thickness.

"Are you on any kind of birth control?" I inquired, praying

she was so I could take her bare. I had condoms readily available, though, just in case.

A quick look of sadness infiltrated her eyes, putting me on guard instantly. "No, but I can't have kids anyway. So...." She stopped talking, a sudden embarrassment stealing the rest of what she was going to say.

"How do you know that?"

"Trust me. I can't get pregnant." She turned her head so I couldn't see her beautiful browns. "Please don't make me talk about it right now," she pleaded.

I would get to the bottom of *that* statement, but I agreed with her, now wasn't the time. Instead, I chose to make sure this was what she wanted, asking her again for her consent.

She turned her head back to look at me and gave me a simple nod, a bite of her lip showing me she was ready and willing.

Pushing myself inside her, inch by agonizingly slow inch, was the best feeling in the world. Her tight walls gripped me like a fist, strangling the pleasure out of me before I even started. Making sure to take it slow so I didn't explode too soon, I stopped halfway in and leaned down to kiss her.

"I can't move right now or I'm gonna be done before I even start." I was in the middle of counting in my head when she thrust her hips up toward me, sheathing more of me than I was ready to give. "Fuck!" I yelled. It was another five controlled breaths before I was ready to stake my claim on her. Possess her with everything clamoring inside me.

"Goddamn it! You're too tight," I groaned, throwing her leg over my waist to open her up some more.

"Does it not feel good?" she worried, her fingers gripping my arms while I bucked into her.

"It feels *too* good. That's the problem."

"That doesn't sound like a problem at all," she said, her

quiet laughter dying when I pulled out and pushed back inside her roughly. "Oooooo... Oh, my God... Do that again," she demanded.

Of course I gave her what she wanted.

Over and over, and over again.

Ten minutes and a lot of exertion later, I could tell she was close to detonating. Her moans had become more intense, her demands on my body more aggressive. I would have never pegged her for someone who would take such an active role during sex, her otherwise quiet demeanor indicating quite the contrary.

Pinning her hands above her head, I thrust deeper, letting go of the last strand of my control, punishing her body with my own, driving out every last cry and plea from her throat. Reveling in her pleasure, a cocky grin spread across my face as I nipped at her bottom lip, demanding entrance into her tempting mouth.

"Sully... I... I can't hold out any longer. Fuck! You're too much," I growled, pushing her further up the bed with my intensity.

"Make me come." She writhed beneath me, flexing her hands in my hold. Wrapping my free arm around her waist, I held her back off the bed and drove into her like some kind of wild animal, shouting out her name as soon as I felt her pussy clench around me, shivers of bliss firing off inside both of us. My vision actually went hazy, chasing after my own goddamn air just so I could breathe.

I buried my head in the crook of her neck, waiting while I came back down to reality. Licking at her salty skin, I realized right then that I would never get enough of her.

Her mouth.

Her skin.

Her pussy.

Just... her.

Everything about her called to me, and not strictly in the carnal way. Something inside her spoke to me. It was unknown what she was trying to tell me, but in due time I knew I would uncover the unspoken messages.

Thirty-Eight

Sully

Lying fully sated in Cole's arms was like a dream, the connection between us more than physical. Granted, we didn't really know each other that well—yet—but there was an undeniable attraction pulling us together. While he was the most beautiful man I'd ever laid eyes on, there was something within him which beckoned to me.

I felt it when he looked at me.

I felt it when he touched me.

I felt it when he called out my name.

The pain he tried to shield from me broke free when he thought I wasn't paying attention, his vulnerability where I was concerned teetering between awareness and obscurity.

My ears pricked to listen to his breathing, trying to determine whether or not he'd drifted off to sleep. He'd taken me twice more, once on top of the bathroom vanity and again in the shower. Each time was more exhilarating than the last, my fear of my new life abandoning me as I gazed into the promise of my future. Although my new husband had upset me with his words on occasion, I knew it was simply because he didn't know how to act.

Was I making excuses for his behavior? Yes.

Did I understand what it was like to have my world flipped on its ass, scrambling around to try and make sense of Fate's warped sense of humor?

Absolutely.

Although Cole Marek was the man who'd kidnapped me, he was the same man who'd essentially saved my life.

He'd forgotten to shut off the bedside light, its soft illumination dancing over his relaxed form. Propping my head on his chest, I stared up into his handsome face. His eyelids fluttered in his sleep, a half-smirk resting on his full and inviting lips. Breaths of soft, warm air hit my cheek, while his heart fell into a steady, easy rhythm. His body heat warmed me. The only thing we had draped over us was a thin sheet, the rest of the blankets were strewn over the bed in a crumpled mess, but I was nice and cozy lying half on top of him.

"If you don't stop admiring me, I'm going to be forced to take you yet again," he muttered, startling me from fantasizing about that very same thing.

"I thought you were sleeping." When I tried to move, he quickly changed positions until he had me pinned beneath him. As soon as I was on my back, I spread my legs wide so he could snuggle in between. The man was insatiable, but I quickly realized I was too.

"How can I sleep with you next to me? I'd be a fool to waste one precious second dreaming of you when I could have the real thing right now." He grinned, his self-assuredness quite the turn on.

To be desired, truly coveted, was the most intoxicating feeling in the world. I'd never had anyone look at me the way he did, even when he was upset with me, or confused about our new situation together. His blue eyes pierced me with the knowledge that he'd come to save me. Whether he was aware of it or not, I wasn't sure, but his soul spoke to mine.

His lips traced a line from my collarbone to my ear, a place he loved to tease with his tongue before making me break out in goose bumps, the contrast of wet skin against warm breath enough to make me squirm in delight.

"I wanna ask you something, and I pray you've come to trust me enough to tell me the truth," he prodded, his soft kisses on my skin a distraction to what was coming next.

Did I trust him?

I was beginning to.

Was I afraid of what he was going to ask me to reveal?

Unequivocally.

He withdrew his body from mine and sat back on the bed, pulling me up until I was in a seated position myself. *I can only imagine what he's going to ask me.*

"Earlier tonight, when I asked you if you were on the pill, you told me you couldn't have kids, to not worry about it. When I tried to ask you to elaborate, you shut down, a sadness filling your eyes I've unfortunately seen before."

I noticeably stiffened, preparing myself for the conversation he was going to force me to have.

I'd only told Cole a few things about what I'd experienced at the hands of Vex and my father, but he didn't know the half of it. Shit, he didn't even know a quarter of it, if I was being honest. He'd seen the scars covering my body, and I'd told him how some of them got there, but there was so much more to my story. A story I was ready to burn in the hottest fire, then watch as the embers of my tragic past floated away on the wind.

Instead of delving too far into the past, I decided to give him part of the truth. Steeling my nerves, my eyes flitted over his face but avoided his eyes. I knew if I looked directly at him,

I would weaken and falter. I'd end up pushing myself back into the darkest parts of my mind, a place I never wanted to venture into again.

"Well," he prompted. "How do you know you can't have kids? You're a young woman, around twenty or so, right?" It was funny he wasn't sure, and I wasn't positive of his age either, yet there we were, sitting across from each other on the bed after a night of passion. Newly married and still discovering the little details about each other. "So what makes you think you can't pop out a few rugrats?" He grinned, his smile softening his callous choice of words.

Wrapping the sheet tighter around me so I wasn't so vulnerable, I fidgeted with my hands while I tried to find the right words. His stare burned through me and I knew he wouldn't wait long for me to respond, patience definitely not his strong suit.

I stared at my hands while I spoke, an action he didn't approve of; his finger moved to lift my chin so he could see my eyes. Taking the deepest breath, my anxiety expelling from me in waves, I mustered up enough strength to start.

"A few years ago, I was bl-bleeding pretty badly, so I was taken to the hospital. My father refused at first because he didn't want any outsiders in our business, but when he saw how bad I was, he reluctantly agreed." I tried to look away again, but his hold on my chin was strong. "The doctor told me there was too much damage, that the chances of me having kids were so minute, I would have more luck being struck by lightning. Twice." A lone tear escaped and trickled down my cheek. I hated that my past still terrified me, but I hadn't been in the company of the Knights Corruption very long. Even if they were basically keeping me safe and sound from my own club.

I hadn't allowed myself to give into the paranoia of what Cole had mentioned earlier, about being on guard and waiting for the Savage Reapers to come and collect what was rightfully theirs.

Me.

"But I don't understand. Why was there any damage to begin with?" His question was sincere, but his eyes told me he knew the worst part of the story was yet to come. By the look of expectancy on his face, he knew *who* was the cause of my dreadful tale.

I couldn't help it.

I broke.

"Cole... please," I begged. "Don't make me...." I couldn't finish, my body shaking while tears streamed down my face. He'd finally released his hold on my chin, his body closing in on me and bringing me in for a hug.

"It's okay, Sully. No one will ever hurt you again," he promised, holding me so close he almost crushed me in his arms. "But I need to know. You have to tell me."

"Why?" I cried, pushing myself away from him. "Why do I have to tell you? Why do you want me to relive it? Why can't you just let it go?" I wanted to run, to barricade myself inside the bathroom for the rest of my life. I was ashamed and mortified that he was going to find out yet another awful thing that happened to me. Pity wasn't something I thought I could bear. Not from him.

He made a move toward me but I only backed up, desperately needing the added space if I was going to continue. Although I didn't think I would be able to.

"Because," he seethed, "when I finally put a bullet between their eyes, I wanna make sure they know *all* the reasons their lives are being snatched from them. Trust me, there's a long list as it stands, but to know their fate was sealed because of the damage they did to one of their own, will sink their souls into the deepest pits of Hell."

He said 'their eyes.' There was no mistaking he was talking about my father and the guy who'd tortured me for six long years. Vex.

Rising from the bed, I walked toward the window, moon-light slicing through and adding to the barest of light already encasing the room. I knew in my heart there was no escape from this.

Like a Band-Aid. Right off.

With my back toward him, I finished my story as quickly as I could. "Vex had gone on a bender for a few days, shoving so much coke up his nose I'm surprised he was still alive. Never mind whatever else he'd ingested to help him fight off his demons. I was tucked away inside our bedroom, keeping to myself, but for some reason he thought I was messing around on him. His paranoia strangled him and no matter how much I pleaded, trying to make him see reason, he was convinced I'd been with someone else. Of course I wasn't, but there was no getting through to him.

"During one of his rants, he attacked me, smacking my head against the wall before shoving me onto the bed. My head was killing me, preventing me from trying to protect myself, but in the end I guess it didn't really matter. He always got what he wanted, no matter how much I fought in the beginning. Screaming at me that he was gonna make me pay for fucking around, he tied me to the bed, the rope so tight it cut into my skin whenever I tried to move." My shoulders trembled, but I steeled my reserve as best I could before continuing. "He raped me over and over. Violently. He left me tied up for two days, and when I'd made a mess because he refused to let me use the bathroom, he... he...." I hiccupped, not thinking I could finish. Thankfully, Cole kept his distance, otherwise, I would have refused to continue. I needed the space. It was just easier that way. Well... 'easier' was probably the wrong choice of word.

"When his body was depleted, he raped me with anything he could find. His beer bottle. An old baseball bat he had in the closet. It went on for what seemed like forever, and no matter how much I begged and screamed, he never relented. I knew my father was aware something was going on because I heard them talking outside our bedroom, Vex telling him he was teaching me a lesson. I tried to call for help, but I was too beaten and broken." The horrific details rushed over me, prickling my flesh like the sharpest of blades.

Tears streamed down my face, my memories like a plague on my soul.

"He left me to bleed like an animal for a whole day, tied to the bed." Turning to face Cole, I needed to see his reaction. I knew he was going to be angry, infuriated even, but I had no idea how much rage one person could muster inside them.

His eyes turned dark, his skin heating like he was on fire from the inside. He stood before me a man ready to kill and right then, I knew he would never let anything bad ever happen to me again. Although he'd forced me to relive one of the worst things to ever happen to me, it made me realize I was no longer in danger, that the man before me would do whatever it took to keep me safe.

Closing the short distance between us, he took me in his arms and vowed to end the men who'd kept me a prisoner my entire life, beating and degrading me for their own amusement, suffocating whatever life burned inside me until they all but snuffed out my essence.

Thirty-Nine

Marek

A month had passed since Sully told me what Vex had done to her. It had taken everything in me not to gather my men and hunt him down like the animal he was in that time.

Realizing I *was* gonna kill him one day—probably sooner than later—gave me solace. It wasn't much, but it was something I could cling to until the day arrived.

"Let's go!" I shouted from the living room. "We're gonna be late, goddamn it!" Not that I should care, but I was a stickler for punctuality, and the fact that the club cookout had started forty-five minutes ago and I was still waiting for Sully to finish getting ready was grating on me.

When I wasn't involved with the club, I spent every available second with my wife, ravaging her and making her scream out my name. She'd finally become comfortable with me, laughing when I playfully teased her, as well as dishing out her own form of medicine. I'd opened up a bit more about my past, as she did hers. I knew she still kept things from me, but I vowed not to push her anymore. Not until she was ready.

That the woman was still alive and going strong was a testament to how strong she was, having faced the Devil and spit in his face.

Every day that passed was one step closer to happiness. I hadn't realized when I snatched her from the pits of Hell that she would change me. It'd been a long time since I'd had a purpose in life, other than plotting the downfall of my enemy and taking my club legit. And while both things drove me each day, they were nothing compared to the woman I'd forced to marry me, thinking at the time it was just the perfect 'fuck you' to the Savage Reapers.

It was the first time in my life I felt whole, if that made any sense. My need to protect and watch over her was sometimes suffocating, probably because I'd never possessed such a need before. Yes, I strived to keep all my brothers alive, watching their backs as they did mine. But they didn't play on a loop in my head, wondering if they were happy, if someone was going to come and snatch them from my life. They were all adults, knew the risk involved, a risk which would hopefully diminish to nothing once we were out from underneath the cartel.

"Woman, if you don't show yourself in the next two seconds, I'm comin' in there and draggin' you out as you are. I don't care if your half-naked or not." I tried to be patient, but it just wasn't in me. I had a temper, and Sully had witnessed it on more than one occasion. Lately, she paid me no attention when I started spouting off at the mouth, our comfort level with each other rivaling those who'd been together for years. It was odd, thinking I'd only known her for a short time, yet I felt as if she'd always been with me.

Like I'd always been waiting for her.

"Don't get your panties in a bunch, Marek," she teased, appearing on the threshold of the living room, a sultry smile lighting up her face. She called me by the name she knew before she was aware of my given name during those times when she was either upset with me, or trying to ruffle my feathers. Like now.

"Oh, hell no!" I shouted, already crushing the distance between us and shoving her back toward our room. Her look of surprise was apparent, but I never gave her an opportunity to question me until she was planted in the middle of our bedroom.

"I thought you were yelling at me to hurry up. Well... I'm done." With her hands on her hips, she asked, "Why are you making us even more late?" She had to know there was no way I was letting her out of the house dressed in that skimpy-ass outfit.

She'd told me about how she was forced to dress when she was with Vex, always wearing baggy clothes for fear he would beat her for wearing something that actually fit. I never wanted to stifle her and make her feel as if she couldn't express herself, and the majority of the time, I didn't have much of a problem with the clothes she wore, dragging many a bag through the front door after a shopping trip with Adelaide. One of my men always accompanied them on their outings and while they complained, Sully knew I was protecting her, still not having heard a peep from the Savage Reapers. Every passing day only put me on guard that much more.

"Are you kidding me with what you have on right now?" I asked, feeling a mixture of incredulity and irritation. Her plain white tank top dipped in the front, showing off the cups of her bra, which were fucking purple. Every bastard's eyes would be ogling her tits, therefore forcing me to mess somebody up.

Her shorts were short, like *really* short, and because she'd thrown on sandals with a huge heel—I think she called them wedges or some shit like that—they made her legs look long... and her shorts minuscule.

252 / S. NELSON

I could only handle one thing at a time.

Taking a quick once-over of her reflection, spinning around to make sure she wasn't missing anything, she asked, "What's wrong with what I have on? It's hot outside, Cole. I'll probably still be dying in what I have on." It *was* rather hot outside, the California summer kicking it up with record highs. Her hair was pulled up into a messy bun resting on top of her head, no doubt preparing as much as she could for the stifling temperatures.

"I can't do it," I said, rifling through the closet to find her something else to put on. "You know I wouldn't normally tell you what to wear, but this is too tempting, Sully. The guys are gonna be drinking, and if any one of them looks at you too long, I'm gonna end up punching them the hell out."

"Oh, you're just overreacting," she admonished, moving to walk away from me. "Come on, let's go. Everything will be fine." When I didn't budge, she turned around and raised her brows at me, waiting for me to come to my senses and follow behind her.

"I'm not budging, woman," I gritted, reaching into one of her shopping bags and pulling out a thin strapped dress which still had the tags on it. While it was short, it was much better than what she was prancing around in. The dress was a cream color with a thick red stripe in the middle. It was nice. She'd obviously liked it if she bought it. Well, technically, I'd given her money to buy it, but who's fussing over logistics? "Here, put this on?"

The Sully who was forced into the Knights Corruption would have never said a word, taken the dress and changed immediately. But the longer she was with me, the more comfortable she was in expressing her thoughts and opinions, which was a good thing.

Most of the time.

But it was times like this when her newly formed strong will was a pain in my ass. And even though she tried my patience now and again, when it boiled down to it, I was her man, her husband, and as such had the final word. Most times I let her go, but when I felt strongly about something, whatever I deemed was law.

And this was one such time.

She stalked forward, stopping when she was a few feet away from me. "Are you serious?"

"Very."

We stared at each other, a battle of wills passing between us. But I wasn't relenting. After twenty tense seconds, she snatched the dress from my hand and stomped toward the bathroom, cursing under her breath the entire time.

"You can change out here, sweetheart," I teased. She slammed the door behind her before I could say anything else.

I thought it was the quickest she'd ever changed, emerging two minutes later. She was trying not to smile, but her sexy lips twitched while she watched for my reaction.

"Motherfucker!" I cursed. "That's almost as bad," I confessed, running my eyes up and down her seductive body. I had no idea the top of the dress was so form-fitting, and while the fabric flared out at her waist, it only came down to mid-thigh, those same damn sandals making her legs look like they went on for miles.

She looked beautiful. Too beautiful to be hanging around a bunch of horny bastards.

"I'm not changing again, Cole. There's nothing wrong with this dress and you know it."

Glancing at the clock, I mumbled under my breath as I took her arm and guided her out the door.

I'm gonna kill someone today. I just know it.

"How long before you decide it's time, Prez?" Zip drunkenly shouted, his body swaying into Hawke, who'd been standing next to him to hold him upright.

"Calm down, man. Not here. Save that shit for Chambers," Stone grated, his patience for the young member's hot temper waning. His cold stare shut Zip up just as he was about to spout off again. The boy was constantly itching to settle unpaid debts between the two clubs, only ever knowing about the destruction they'd caused in the past couple years against his brothers. He had no idea just how far back it went.

Motioning to Hawke, I tried to dispel any further rantings from Zip. It was a day for relaxation, a cookout in full swing as the sun dipped low in the horizon. "Go find him someone to occupy his time," I demanded, jerking my head toward the small group of females huddled together across the compound. "And make sure you don't offer yourself up as well, seeing as how Edana will be here any second." He laughed, but I gripped him by his collar. "I mean it, Hawke. I don't need her freakin' out. Can't handle that today."

"Don't worry. I'll be on my best behavior." He saluted, winking as he turned a staggering Zip toward the laughter of one of his future bedmates.

"I'll believe that when I see it," I muttered, taking a pull of my beer while I watched them walk away.

It was days like this that reminded me of who I was, what I was in charge of. Looking around the wide open space, the confines of the large metal gates keeping us safe, I watched as people enjoyed themselves, filling up their plates while they caught up with people they hadn't seen in some time.

Our cookouts were a time to chill and appreciate what was real in life, family and friends being the most important.

Although, in our crew, friends *were* family. We had a few people who didn't always see eye to eye—Trigger and Stone being the two men who jumped to the forefront of my mind at the moment—but everyone here would take a bullet for the person standing next to them. Women included.

To be an old lady of one of the men, they had to love and embrace the club, and everything that went along with it. Good and bad. And that was a hard thing if someone didn't grow up in this life, which was why most outsiders weren't built for it. The only person I knew of who wasn't fully integrated, yet was around us from time to time, was Adelaide.

I knew something was brewing between her and my VP, and the best of luck to them for trying to figure it the hell out. There was many an obstacle in the way, her uncle only being one of them. But my boy deserved to be happy.

Speak of the devil and he shall appear. "Hey," Stone greeted, bumping my shoulder with his as he took a seat next to me. "Party's good. Weather's nice," he assessed. "And Sully sure looks hot as fuck."

It took me a quick second for his words to penetrate, and when they did I offered the only retort that would hit him right back.

"Adelaide sure looks tasty," I said, watching his expression fade from amusement to shock.

Then controlled anger.

The smirk I threw his way played with him until he cursed out loud and rose from his seat, making a quick beeline toward the woman I'd teased him about. He was becoming so predictable when it came to her, and if he wasn't careful, it was gonna bite him in the ass.

My eyes roved through the large crowd, men laughing and drinking, women gathering together to no doubt talk about the men, and children zig-zagging between the adults as their screams of happiness broke through the air.

A light tap on my shoulder made me turn my head to the right. Sully sat beside me before I fully realized it was her who'd called my attention. "Are you having fun, *Prez*?" She laughed, her beautiful eyes studying my face as if she were never gonna see me again and wanted to remember every line. When her gaze landed on my mouth, she bit her lip and fidgeted in her seat. The heat from her body warmed me, even though we were both already baking in the sun.

Her hands rested in her lap, her fingers clenched tightly to the hem of her short dress. Daring to sneak a peek at her exposed legs, my pants had suddenly become quite the hindrance. All I wanted to do was whisk her away and thrust inside her, making her scream my name, no matter if she was heard or not. But I'd not taken my hands off her for the past month, and it was as good a time as any to practice restraint.

"I'm good," I answered, finishing off the last of my beer. "Are you?"

"Yeah," she said, taking a quick look around. "I really am." She smiled wide and my heart flipped. Sully had been so reserved when she'd first come here, and rightfully so. I'd plucked her from her life and shoved her into a world she'd feared as long as she could remember. But my actions, as well as my club's, had proved she was safe with us, and every day since I'd seen her come alive. Breathing in the air as if it were truly a gift. I saw the world differently through her eyes. I appreciated the little things because, in a way, she was experiencing them for the first time herself. No matter if it was a walk along my property on a nice day, or running a mundane task such as grocery shopping, she treated each excursion as if it was the biggest deal. And for her, it was. She hadn't been allowed off her compound much at all, the world around her taunting and excluding her from a life she would never know.

Leaning in to give her a lingering kiss, her tongue captured mine and for a brief moment, our surroundings faded into obscurity. When we finally pulled back, I heard a round of gasps and someone whistled off in the distance. Turning toward the noise, I shook my head and huffed, the eyes of everyone attending glued to me and Sully.

"The hell you all lookin' at?" I yelled, a genuine smile on my face for the first time in what seemed like forever.

The woman to my right the sole reason for it.

Forty

Sully

"Come on, Sully. We'll be right back," Adelaide promised, snatching my hand in hers and pulling me toward her car. The sky had darkened, most of the KC members well on their way to not remembering the gathering. "It's just two little blocks down that way." She pointed to her right. "We'll be back before they even know we're gone." She smiled, and her expression was contagious.

"I don't know. If Cole finds out, he'll be pissed, not to mention it's still not safe." I bit my lip on the last word, watching my friend closely.

"Not safe from what?" she asked, tipping her head to the side.

Even though Adelaide and I were fast becoming close, I still held how I'd come to be there safeguarded. She would inundate me with questions, ones I couldn't even begin to know how to answer. Not wanting to taint her image of me, or put her in harm's way, I chose to keep my mouth shut.

"Just in general," I lied. "It's getting dark, and there are unsavory people lurking around every corner."

She shook her head in amusement and dragged me toward her car. "Come on. I have an unhealthy craving for nachos and cheese and they ran out a while ago. Plus, we could use a couple more bags of ice." Trying to convince me to go with her, she added, "Wait and see. They'll all be happy we had the foresight to think ahead, their beer warming as we speak."

"It's only two blocks away? And we'll be right back?" I prompted.

"Promise."

"Okay," I conceded.

She had to threaten the men guarding the gate, using her uncle as bait. I laughed every time she did it because the expression on the men's faces never failed to be priceless.

In my nervousness, I continually played with my wedding band, twisting it around and around, counting the seconds until we were back inside the KC compound. Uneasy about upsetting Cole was second only to the fear of my club kidnapping me right back from their sworn enemy. Then I could kiss everything good-bye.

Cole.

Adelaide.

My life.

Pulling into the parking lot, we both quickly exited the vehicle, my eyes searching our surroundings to make sure we were safe. We walked into the store and immediately noticed only two other people inside, and they were both women. "I'll grab the ice while you get what you need," I told her, making a beeline toward the freezer area. Opening the door, the cold waft of air hit me, instantly making me shiver. As I searched, I heard the ding of the bell over the front entrance. Tossing some damaged ice bags aside, I finally found what I was looking for.

Standing up, I allowed the freezer door to slowly close in front of me, gripping a bag in each hand and thinking about how much better I'd feel once we joined the party again.

Raising my head, I caught my reflection in the door, and in that split second I saw a man standing behind me. The image was quick, but there was no mistaking the one person who'd damaged me for years, torturing me for his own sick amusement and making me wish every day that fate would step in and take me from this cold world.

"Hello, *sweetheart*," he rasped, his voice pure evil. There was no time to defend myself, or to even scream for that matter. Painfully bruising my arm with his fingers, Vex leaned in closer and threatened me—not that his mere presence wasn't making me tremble already. A sharp pain erupted in my midsection, and it only took me a moment to realize he'd roughly shoved a gun into my ribs. "Make one sound and I'll kill that little bitch you came in here with. First, I'll make you watch me torture her, then I'll blow her fucking brains out."

I reacted quickly. "I don't know her. We just walked into the store together." Having no idea how long he'd been watching me, I tried to call his bluff.

"Nice try. But I've been watching you for quite some time. I know she's a friend of yours, just like I know it'll rip your heart out to watch her life slip from her... all because of you."

Shit! What was I going to do? The last thing I wanted was to put my friend's life in danger, but I knew if Vex walked me out of this store, I'd end up dead by his hands.

Or my father's.

The bags of ice dropped to my feet and hit the ground, barely making a noise. Adelaide was not where I could see her. I prayed she didn't show herself because, if she did, my situation would certainly become more precarious.

"Vex, please," I pleaded, which only earned me instant

bruises on my arms from his grip as well as my side from the muzzle of his gun.

"Speak again, bitch, and I'll shoot you where you stand," he sneered. Tears instantly welled and my thoughts ran a million miles a second. More people suddenly filtered into the small store, and it was then he chose to make his move. "Don't come willingly and I'll make good on killing her. Test me."

The thing was I didn't need to test him. He was crazy enough to walk right up to her in front of witnesses and shoot her dead. Sanity had left Vex a long time ago; in its place was madness, worsening every day.

I had no idea why my father kept him around as long as he did. Actually, that was a lie. I *did* know why, but it still wasn't a good enough reason to excuse his recent behaviors.

Vex's father, Manny, had been my father's best friend, until he went and got himself killed, dealing on the side and hiding the profits away from the supplier. When my father tried to right the wrong and exact revenge for Manny's death, he put himself right into harm's way. It was Vex who'd rescued him, hence making him put up with his crazy shit for years. There were times I thought my father would say fuck it and put a bullet in Vex, but he never fatally punished him. It was during those times, where there didn't seem to be any consequences, that I used to think crazy needs crazy, and that my father would be lost in a way without Vex's instability.

Hell, Vex's unsettling nature probably made my father feel somewhat normal.

Yanked back into the horridness of the situation, I prayed for more time to come up with a plan of escape. But it wasn't to be. Vex found his chance to steal me when three young kids tripped into the store, drunk and causing a much-needed distraction. Ushering me quickly toward the front door, he shoved me through first, his gun still digging into my sensitive flesh. I never even tried to look for Adelaide, for fear she would see me and jump to my defense.

Once we'd made it outside, we walked toward the back of the building and straight toward a beat-up car. Throwing open the trunk, he shoved me inside before I could even think about protesting, even though I knew any resistance was futile.

I decided right then and there to save all of my strength.

I was going to need it if I hoped to die with any kind of dignity.

Forty-One

Marek

"Let me in!" I heard a woman scream, her voice becoming shriller the more she was denied access into Chambers. Everyone knew women weren't allowed behind these closed doors, the only exception being when we made a back room into a makeshift operating area for Tripp, and Adelaide was the only one attending to him. Once he was well enough to reside in one of the regular bedrooms, he'd been moved.

"You know you're not allowed back there," one of my men called out, but the thickness of the doors muffled their voices enough that I couldn't tell who'd said it, nor who the female was who was trying so desperately to push past them.

I heard scuffling, then a fierce pounding on the door, followed by more shouting.

"What the hell?" I grumbled, catching Stone's focus while I rose from my seat. I'd pulled him behind closed doors a few minutes prior to discuss the phone call I'd received from Yanez. He told me they would be stopping by our club in the next week to finalize all details, something I thought we'd already done through him, but I guessed his boss wanted to speak to us face-to-face. I wasn't opposed to talking to Carrillo, finally being able to see his face while he promised me once again that my club could walk away from the cartel. It was just one more thing I had to oversee and handle to ensure the safety of my men.

But that was what I'd signed on for when I accepted the gavel, I supposed.

The handle turned with such vigor I was surprised it hadn't popped off altogether. Whoever was on the other side was adamant about getting in, and my curiosity as well as my anger rose with every heartbeat.

"Adelaide, calm down!" the man shouted, who I soon realized was none other than her uncle, Trigger. And for him to be restraining her from entering meant something serious was going on.

My mind instantly shot to Sully for some reason, if only because I knew how close the two women had become. Calming my thoughts, I settled on that she was probably trying so hard because Stone was with me. As soon as the thought breathed to life, I shoved it aside, realizing Adelaide wasn't like the women I'd had normal dealings with. She didn't seem to overreact to situations, instead being the calm one everyone gathered around to seek the same kind of serenity in times of panic. Tripp's situation being one such time.

As soon as her name drifted out of Trigger's mouth, Stone jumped to his feet and flew toward the locked door, twisting the handle and throwing it open. Adelaide looked frenzied, her wild eyes searching for someone. They landed on Stone first, passing him an unspoken message before shoving past him and toward me. My heart raced, the hairs on the back of my neck bristling with worried anticipation.

"Marek," she cried out, crushing the rest of the distance

between us until she stood two feet from me. "Sh-she's g-gone," she hiccupped, tears breaking free and trembling down her reddened cheeks. "W-we were in the store... th-then she was gone." Her hysterics heightened my worry, but she was speaking so fast I could hardly make out what she was saying.

Grabbing her arms, I steeled her shuddering body and tried to calm her enough for her to make some goddamn sense. "Who's gone, Adelaide? What the hell are you talking about?" As far as I was aware, she hadn't gone off the compound, so talk of a store was ludicrous.

"It's all my fault," she offered, a hint of hysterics washing over her while she continued to plead with me. "You have to go find her, Marek. You have to go now," she urged, pulling from my grip and taking a step back. Stone was at her back. As soon as she sensed he was near, she turned around and wrapped her arms around his waist, finding comfort in his embrace. Trigger noticed and took a step forward, his fists clenched like he was ready for battle.

One look from me, however, and her uncle stopped all movement. He was smart enough to realize his temper wasn't welcome right then. Reservation smothered him as he kept his fury in check, forcing himself to focus on the bigger threat.

Turning Adelaide around in Stone's hold, I held her gaze while I asked for the last time, "Who are you talking about?" I knew, but I needed to hear her name fall from Adelaide's mouth to unfortunately confirm it.

"Sully." She tried to wipe away her tears but they kept falling. Finally, she gave up, her shoulders slumping forward in defeat. "I'd convinced her to run to the store with me and now... she's... she's gone. I couldn't find her anywhere." Her lips quivered. She was trying to be strong but she failed. Big time. "I'm so sorry, Marek," she confessed.

"Why did you go off the compound, Adelaide?" I yelled, all

of my reserve suddenly gone. I could no longer control my rage, taking a single step toward the woman telling me the horrible news about my wife. Both Stone and Trigger stiffened, prepared for anything now that my stance threatened their woman, their family. "I specifically told you she wasn't allowed to go ANYWHERE without one of us. What the FUCK!" I'd never been so incensed and so frightened all at the same time.

"I'm sorry," she repeated. "The store was only two blocks away, and I really didn't think there would be any harm. We'd be back before anyone even knew we were gone."

"And now they have her!" I roared, my entire body set to explode. Stone stepped forward, shoving Adelaide behind him toward her uncle. Jerking his head in the older man's direction, Trigger ushered his niece out of Chambers, slamming the door behind him before I really lost it.

"Shit!" Stone rumbled, shoving his hand through his dark blond hair. His distress was enough to put me even more on edge, realizing the direness of the situation. I knew the Savage Reapers weren't gonna let this go. And now that they had her back in their grips, not only would they torture her, but they were most likely gonna kill her, especially after finding out I made her marry me.

It took me all of one minute to devise a plan, albeit a haphazard, careless one. But it was a plan nonetheless. We would storm into wherever she was being held and kill every fucker we came across. It was gonna be a bloodbath.

As soon as I shared my plan with Stone, he froze.

"Marek, we can't go in there guns blazin'. For one, we have no idea where they took her. Second of all, we can't risk the lives of every brother here just to get her back." The last word hadn't left his lips before I slammed him against the wall.

"She's my wife," I seethed, pushing my forearm further into

his throat. Stone was a big guy, and although I didn't want to hurt my best friend, I needed for him to feel my rage.

"Yeah? So what?" he dared to retort. "She's your wife because you forced her to marry you. You're just pissed because those bastards bested you." Pulling back, I straightened myself until I was no longer leaning into him, but instead standing tall in front of him. Toe to toe. His eyes widened at my reaction. A swift tick of the clock passed before my right fist connected with his face. His head turned, but of course the force of my punch didn't hurt him. It was times like this when I hated that he couldn't feel any pain.

His shock, however, was satisfaction enough.

It had to be.

Pinning me with his glare, he said, "What the hell was that for?" There was no rubbing of his jaw to soothe the pain, but there was a trickle of blood which covered the corner of his lip. He felt the moisture, wiping it away before it dripped onto his white T-shirt.

"She's my wife," I repeated. "Therefore, she belongs to me." So many emotions battled together. Hurt, anger, confusion... but mostly fright. I was scared for Sully, and the longer we stood there arguing, the longer she was subjected to her club, mainly Vex and her father, Psych.

A pained expression washed over me. My eyes had become glassy, a reaction I had no control over. Fists clenched and nostrils flaring, I retreated until my back hit the wall. I hung my head so my VP couldn't see the expression on my face. Hell, I wasn't even sure what was happening to me. Clutching my chest, I tried to assuage the tightness, instinctually rubbing the area closest to my heart.

"Oh, no!" Stone called out, instantly garnering my attention. A knowing smirk appeared on his face. "You love her," he proclaimed, brushing his hair off his forehead. "Fuck, Marek. Why didn't you say something before?"

"Because I didn't realize it until right now," I affirmed, running my hands through my own hair in frustration.

"This changes everything," he said.

I quickly nodded.

"I'll gather the men. You start figuring out how we're gonna find her." He advanced toward the door, but before he disappeared from sight, I said something which stopped him right away.

"I had a tracker put in her wedding ring. If she still has it on, we'll find her."

I prayed whoever took her hadn't noticed the band, because they would have taken it from her. It was the biggest reminder that she was no longer a part of their club, the biggest 'fuck you' their enemy could shove down their throats.

Forty-Two

Sully

Twisting the ring around my finger over and over helped to soothe me. It was funny how things turned out. At first, the ring had been something that had shackled me to Cole, and his club. But now, I found solace in the gold metal band, as if in some way I was still connected to the man I'd ended up falling for.

I had to make sure Vex didn't see it, though. Otherwise, his rage toward me would be off the charts, and he'd probably kill me before returning me to the Savage Reapers.

Slipping the band from my finger, I quickly placed it into the cup of my bra, tucked securely under my left breast. No sooner had I pulled my hand from my clothing than the car came to an abrupt halt, jerking me forward in the trunk. Bracing for what I knew was coming, I prayed Cole would be able to find me. I had no idea how, but I prayed nonetheless.

A light humming noise filled my ears, the only one of my senses on high alert. My eyelids were closed, too heavy to open even if I wanted to. My hands and legs were numb, and it wasn't until I tried to move them that I realized I was restrained. The shock of it wore off quickly, as soon as my memories flooded over me.

Vex had taken me. Shoved me in the back of a rundown car and driven for what felt like hours. It was the last thing I remembered before groggily waking up wherever I was now.

Was I back inside the Savage Reapers' compound? Or did Vex take me somewhere completely different? Instinctually, I knew if he'd taken me back to my father, I'd be dead before Vex could exact whatever revenge he felt he was entitled to.

Wriggling my hands behind my back, I heard movement behind me. "Good, you're awake," Vex said. "I thought maybe I gave you too much."

I opened my mouth to speak but no words came out. The only noise to escape was a low groan. My tongue felt like sandpaper, my lips cracking from the lack of moisture.

I had no idea what he'd drugged me with, but it obviously wasn't meant to kill me.

His finger lifted one eyelid, the light above my head infiltrating my pupils and causing me a great deal of pain. It was like tiny shards of glass poking at me, and it only stopped once he'd withdrawn his hand and my eye closed into darkness again.

"It'll take a few minutes for the drug to wear down enough for you to open your eyes. It's a bitch, isn't it?" he grated, happy with himself that he was able to impose pain on me yet again.

He rambled on for the next ten minutes about how much he was going to enjoy hurting me, that while I was away he had to resort to taking out his aggression on the countless club whores who were only too eager to jump all over him. That was, until he'd beaten most of them to within an inch of their lives. He'd even sliced up a few of them for added enjoyment.

Just when I thought I was going to throw up from the details of his rampage, my eyes flitted open. I tried to focus on something in front of me to calm my rising nausea, praying he wasn't the only focal point in the room. Thankfully, he was behind me. I'd chosen a spot on the wall in front of me, inhaling long, slow breaths. Silently blowing them out through my nose. Within seconds, my stomach calmed.

A shadow moved at my side then quickly in front of me as Vex crouched until he was at eye level. I tried to lower my head but he wasn't having any of it, his fingers roughly pinning my chin in place. He dug into my skin, instantly bruising the sensitive flesh.

I winced... and he laughed.

He had always enjoyed my pain.

His soulless green eyes pinned me, narrowing his gaze as if he was trying to read my mind. Funny thing was he was so far gone from reality that he probably thought he could. Whipping my head to the side before he stood, he cursed under his breath and walked away before uttering another word.

"Where are we?" I rasped, the vibrations in my throat instantly alarming me. I didn't sound like myself, and it scared the hell out of me.

"Somewhere nice and safe, *sweetheart*. Don't you worry about that." Clanking sounded behind me, and my heart raced the longer he stayed hidden from sight. "You see," I heard him say. "Your father wanted me to bring you back to him so he could do with you as he saw fit. But I couldn't do that." He tsked. "I needed to do my own thing first." More clanking. "He can have whatever's left of you when I'm finished. Or maybe I'll go back and tell him I couldn't get to you. Keep using that excuse day after day. Week after week. Hell, year after year." He slammed something down on a metal desk, whatever objects were on top crashing against each other and creating a loud noise. "I watched you for weeks, Sully. I only needed to find the right time to take back what rightfully belonged to me."

Following weeks spent with a man who let me speak my mind whenever I had something to say, I'd forgotten my place when it came to Vex. The words flew from my mouth before my brain could warn me against it.

"I don't belong to you. I never did."

There was no sound in the air around me before I felt his fingers around my throat. My body smarted at the aggression, my eyes bulging, my chest constricted the longer I was unable to take in oxygen. Just when black dots hazed my vision, he released his hand and backed away. Instantly, I went into a frenzied coughing fit, inhaling air as quickly as I could muster.

"You've always belonged to me. You were always mine. And nothing's changed," he sneered, his malevolent smile making my heart skip a rampant beat.

For someone to be so young yet so calculating—and dead inside—was something which had always baffled me about Vex. My father, I could see. He was much older, life having beaten him down. The only thing he had to cling to was his ruthlessness.

But nothing had happened to Vex to make him the way he was.

He was simply born bad.

Forty-Three

Marek

Forty-five minutes we drove. Even though the odometer read a hundred miles an hour, it felt like we were driving at a snail's pace. My fingers curled around the steering wheel while my stomach twisted the further away from the club we ventured. I couldn't stop my mind from drifting to the image of Sully being hurt at the hands of that bastard, Vex. I tried my absolute best to keep her safe, always making sure either me or one of my men was watching over her, impressing upon her how important her safety was, yet she'd still made the decision to go off the compound without protection.

But I couldn't blame her alone. Adelaide was the other half of the equation, although she didn't know about the circumstances behind why Sully needed such protection. She probably just assumed I was being an over protective, possessive man, wanting his woman heavily safeguarded. While all that was in fact true, there was more to the story. Way more.

For as much as I wanted to point the finger at Sully and at

Adelaide, I knew in my heart there was only one person responsible.

Me.

I should have paid more attention to her whereabouts during the party.

I should have drilled it into her how imperative it was that she not leave the compound without my permission.

I should have....

Punching the dashboard, an immediate pain radiated through my hand, but I welcomed the quick distraction. It took my mind off the fact that if anything happened to Sully, I didn't know what I would do.

Wait... That was a lie.

Yes, I did.

I'd rip through the Savage Reapers with the vengeance of the Devil, and I'd snatch every last one of their lives. If I perished in the process, then so be it.

"We're gettin' closer," Stone confirmed. Sitting beside me, he studied the tracker to make sure we were headed in the right direction. I prayed her wedding ring was still on her hand, or at least somewhere on her body. I knew she was aware of the significance of the round piece of metal. Not only because it tied her to me, but if her club knew she'd married the president of their enemy, her life would be in even greater danger.

Hopefully, she'd had the foresight to hide the damn thing, all the while keeping it close.

Ryder and Hawke accompanied us, their silence in the back of the van a sign they knew how serious the situation was. I wanted to bring more men in case we ran into a few of the Reapers, instead of the single man who I believed had taken her, but I couldn't leave my club unprotected. While I believed Sully was in extreme peril, it could also have been a setup of sorts.

Either way, we were heavily armed, never mind that we had the element of surprise on our side. There was no doubt they knew we were coming, but I doubted they expected us to find her so soon.

"It's up ahead," Stone called out. "Turn here and shut off the lights," he demanded. I obeyed, not giving him shit for the first time in our lives.

He took our situation seriously, and I couldn't have been more thankful. The second he found out she was missing he was by my side, firing off question after question and gathering a couple of the men to come with us.

The creak of the sliding van door screamed into the silence of the night. Looking around quickly, we noticed a large plot of land surrounded by vast emptiness. There were no houses. There were no cars. Hell, there weren't even any people anywhere in sight. The further we walked, the closer we came to a small building set back in the middle of the wide open space, a tall chain-link fence barricading the structure into some sort of privacy.

The sun had long gone down, and in the absence of street-lights the only thing guiding us was the moon. We knew instantly we were in the perfect place to kill, or be killed, and no one would be any the wiser for days. Weeks even.

With the seemingly abandoned building a few hundred yards in front of us, we stealthily crept forward, the shadow of night cloaking us enough that we were able to sneak around without the fear of being caught.

I still had no idea what we'd walk into. Their entire club could be hidden inside, and although I had rage on my side, I was no match for the likes of an entire club. Or we could walk in on nothing, Vex having figured out we were tracking her, this stop-off point merely being a ghost hunt.

"Go left," I instructed Hawke and Ryder. "Stone and I will

go around that way." I pointed to the right of the rundown building. Silence screamed all around me and the more the eeriness deafened me, the more alarmed I became. Pricking my ears, I listened for any signs of someone else there with us, but there was nothing.

Securing the perimeter, we'd all met up around the back and searched for a way inside. A busted-out window toward the middle was our best choice.

"I'll go first," Stone offered. When I tugged on his jacket, he wrenched his arm free. "I'm the obvious choice and you know it." He winked. "Besides, if anything happens, at least I won't feel a thing," he tried to joke. Under any other circumstance, I would have laughed, but the precariousness of what we could potentially walk into still had me on guard. No time for carelessness.

I moved to go first, but he shoved me back, a stern look in his eye only he could get away with flashing my way. "I mean it, Marek. Let me go first. I'll check things out and see if there's another way in. One where we aren't standing on each other's shoulders to get inside." His eyes gleamed as he tried to lessen my worrisome mood.

But again, nothing.

Just impatience... and fear.

Fear I would walk in and find Sully dead.

Fear I would walk in and not find her at all.

"Then go if you're goin'. Stop blabbering on and get in there." I cradled my hands together to make him a foothold. Raising him up, he took a quick look inside, as best he could with no apparent light, and lifted himself further until he was able to shove a foot into the corner of the window frame. Thankfully, the opening was wide enough for a man of his size, his broad shoulders skimming the sides.

We heard a thud, followed by a stream of cursing. At first, I thought he'd seen someone, but quickly found out a large piece of glass had cut his hand when he'd landed. The only reason he made any noise was because he had to rip a piece of his shirt to cover the wound.

He'd found a side door and beckoned us forth before we were caught like sitting ducks. Again, we had no idea if we were the only ones there, or if people were waiting to ambush us.

Twenty minutes it took the four of us to search around in the dark.

Twenty minutes of my heart in my throat.

Twenty minutes of agony while I searched for the woman who'd flipped me on my ass.

The vast space was cut into multiple sections, rooms disappearing into each other, plenty of hiding places to search. I wasn't even sure what kind of building we were running around in, what type of business it could have been used for. And I didn't give a shit either. All I cared about was finding Sully.

"Are you getting anything?" I asked Stone, pointing to the tracking monitor.

"Not really. Just a weak signal that keeps fading in and out, depending on where we are inside this shithole." The place smelled rank, a mustiness mixed with the scent of dead animals filling our nostrils.

We'd quickly discovered there were two levels to the place, the one we were currently searching and a lower one. Hawke found a door with steps which descended below. Was that were they were all waiting for us? Were we walking into a trap?

With the meager light of his phone, he opened the door and started his way down the steps, careful not to shout anything back to us. But he didn't have to because we were right behind him.

278 / S. NELSON

It was the last place we had to look and I prayed we found her or, at the very least, a clue as to where she could have gone. If she was even there at all.

Once we'd reached the bottom of the crumbling staircase, concrete falling away with every step we took, my eyes tried their hardest to adjust to the lack of light. It was even darker down there. Ryder flicked his lighter and as soon as the flame caught, we walked close to each other, huddled around that damn sparse source of light. My phone was well on its way to dying, as charging the device was the last thing on my mind before I rushed out to search for Sully. Hawke still had his cell out, but even with all three sources of illumination, the dank cellar was intimidating.

Fifteen minutes later, we concluded no one else was hiding away in the old abandoned building. As we headed toward the steps, I kicked something, sending the object rolling across the hardened floor. The metal *clang* instantly raised my hackles, and for some reason a feeling of dread settled down deep inside me.

Following the sound, I snatched Ryder's lighter from him and bent down to retrieve the item. Between my fingers was a ring. A thin yellow band.

Sully's ring.

She *was* here.

But where is she now?

Not having the concentration needed to drive, Stone took the wheel once we'd approached the van. We were on the road and headed back when Hawke's phone started buzzing.

"Yeah?" he sharply answered. "Hold on." Tapping me on the shoulder, he passed me his cell. "For you. It's Cutter."

"Yeah?" I answered, giving the same curt greeting.

"Prez, we think we have a lead on Sully," he rushed. "One of those fucks dared to show up at Flings, spouting off at the mouth to anyone who would listen about how the Reapers were going to own this town soon enough, so everyone better watch out. He was definitely high on something, which worked to our advantage because we grabbed him quickly and threw him in the back room. I have no idea where he ranks in his shithole of a club, but I figured it couldn't hurt to try and extract some information from him." Cutter was a man of few words, so his continued rambling was certainly telling.

"Fuck, Cutter, get to the point!" I shouted, losing any and all patience. "What do you know?"

"Sorry. After a little *convincing*, the punk sung like a canary." I rolled my eyes at his obvious enjoyment. Cutter wasn't shy when it came to making people talk. I wouldn't say he *enjoyed* what he needed to do from time to time, but I know that shit didn't bother him too much either. "He told us Vex might be holed up in some shitty motel somewhere on I5, maybe near Tulare. He's not sure where he's going, but he told us Vex was overheard telling a few people he was going to 'end the embarrassment once and for all.'" He took a short breath before continuing. "Are you guys anywhere near there?"

Catching a passing road sign, I concluded we were close to an hour from where Vex might be. "You don't happen to know what he's driving, do you?" I held my breath and prayed for the information to keep on flowin' my way.

"A red '75 Impala. Beat to shit but still good enough to keep runnin'."

"Thanks, man," I said, ending the call before shouting directions to Stone. I felt the van pick up speed, the engine whirling with the force of my VP's determination.

It seemed like an eternity before we came upon the first shitty motel we could find, but after a quick scouring of the small parking lot, we deemed it wasn't the right place. For all we knew, the information given to Cutter had been utter bullshit.

So it went, crappy motel after crappy motel, until my hopes were dashed. At the rate we were going, there was no way I would ever find Sully. The only link I had was her wedding ring, and it either had been taken from her to be left behind at the abandoned building to taunt me, or she'd somehow dropped it.

My money was on Vex having figured out there was a tracker in it, leaving it behind on purpose. And who the hell knew how long they'd been there. I knew it couldn't have been too long, though, because as soon as Adelaide told us she was missing, we took off. But one *minute* was an eternity, knowing she was being subjected to God knew what.

The long stretch of highway had my mind all twisted up. Thoughts of Sully consumed me. She'd brought out parts of me I hadn't even known existed. The need to protect a woman so fiercely was beyond any scope of reality I'd ever lived in. She drew my attention, as well as those around her. If anyone's eyes lingered too long, I would become instantly engulfed in fury, threatening their very life until they looked away. And that just wasn't like me. I was a pretty laid-back guy. Normally. Before she'd come into my life, anyone who knew me would have attested to such a thing.

But I was possessive over Sully. I wanted all her time and focus. I hated when she was out of my sight, mainly because I didn't trust anyone to protect her the way I could, but also because I couldn't stand when other people made her laugh, or felt joy in a world where she belonged to me. I should've been the one putting those smiles on her face, enticing those intoxicating laughs from her lips.

And I did.

But others shared in that glory as well.

My bombardment of irrational thoughts was yet another one of her effects on me. They were unexplainable, and I wore myself out mentally trying to dissect my feelings.

Slowing the van, Stone jutted his arm out in front of me, startling me from my brief escape from reality. "Is that the car?" he asked, trying to lean over me to get a better look, all while doing his best not to veer off the road.

A small sign for a Motel Nine flashed in front of us and, sure enough, in the small dirt parking lot was an old, beat-up red Impala. "That has to be it," I affirmed, more to myself than anyone else. "Keep driving," I instructed, hitting the dash in anxiousness.

Stone read my mood quickly. "We'll get her, man," he said, tapping the wheel before proceeding further down the road, easing his foot off the accelerator so we didn't miss a good spot to hide.

We parked and slinked around the building. Hawke and Ryder walked toward the office to find out some more information. We had to make sure we had the right place; barging in on innocent people with guns blazing and murderous intent probably wouldn't be the best thing right now.

Grinning like a fool, and with bloody knuckles, Hawke came strolling out of the front of the building, Ryder quickly in tow. "He's in number three," he said, brushing past me toward the room.

All four of us rushed across the lot, guns drawn and prepared to kill if and when we deemed it necessary.

There was a good chance Vex had acted alone, stealing Sully like the true coward he was. Swooping in and kidnapping her only when he knew she was alone and defenseless. The only time he would ever be able to overpower her was when she was without protection. At least when I'd done it, we'd attacked their club like men, killing as many of those worthless bastards as we could.

"Vex is mine," I growled, gun cocked and aimed at the flimsy door ahead, prepared for anything. I prayed Sully was all right, but only time would tell what he'd actually been able to do to her. It only took a split second to end someone's life, and if that was the road he'd chosen to travel down, then he would be following her into the afterlife sooner than later. Although, before he stole his last breath, I'd make him beg me for death.

As soon as Ryder's big black boot made contact with the door, all four of us filtered into the room, no light inside except for a small table lamp in the far right corner. I'd never surveyed an area quicker than I did right then. Floral wallpaper from the seventies covered the walls, an old box-style TV sitting on a metal stand, half of it bent from the weight buckling it. Two separate areas on the walls were faded, indicating a picture had once hung there. A queen-sized bed sat in the middle of the room with covers, which conveniently matched the wallpaper, crumpled into a ball. In the middle lay the woman I'd come to save.

There was a split second, the time between one breath and the next, when Vex looked stunned. Sitting hunched over the only chair in the room, he snorted a line of coke off the corner of the long dresser. His eyes were bloodshot and his nose was bleeding, but it didn't stop him from shoving that shit up his nostrils. A coked-out fucker was dangerous, and we all knew it.

They were unpredictable.

Jumpy.

Paranoid.

Hawke and Stone rushed forward, attempting to reach for Vex while I ran toward Sully. Her limp body was sprawled across the bed, her head lolled to the side so I couldn't see her entire face. At first glance, she looked dead. Her hair covered the only visible side of her face, so I was unable to assess any immediate damage. But the further down her body I scanned, I knew right away he'd injured her. But how badly was the question.

The cream dress she'd been wearing had turned one color.

Red.

Blood red.

Rushing forward, I said a silent prayer she was alive, that the illusion she cast was just that. "Fuck," I cursed loudly, jumping on the bed and cradling her head in my hands. Pushing back her hair, I gasped at what I saw. Both of her eyes were swollen, her right one on the way to being sealed shut because of all the damage. Her bottom lip was split and there was dark bruising around her entire throat. She'd been strangled.

My hands ran all over her body, searching for the cause of the crimson river. Before I could lift her dress to check, I heard a shuffle behind me, then a gunshot. Whipping my head around, I saw my VP on the ground, holding his side with one hand, his other propping up his upper body. Blood trickled over his fingers, hitting the faded, light green carpet.

"Goddamn it!" Stone roared. "Like I don't have enough fuckin' scars as it is." Yeah, that's what he was concerned about. I knew damn well he wasn't feeling any pain, instead worried about the vanity of it all. I would have laughed at him if our situation weren't so dire.

While I was on the bed with Sully, and Stone was holding his weeping wound, Hawke had tackled Vex and had him restrained on the ground, his knee pushing into the bastard's back to help keep him still. It worked in our favor that he was drugged out of his mind and although he got off a lucky shot, his reflexes were otherwise impaired.

Once I knew he was no longer a threat, I focused on Sully, the rampant beat inside my chest pushing fear into my heart.

"Ryder, come help me!" I shouted. He was next to me before I took my next breath. "Sully," I called out, reaching for her face and trying to wake her. Placing my hand on the side of her neck, I'd been able to find a pulse, but it was extremely faint. I knew it was only a matter of time before she drifted away from me for good, so I had to think fast.

With Ryder taking over and cradling her neck, I'd finally been able to push her dress up. Sections of the material stuck to her skin, which was not a good sign. After carefully separating the dress from her body, I discovered she'd been stabbed. A deep gash between her upper ribs. The warm stickiness of her life coated my hands, while I tried to find something to push down on her wound.

"We have to get her to a hospital. Now!" I felt myself starting to panic, something I never did.

"What about me?" Stone yelled. "I need a hospital too, man. Just because I don't feel it doesn't mean that damn bullet isn't ripping apart my insides." He slowly rose to his feet, wobbling a little before catching the edge of the dresser for support.

I scrambled off the bed, carrying Sully in my arms while I debated what to do. I knew she needed immediate medical attention, and lots of it, but so did my VP. Explaining a knife wound *and* a gunshot wound would surely bring in heat we didn't need.

We were close to a two-hour ride away from the club, and I wasn't sure if she would make it. But what choice did I have? I couldn't just drop her off at the hospital, all alone, but I couldn't very well carry her in there myself either. No, if I left her all by herself, the authorities could take her from me, or worse, her father could somehow find out and steal her right out from under their noses. Then I'd never get her back alive.

"What about the safe house, Prez? It's only an hour from here. Surely they'll both make an hour's ride," Ryder said hopefully.

I knew I brought him along for a reason.

Quickly glancing around the dreadful scene in front of me, I made the decision that the safe house was our only bet. It was a place we kept on the side in case of emergencies, and today it was going to serve a dual purpose.

To treat Sully and Stone... and to finally end Vex once and for all.

"Stone, are you okay to get to the van with Ryder?" He looked paler than he had a second ago, and I wasn't exactly sure how bad his damage was.

He stumbled again, but righted himself while he walked toward the busted door, fending off any help from Ryder. "Yeah, I'm good. We'll be right back."

"Hurry up," I yelled to their retreating backs. Stone was hurtin'. Maybe not physically, but his body was taking the brunt of his trauma.

I heard the screeching tires in no time, rushing out to place Sully in the back of the van. I'd swiped the comforter from the motel room to help make her as comfortable as possible, even though it was covered in blood. *Her* blood. But I didn't want to lay her down on the cold, bare floor of the vehicle. Rushing back inside, I grabbed my VP's gun, which had fallen out of his hand when Vex had shot him.

"Hawke, go out and get in the van," I demanded.

"What do you wanna do with him?" he asked, pushing his knee further into Vex's back. I'd insanely thought Vex was choosing to remain silent all this time. What I hadn't realized was that when Hawke had tackled him, he'd inadvertently knocked him out.

"He's gonna meet his maker tonight," I sneered. Hawke moved away from his body, allowing me to kick Vex then roll him over. I expected the unconscious bastard to wake up, throw some attitude my way, as if he were invincible, and then eventually plead for his life.

I wasn't particularly fond of torture, or at least being the one to do it, but I would thoroughly enjoy what I had planned for the man who'd made Sully's life a living nightmare. Day in and day out. I knew she chose to still protect me, or herself, by not divulging a lot of the things that went down when she was living with him, and because of that my imagination was my worst enemy.

Time quickly escaped me, and if I was gonna do something, now was the time. I had to make sure to get both Sully and Stone to the safe house as soon as possible.

A bullet to the head while he was unconscious seemed unfair. No, I needed for the bastard lying before me to suffer in ways I hadn't even thought of yet. Making the quick decision to bring him with us, although the thought of him breathing the same air as the rest of us tugged at the unraveling string of my sanity, I picked him up off the floor and threw him over my shoulder. Taking one last look around the disheveled room to make sure I wasn't missing anything, I closed the door and walked the few feet to the vehicle waiting for me.

Once we were on the road, I instructed Hawke to place a call to Trigger, asking him to bring Adelaide to the safe house right away.

Hopes were high that both of the people who meant the most to me would live to see another day.

Forty-Four

Marek

Hunching over Sully in the back of the van, I cradled her head in my lap, securing her to me while making sure she was as comfortable as she could be, given the circumstances. She was still out cold, her motionless body making my own tense in sorrow.

"She'll be okay," Stone assured, turning around in the passenger seat to look at me. Clutching his side, he tore his hand away to assess the damage, blood coating his entire side. It looked pretty bad, and I was extremely grateful my friend didn't feel an ounce of pain. His body's reaction to the intrusive bullet, however, was less than desired. All signs of life seemed to drain from his face, a pale shadow of disbelief coloring his features. His sitting form wavered, unable to fully control himself while Ryder drove like a maniac. I think it was the only time either one of them used their seatbelts.

"Are you okay, Stone?" I asked, not doing my best to hide the worry in my voice.

"All good, bro-brother," he stammered slightly. A deep

breath later and his head lolled to the side. Ryder took a corner faster than he should have and Stone's body tipped over, his head hitting the passenger window with a thud.

"Goddamn it, Ryder!" I shouted. I wanted so much to berate him for driving so carelessly, but at the same time I wanted to urge him to go faster. He never said a word, all the apology I was looking for pouring forth from his reflection in the rearview mirror.

The rest of the trip was executed in silence. Stone had come to only to pass out once more before we arrived at our destination. Sully's body still lay across my lap, unmoving except for the shallow breaths of air she took into her lungs. And Vex form still laid in a crumpled mess across the back of the van, stuffed into the corner so Hawke could keep a closer eye on him. Primed to make a move in case he woke up and tried something.

So lost in my own head, I hadn't even realized we'd pulled into the garage at the safe house. The place was located in a normal residential area, hiding right out in the open.

Throwing open the side door, the first person to greet us was Adelaide. At first her composure calmed me, until she moved closer and was able to witness the destruction we hid inside the vehicle. Reaching forward, she touched Sully, her hands roaming all over her body to locate the source of the damage. When she skimmed her fingers over her friend's ribs, she jerked them back in horror.

"Oh, my God!" she cried. "Who stabbed her?" Her eyes were on me instantly, silently pleading for an answer, but there simply wasn't any time.

Jerking my head toward Ryder, who'd come around the back of the van, I indicated I needed his assistance. He carefully cradled Sully's body until I was capable of extracting her from the vehicle myself. With my wife in my arms, I shouted for whoever else was around to attend to Stone. I didn't need to tell Hawke to stay with Vex—he knew what he had to do until he was told otherwise.

Before I disappeared inside the house, I heard Adelaide's cries once she realized Stone was out cold inside the van, but I couldn't falter. I needed to ensure Sully was taken care of before I gave my attention over to my buddy. Being torn between two people was the worst feeling in the world, but I knew the woman lying lifelessly in my arms was my first priority.

If the roles were reversed, and it had been Stone carrying Adelaide and me bleeding out, he would make the same decision. I knew he cared for her as I did for my wife; I saw it in his eyes, and in the way he reacted to situations where Adelaide was concerned.

There was a flurry of activity inside the makeshift hospital room, aka the living room. Adelaide had set up rather quickly, calling in the assistance of her doctor friend, the one she'd relied on to help Tripp when we'd found him dumped outside the gate. They both worked diligently to repair the two broken people placed before them.

After what seemed like the longest five hours of my life, they were both on their way to recovering.

Luckily, most of Sully's wounds were only superficial, although her knife wound was certainly going to leave a nasty scar to match those already marring her beautiful skin. I viewed the newest addition as a testament to how strong she was, but I knew she would see it as yet another possibility for me to pull away from her, thinking such imperfections would make me change the way I saw her.

The way I felt about her.

Stone's wound was a bit more damaging, nicking his liver before it passed through his body. Thankfully, I'd been informed he wouldn't sustain any long-lasting effects because of it, the liver being one of the organs which rejuvenated itself rather quickly. The other plus to that was Stone didn't feel anything, other than Adelaide's anger when he'd tried to get up and move around too soon. We transported them both back to the clubhouse the next evening. I gave strict instructions not to allow either one of them to leave the confines of the compound, needing as many people around them for protection until they were both completely out of harm's way.

Plus, I needed time to deal with Vex before I followed them home.

I needed someone with me who wouldn't think twice about what I had planned for Vex, so I placed a call to Cutter to meet me at the safe house. Any one of my men would have helped me out, but Cutter was fashioned from a different cloth. He didn't get off on torturing people—it wasn't an unearthed desire he had brimming below the surface. He was just able to switch something off and do whatever was necessary without a second thought.

Waiting in the hollows of the vast basement, I heard the garage door followed by the door to the kitchen creak open then close, the deadbolt locking in place soon after. Our safe house was a well-guarded secret, but just in case we'd been compromised, I cocked the gun resting in my hand, ready and able to take down any intruders who thought they could get one over on me.

I waited in anticipation while footsteps drummed down the wooden stairs, followed by unhurried walking down the short corridor. Not having to give direction to which room I'd be in, mainly because it was *the* room we used whenever we found ourselves in this predicament, the handle turned and very slowly, the door swung open.

Cutter loomed on the threshold, his short, graying hair perfectly styled in place. He'd come wearing all black, as was the necessary required uniform for someone about to torture another person.

A quick nod between us was all the greeting we gave each other before he moved further inside. Years ago, we'd transformed the room into a soundproof area. For obvious reasons. We didn't need to alarm any of the neighbors because otherwise, we'd have to find another location for our safe house. And, well... that was just a pain in the ass.

Vex had woken the previous night while Adelaide was tending to her two patients, but since he'd been confined to this room, which was directly below the living room, no one heard him when he started yelling obscenities to no one in particular. The only people who even knew he was there were me, Hawke, Ryder and Cutter. Maybe Stone knew, but he was so out of it for the majority of the night I doubted he'd paid any attention to what was going on around him. Other than Adelaide tending to him, of course.

Naked and bound to an old wooden table with coarse rope, Vex's crazy eyes followed me as I moved around him, making sure his restraints were still properly tied. I didn't need him busting out of them during what we had planned. A small piece of me wanted to free him, to best him with nothing but my brute strength, ending his life with my bare hands, but I didn't have time for it. I needed to save whatever reserve I had left for Sully.

She needed me whole.

Physically as well as emotionally.

The one thing I allowed Vex to have was his voice. I wanted to hear him beg for his life, all while I explained what was coming next. I wanted to hear his excuses, his reasoning for tormenting Sully for however long he had access to her. To hear why he chose to treat her like he had.

Did he have any regrets?

Was he sorry in the least for what he'd done to her?

Would he beg for forgiveness before pleading for his life?

We were about to find out.

Cutter stood off to the left while I remained close to the table, Vex continuing to follow me with his stare.

"So," I started. "Although I'm gonna snatch your life from you today, yours won't be a quick death." He closed his lids and exhaled a long breath, but remained silent. When his eyes connected with mine again, he looked... crazier? If that was even possible.

Whatever he'd told himself inside that fucked-up head of his was enough for him to hide his fear from the two men who would be the last to see him alive.

Going against my better judgment, I asked him a question. "Do you have anything to say before we get started?"

Glancing first to Cutter wielding one of his favorite knives, then to me standing directly beside him, he cracked his neck from side to side as if he were preparing to do battle himself.

"You stole my property. You barged into *my* club and stole what belonged to *me*. I saw you. I saw the way you looked at her, the way you tried to make sure she was safe when she wasn't with you. I've been watchin' for weeks. You have a soft spot for the whore, but know this. Even when I'm dead and gone, Psych won't rest until she's back inside our club. And how you found her at the motel will be nothing to what he's gonna do to her once he gets her back."

Though I tried not to react to whatever he said, he'd been able to rattle me. He'd been able to play on my fears. Vex was only *one* of the threats toward Sully, and we both knew it. Her father was diabolical, and if he ever got his hands on her, there was no way he wouldn't kill her soon after. Vex had only allowed her to live so long because I was sure he was gonna use her until he'd had his fill.

Deciding not to give the bastard any satisfaction, I steeled my posture and made sure my face was expressionless when I uttered one word.

"Cutter."

And just like that, his torture began. Neither one of us had a specific plan as to what we were gonna do to him. I simply knew it would be drawn out and painful.

Over the course of the next hour, my man went to work carving up Vex's chest, inch by inch. Some cuts were shallow, some were deep. Some were long, some were short. But each one was precise.

Stepping back after Cutter had finished, I could clearly make out the letters 'K C,' even with all the blood seeping from his open wounds. To have the initials of a rival club carved into the chest was one of the highest insults. The only thing equaling it was integrating one of their own, which I'd already done when I made Sully my wife.

While I thought Vex would beg and plead, scream and holler, cry and break down, he did none of those things. He grimaced every time the tip of the blade cut through his flesh, but not once did he say anything.

Which led me to believe one of two things.

Either he was strong-willed and brave.

Or he was certifiably insane.

I was leaning toward the latter.

Walking around the table until I stood next to his head, I leaned in close so he wouldn't mistake what I had to say. "We're just getting started, you fucker. Hope you like what we have planned next." His bloodshot eyes glared at me, his lips drawn so tight they'd lost all color. Although he chose not to utter a scream, the stress of keeping all his pain bottled up was wearing on him. His brown hair was matted to his forehead, his body's one indication he was indeed panicking on the inside.

He looked haggard.

He'd aged years in just minutes.

"Cutter, help me turn him over." Having no idea what I was thinking, he acted as instructed. No questions asked.

I debated on whether or not to knock Vex out before loosening his restraints, or to allow him to fight one last time.

What the hell. I enjoy a good challenge.

As soon as I loosened the ties around his feet, his body went into full fight mode, kicking and thrusting his legs every which way. His entire body twisted, his back arching off the table while he continued to thrash about.

Realizing he was gonna be quite the handful, I brought the butt of my gun down quickly on the side of his head, a lump swelling on his temple almost instantaneously. The blow was enough to stop him from freaking out, but not enough to halt him entirely. Which I welcomed.

What fun would it be if he complied completely?

Cutter held down his lower half while I freed his arms, flipping him over quickly so we could restrain him again. A low groan escaped his mouth as soon as his carved-up chest hit the surface of the table, blood steadily pouring from him and hitting the ground at our feet.

Widening his legs, I tightly fastened each ankle to the bottom of the table. He was most certainly going to resist his next and final punishment, so I had to ensure he was secure before making my next move.

Beckoning Cutter over, I leaned in close and whispered something into his ear, Vex's head turned to the side, his eyes roaming over the scene of his two assailants with vigor. There was no way he would know what was coming, and while I wanted nothing more than to surprise him directly before inflicting his much-deserved pain, I decided to give him a hint.

Let him sweat a bit beforehand.

Once Cutter had ascended the basement steps, I leisurely walked around the space, pacing and slapping my hand on various objects placed around the room. First it was a set of chains. Picking up the heavy objects, I tossed them into a tin tray, the noise startling even me, and I was prepared for it. Then I fingered the many knives lined up next to one another on the far side table. In view so he could see, but not so close he could make out the intricate carving details of each.

"Sully told me all about what you did to her." Choosing to remain silent while my words resonated, I waited to see if he would banter with me. A few moments passed... and nothing. So I continued. "She told me how you abused her for days before leaving her tied up to bleed out like some kind of animal." Footsteps sounded overhead. "And I'm gonna do to you what you did to her." Rounding the table so I could lean in close, I threatened, "Let's see how you like being fucked with a bat."

The last word left my lips and, as if on cue, Cutter strolled into the dank room holding an old, beat-up, wooden baseball bat. I kept my eyes on Vex the entire time, waiting for it to register just what was gonna happen to him. My satisfaction came when my fingers curled around the larger part of the bat. His eyes shut tightly before his body twitched on the table, his muscles locking up the closer I moved toward him with the weapon in hand.

"If you believe that lying whore then you're the idiot!" he yelled, breathing hard as he waited for my next move. "I never did any such thing to that bitch," he seethed.

"Maybe you just don't remember it," I countered. "Enough

talk. Let's get down to it." I tapped the wood against his upper thighs, tormenting him before I even started. "Who knows, Vex, you might actually enjoy this." My laugh was sinister. I had no qualms about dancing with demons that night, every punishment I deemed appropriate as payback for all the years he'd tortured Sully. Not givin' a shit about her well-being, physically or emotionally. Tapping the bat against his ass that time, I finished with, "Or maybe not."

His howls were music to my ears; he'd finally broken. He was a soulless sadist who deserved every bit of pain I inflicted on him. After an hour, I blessed Cutter with the authority to finish him off however he deemed necessary. I gave him strict instructions to drop off Vex's rotting corpse somewhere his club would find him, and to leave the bat in place so they knew exactly what had happened to him—among other things.

Forty-Five

Marek

Two weeks had passed and both patients were doing quite well. I'd taken Sully back home to my house—*our* house—and let her recoup under my watchful eye.

I'd forsaken the club to a point, vowing to care for my wife until she was completely healed. The area surrounding her wound remained red and puffy and she still experienced a bit of pain, but not nearly like she had. Every time she moved too quickly, or twisted the wrong way and winced, it sliced right through me. As soon as she witnessed the pain in my eyes, she was the one trying to comfort me.

Our affections for each other only grew stronger, and it was on a mundane Thursday evening when I decided I needed to finally tell her how I felt once and for all. Expressing myself wasn't necessarily my strong suit, unless, of course, I was angry about something. In those cases, I had absolutely no problem letting anyone know what was brewing inside me.

"Can I get you anything else?" Sully reclined on the couch, taking a small sip of water to wash down her pain meds. She was getting better with each passing day. Physically, anyway. Emotionally was a different story. Almost every night, she'd woken from nightmares, choosing each time to remain tight-lipped when I asked her what exactly plagued her. The only thing she would mumble was "Vex."

I saw the effects of what he'd done to her body, but I still had no idea about what had happened during the time she was with him, which had led to each and every bruise... and to the stabbing. My body clenched in rage every time I looked at the remnants of her abuse, but I always made sure to keep my fury in check so she didn't think it was directed at her in any way.

She'd asked me a few days after I'd rescued her if I'd killed Vex, the whimper in her voice almost indecipherable. I warred between thinking she was fearful he was still alive, and her expressing her sadness because she still felt something for him. Something akin to Stockholm syndrome, or some shit like that.

When I fessed up that he'd been taken care of, that he was no longer a threat, she breathed a sigh of relief. An action which immediately put all my fears to rest. I didn't go into detail over what we'd done to him, however. She didn't need to hear any of it.

She was relieved Vex no longer breathed the same air, and that was good enough for me.

Now, the only other person I had to worry about was her father.

I'd been in touch with Rafael, making sure our deal was continuing as promised. Soon enough, the Savage Reapers would be without a steady flow of income, and as soon as Psych and his men were vulnerable and desperate, my men and I would swoop in and end him and his filthy club once and for all.

"No, I'm fine," she answered. "Thank you." She turned her head and looked up at me as I approached. She smiled, her entrancing brown eyes beckoning to me. "You know you don't have to dote on me, don't you?" She licked her lips and waited for me to sit next to her. Once I was close, I reached for her hand and entwined my fingers with hers, the warmth of her touch calming my erratic nerves.

"I don't mind. Whatever I can do to help you, I will. Always." I meant to smile, but my face remained expressionless. There were so many things I wanted to say, so many questions I had, about everything, that curving my lips was the last thing I thought about.

And she noticed.

Turning slowly to face me, her hand covering her newest wound out of habit, she looked worried. "Is there something wrong, Cole? Why do you look so serious?" When the only response I gave her was silence, her eyes widened and she had a mini panic attack, as if I were about to ruin her with whatever was gonna come tumbling out of my mouth.

Clutching her hand tightly in mine, I leaned in and kissed her lips. It was gentle at first, then the more breath we shared, our entanglement became something else.

Raw.

Carnal.

Promising.

I love you. I think I fell for you the first time my world crashed into yours. There hasn't been a moment that's gone by when I haven't thought about you. About what you were doing. About how you were dealing with your new life. If you were attracted to me. If you thought about me as much as I thought about you. My life had very little meaning before I met you, and now... Shit! I have no idea what I would do without you. When you were stolen, my soul was crushed, the very thought of never seeing you again too much to bear. I exist because you exist. I hate when other men look at you, let alone dare to talk to you. I want to rip their eyes out of their heads, their tongues from their mouths. My heart hammers against my chest in anger when I'm not the only one who makes you laugh, who puts you at ease, for however long that might be. When I'm inside you, it's the best feeling in the entire world. Nothing else matters. The only sounds I want to hear for the rest of my life are the sexy-as-hell moans you make when you're coming. Whether it's from my mouth, fingers or cock. I could live with you, here, all alone, just the two of us, naked and satisfying each other for the rest of our lives.

I wanted to say all of that to her, but I didn't. Pulling back from her mouth, I said, "I'm fine. Just worried about how you're feeling."

Her face relaxed a little, short pants of air hitting my face while she tried to calm down from our kiss. "I'll be okay. Really. I've been through worse." She cringed at her own words, which in turn made me stiffen.

A few precious moments passed while be both studied each other. I knew what was rumbling around inside my head, but I had no idea what *she* was thinking. I knew she cared for me, deeply even, but she'd never really told me how she felt, only ever giving me whatever I craved, whenever I was craving it. Her. Always her. And she gave herself to me freely, each and every time since I'd officially claimed her as my own.

"Are you tired?" I asked, watching her face carefully.

"I think so. Yes." Her fingers danced over her shirt, mindlessly playing with the part of her that was bandaged. She'd needed twenty-five stitches to close the wound. While that was bad enough, it could have been worse, I supposed.

"Okay," I said, pulling her to her feet very gently. "Let me change your bandage and we'll go to bed."

"That's okay. I can do it. You've done so much for me

already." For some reason, she looked down at her feet when she spoke.

"Look at me," I instructed, tilting her chin up with my finger so I could see her face. "I want to do everything for you. Please don't take that away from me." *I sound pussy whipped for sure.* But I wouldn't have it any other way.

She remained quiet.

"Okay?" I asked, my brow arched in question.

"Okay," she whispered, before leading me to our bedroom.

Once I helped her undress, a task which was painful for me because I hadn't been able to sink inside her in weeks, I crawled into bed next to her, careful not to push against her side. I was overly cautious around her recently and I knew it drove her nuts, but the last thing I wanted to do was cause her any kind of discomfort.

"I won't break, Cole," she mumbled when she saw the reservation on my face while I held myself back.

"I know. I just... I don't want to hurt you. Not after everything you've been through." I tried to smile but I failed. Again.

I was painfully hard as it was, and her writhing under the covers, even though it was simply to get better situated, was driving me insane. I couldn't help it. I felt like some kind of creeper the way my eyes roamed over her entire body, heat exploding in my veins at the very thought of how she felt underneath me. Over me. Next to me.

Thrusting inside her tightness, tasting her essence and exploding together had become my new favorite things in the world.

"If you keep looking at me like that, I'm gonna be forced to jump you. And since I can't put that kind of pressure on my body yet, it would be wise for you to stop." There was a playfulness to her tone, although I knew she was being serious.

Apparently, I was torturing her as well as myself.

"Sorry," I said, lying on my back and staring at the ceiling. The light next to her was still on, and it didn't take her long to ask me to lean over and shut it off. Carefully, I moved over her body and stretched for the lamp, my chest brushing against hers as I did so.

A soft groan fell from her lips. Shit! I hadn't meant to touch her afflicted area, but I was too big not to. "Sorry," I repeated, that time for a different reason. Before I pulled away, she put her hand on my upper arm and squeezed. While I remained frozen in place, she moved her legs apart, kicking one over mine so quick I was surprised she had the strength.

"What are you doing?"

"I said I can't jump you. That doesn't mean *you* can't jump *me*." A sexy smile appeared on her face, her tongue parting her mouth and licking her lips while what she'd just said registered.

"I don't want to hurt you, though."

"You won't," she assured me, spreading her legs wider. "Just be gentle," she urged, her night shirt riding up her body until I could see her pink lace panties.

Fuck! She was so beautiful. I should have declined. I should have lain back down and fallen asleep, allowing her more time to heal.

But I was greedy.

And I needed my fix.

Hovering until my body was completely covering hers, I grinned wickedly before taking her mouth, her sweet tongue unraveling the last of my restraint.

"The way I'm feeling right now, I can't be gentle. So I think it's best if we just go to sleep."

I thought I'd had my say, kissing her one last time and trying to remove my body from hers. But a firm grip on the back of my neck halted me. Her foot caressed the back of my thigh, digging in when she thought I was going to retreat.

"Then I challenge you to take me slow. And gentle. I want you to draw out my release. Make me lose my mind, Cole," she pleaded. To say I was stunned was an understatement. I was usually the one who talked during sex, telling her over and over how good she felt, her moans affirmation she loved the way I fucked her. But in all the times we'd had sex—and there were numerous occasions during the short time we'd known each other—she'd never openly expressed herself as much.

Never mind that she'd just challenged me. It'd been a long time since anyone had challenged me to do anything. How did she know I could never turn down such a thing?

"You dare me, do you?" I asked, amusement dripping from my tone.

"I do," she answered, both of her legs pinning me in place. Our lower bodies were still covered by thin material, hers by a flimsy scrap of pink lace, and mine by the fabric of my boxer briefs.

Reaching behind me to unlock her legs, I backed up until I could grab her panties, drawing them down her thighs and discarding them somewhere behind me. When I made a move to lie back on top of her, she stopped me with a confused look on her face.

"What?"

"Aren't you going to take yours off too?" she asked, pouting that I wasn't already completely naked.

"Don't worry about me, sweetheart. You'll feel me. Trust me." I moved to cover her once more but she stopped me. Again.

"Cole, I want you naked. I want to feel every part of your body on mine. I don't want a piece of clothing in the way." My woman sure was feisty, and I found I absolutely loved it.

Without another word, I quickly peeled off my boxer briefs before lying over her one more time. "Better?"

"Better," she responded, closing her legs tightly against my waist. "Much better."

Resting on my forearms, I captured her mouth, simultaneously running a finger through her swollen folds to make sure she was ready for me. It took me only seconds to find out she was indeed primed to go.

I lined myself up and gently pushed inside her, as slowly as I could manage. Her breath caught in her throat, the look on her face one of pure lust. While I wanted to quickly sheath myself, I made sure to adhere to her challenge. If she wanted it slow, I would give her what she craved.

Thrusting in a few more inches, I stopped to seize her hip, my fingers digging into her soft skin while I withdrew until only the tip of my cock remained inside. I felt her frustration when she ran her nails down my back, the slight sting of pain affirming I was driving her insane. Little did she know she was affecting me the same way. The softness and warmth of her body was pure torment. Pleasure spiraled through me when I pushed back inside, her tightness clenching around me until I thought I was gonna explode.

"You like that?" I rasped, barely able to hold onto the sliver of control still in my grasp. "How do I feel?" Sucking her bottom lip into my mouth, I swirled my tongue with hers before she could answer. I thrust in further, faster than I'd intended. "I could fuck you forever," I growled, dangerously close to throwing caution to the wind and taking her rough and hard. Thankfully, I didn't allow my baser instincts to take over because I would have surely hurt her. But gone was the need to prove a point, her dare flying right out the window as I forged ahead and rocked my body into hers.

My hand moved from her hip to her tit to roughly pinch her nipple, a satisfied moan falling from her gorgeous mouth as soon as my fingers released her. My lips closed around the puckered area, my teeth gently biting her before withdrawing. I knew what she liked, and it was my goal to make sure my wife was completely satisfied.

"Cole!" she cried out, her fingers gripping my hair tighter the more our bodies moved as one. Her eyes fixated on mine, her teeth capturing her bottom lip when she couldn't take it any longer. I knew she was close, could feel it in the way her muscles clamped down on me. We'd only known each other a short while, but I knew her body inside and out, and I knew when she was ready to lose herself into oblivion.

"Do you love how I fuck you?"

"Yes," she moaned.

"You like how my cock fills up that tight pussy?" I breathed hard.

"Yes."

"Fuuuccccckkkk! I'm not gonna last long. I need you to let go. I need you to come all over me, Sully," I demanded with ragged breaths. I swallowed her screams as she gave in, her body locking down tight underneath me. She threw her head back and broke our kiss, her moans filling the air around us. She was so incredibly sexy like this, lost to what her body needed.

I couldn't take any more torture. Wanting to draw out my pleasure simply wasn't a reality. Our harsh panting melded together, our bodies as one driving us both toward the edge of insanity. I captured her mouth, our kiss hard and unforgiving. When I felt her teeth pierce my lower lip in urgency, I simply lost it. I slammed into her over and over again until I felt the pull of bliss rock through me.

Grunting out my own pleasure, I filled her with my release, and it took everything in me not to collapse on top of her. I was spent, fully sated, but I remained mindful of her condition.

When I stopped twitching inside her, I withdrew from her body and fell onto my back, my arm quickly searching for her to pull her closer. Once her head rested over my heart, I breathed easily, counting my heartbeats because I knew every one of them belonged to her.

"I love you," I whispered. My resolve had snapped, but I wouldn't take back the words for anything. Busting inside with the overwhelming feelings, a first for me, I just had to let her know how I felt. I'd almost lost her once without her knowing. I wouldn't make that same mistake again.

No more holding back.

Instead of feeling her relax against me, she stiffened, rolling over on her back quicker than I could stop her. Did she not feel the same way? Had I made a mistake by telling her? Instead of regret washing over me, waves of anger at her blatant denial forced me to say something I should have kept quiet.

I felt vulnerable right then, and when I felt out of my element, I lashed out.

"What's wrong with you?" I practically shouted. "Can you only love someone who beats the shit out of you?" Dick move, but what could I say? I hated feeling cast aside. I sat up in bed, throwing my legs over the side and giving her my back. I regretted the words as soon as they'd left my lips, which I knew would happen the second she moved away from me, but I couldn't help myself.

Silence tortured me, so many thoughts and regrets running through my brain. I screamed at her in my head to say something. Anything. Finish her rejection of my words if that's what it came down to, but make a fuckin' move.

She rose from the bed and walked toward the door, dragging the sheet to wrap around her. Jumping up to stop her, I gripped her arms and shook her. Not hard, but enough to garner her attention. There was no way I was letting her leave me right then, not without some kind of explanation.

"Answer me," I growled, my anger still simmering from her

refusal. Instead of telling me I'd hit the nail on the head, she started shaking, lowering her head until I could no longer see her face. She kept sniffing, and I knew right then she was crying, trying to hide her emotions from me. Was my declaration so unwanted I'd upset her to the point of tears?

Just when I thought she would remain close-lipped, she spoke. "Why are you lying to me?" She kept her head down while her body continued to shake, her long hair shielding her from me.

My grip on her arms tightened, although I was far from hurting her. "Sully," I called, but still she didn't look up at me. I tried once more. "Sully, let me see your face. I won't ask you again." She shook her head, refusing me.

Quickly walking her backward, she hit the wall with enough force to snap her out of whatever she'd just lost herself to. Conscious of her bandaged area, I took care not to jostle her any more, just enough to pull her focus back to me.

"Why do you think I lied to you?" I asked, pure confusion muddling my overactive thoughts.

She drew a quick breath before answering. "Because no one has ever told me they loved me before. Not even my father." Imploring me with her eyes, she continued spewing garbage from her mouth. "I'm disgusting. I'm riddled with scars and marks. I know you're trying your best to be nice to me because you pity me, but you don't love me. So please don't torment me with such words."

My heart broke because I knew she truly believed everything she'd said, her self-image more damaged than I could have ever imagined. If there were any possible way for me to go back in time and snatch her from her club years ago, I would have done it. It was unreasonable, but I felt responsible for her, even before I knew her.

Yeah, how fucked-up was that line of thinking?

Holding her face so she had no choice but to continue to look at me, I poured out my feelings for her. Again. Only this time, I hoped she didn't reject me, instead choosing to believe me and accept my words as the truth.

"I *do* love you. That is the God's honest truth. You might not believe me now, but in time you will. I can't promise I won't say something that might hurt your feelings, or do something which would make you question my loyalty to you, but at the end of the day, you are the woman I want to spend my life with. I will never physically hurt you, but the heart is another matter altogether."

I knew I was about to touch on a subject I barely even gave thought to, much less voiced, simply because it was still too painful, but it was the perfect time to bring it up. "I'd seen the way my parents were toward each other and, while they loved each other deeply, jealousy ran rampant between the both of them. They would sometimes say things they would instantly regret, but their love was what got them through, the glue that held them together until...." I stopped speaking, suddenly questioning whether or not I wished to delve into that part of my life. I thought I wanted to, but saying the words out loud was a completely different story.

With everything I'd just spoken, the part she chose to hang on to and question was the part about my parents. Maybe it was easier for her to digest than the feelings I harbored for her. In time, maybe she would come to believe me.

"What happened to your parents?" she asked. "Are they still alive?" She held her breath while she waited for me to speak again.

"They're both dead." The words cut me, even though I'd come to grips with their death. Reaching for her hand, I pulled her back to the bed and sat her on the edge, taking the seat right next to her. I wanted to get this over with, and then hopefully she'd allow me to lose myself in her for the rest of the day.

"Can you tell me what happened? Do you want to talk about it?" How the hell had our conversation started off with my telling her I loved her, to her rejecting my affections and calling me a liar, to talking about my deceased parents? Funny how life works, switching from one thing to the next in mere seconds. Sometimes without any warning whatsoever.

"My mom passed away in her sleep six years ago. The doctors said it was a brain aneurism." My eyes became glassy at the memory of her, but I pushed the thoughts aside. No time to dwell on that now.

"And your father? What happened to him?"

"Three years ago, my father and his VP, Stone's father, went on a run. Everything was going according to plan until the Savage Reapers interfered. Long story short, both my father and Stone's were killed during the battle. Hence one of the many reasons we're at war with those bastards."

It had always been difficult for me to discuss my father, mainly because I missed him immensely. Plus it was too much of a drain that evening, having other issues which required my attention.

Sully's body shook. "I'm so sorry," she cried. *Yeah, me too.*

After some time had passed, we were back in bed, lying next to one another in complete silence. I'd revealed a lot of things and it was best I let it sink in, giving her time to come to grips with the revelation of my feelings for her as well as the background as to why it was my ultimate goal to destroy the Savage Reapers.

"Cole," Sully whispered, breaking the silence of the room.

"Yeah," I answered, shifting over on my side so I faced her. Trailing a finger along her belly, I enjoyed the moment until she decided to continue.

"I told you I hated Vex, and I do. Well... I did, when he was alive. But there was a time when I told him I loved him. Once. I thought if he heard the words, he would have a change of heart and start treating me better. But the only thing my words got me was a black eye." Her body shook under my touch. "He told me I was trying to trick him, and if I ever told him that again he would kill me."

She turned on her side so we were staring at each other, her warm palm resting on my bearded cheek. "So you can see why I reacted the way I did when you told me you loved me. Rejection was all I'd ever known, but I see now with you it's different. While it might take me some time yet, for it to fully sink in, I do believe you love me." A lone tear trickled down her cheek, her eyes so full of acceptance, but there was a trace of fear still wedged beneath her stare. "As I love you."

My mouth was on hers before she could take her next breath. This whole sharing feelings and loving someone was a whole new world for me. Yes, it would take her some time, but I was willing to stick by her until she was completely mine.

Mind, body and soul.

Epilogue

Marek

"Are you sure you want me to come with you? I know how you get," she teased, walking toward me in a pair of jean shorts and a modest pink tank top. I say modest because her tits were concealed... well, as well as could be expected while still wearing a flimsy piece of material. My jealousies where she was concerned only seemed to worsen, not get better. I trusted her; it was everyone else I had a problem with.

Jagger knew to stay clear of Sully. I knew of a few occasions when I'd been in Chambers and she was helping some of the other women cook, or clean up around the clubhouse, and she and the prospect had run into each other. But from what I was told, their encounters were always kept short, and they never happened when I was present. I made sure of it, for all of our sakes. Sully had tried to plead her case every now and then that the two of them were just friends, but I shut her down every time, dismissing her rants as naivety. On one occasion, we'd gotten into such a heated debate over it I dropped her off at the house and stayed at the club for two days. It was my way of telling her to drop it, or else.

Was it mature?

No.

Did I get my way?

Abso-fuckin-lutely.

"Of course I want you to come. Stone and I have a quick meeting about club business, and then you and I are takin' off for a few days." Pulling her close, I pushed her long hair over her shoulder and nuzzled into her neck, inhaling her scent and dreaming of the exact second I could lose myself inside her again.

Kissing the sensitive spot below her ear, she laughed before flinching, but not before gracing me with one of her sexy moans. "Where are you taking me?"

"It's a surprise, so stop trying to ruin it." Giving her one more quick kiss, I turned toward the door and pulled her behind me.

We made it to the compound quickly, spotting Stone as soon as I parked. Having Sully on the back of my bike was amazing. The way she held on to me, clutching on for dear life sometimes, was extremely satisfying. She wasn't too familiar with riding, her father and that bastard hardly ever taking her off their property, let alone on the back of a motorcycle. A fact I relished more than I let on.

The more we rode together the more she relaxed, although she still had her moments, especially when I kicked it up a notch, traveling faster than was safe sometimes. But I couldn't help it; when I was on the open road with the woman I loved behind me, I let time and speed escape me.

She handed me her helmet as soon as she planted both feet on the ground, sidling up to me to give me a quick kiss before disappearing inside. "I'll be in the kitchen when you're done," she called over her shoulder. I was still staring after her when Stone punched me on the arm.

"Earth to Marek," he jested, a goofy smile on his face while he waited for my reaction. I didn't give him one, instead brushing past him to walk inside as well.

"What time will he be here?" I asked, rounding the table in Chambers and taking my seat at the head. We had a few other things to discuss before Yanez showed his ugly face. But it was necessary—vital, even. The encounter should be the last one we would need to have with the cartel before we were separated from them for good. I wanted to confirm everything else was in place, mainly the beginning of the inevitable demise of our biggest enemy.

"They," my VP corrected. Lifting my head, I tilted it to the side and questioned him with a furrowed brow. "Rafael is coming with Rico this time. They should be here within the hour." He smiled wide, knowing damn well I preferred talking to Carrillo than Yanez. It appeared my day was looking up.

"Good. Happy to hear it."

Leaning back in my chair, the soft leather of the seat conforming around me, I interlocked my fingers behind my head. Smiling wide, I couldn't help but feel as if my life was on the right path. My relationship with Sully was progressing in the right direction. The final piece of the puzzle of taking my club legit was falling nicely into place, and those around me seemed to be happier because of it.

Life was good.

Or so I thought.

Want More?

Are you ready for more? Then dive back into the Knights Corruption with Stone, book 2, available now.

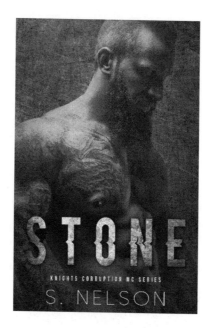

Stay Informed

Did you enjoy Marek?

Want to find out about S. Nelson's next novel?

Each month she sends out updates on upcoming books, sales, cover reveals, and awesome giveaways.

Get her FREE monthly newsletter by going to:
www.subscribepage.com/snelsonnewsletter

WANT A STORY THAT WILL LEAVE YOU
BREATHLESS? THEN GRAB YOUR COPY OF
ADDICTED, BOOK ONE IN THE ADDICTED
TRILOGY

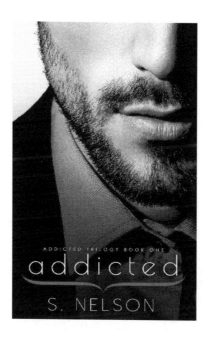

She intrigues him.
She challenges him.
She threatens the secret he's been hiding for years.
Will a promise made long ago be the very same thing that
destroys their chance for happiness?

About the Author

S. Nelson grew up with a love of reading and a very active imagination, never putting pen to paper, or fingers to keyboard until 2013.

Her passion to create was overwhelming, and within a few months she'd written her first novel. When she isn't engrossed in creating one of the many stories rattling around inside her head, she loves to read and travel as much as she can. She lives in the Northeast with her husband and two dogs, enjoying the ever changing seasons.

If you would like to follow or contact her please feel free to do so at the following:

Website: www.snelsonauthor.com
Email: snelsonauthor8@gmail.com

Also on Facebook, Goodreads, Amazon, Instagram and Twitter

Note to Reader

If you are a new reader of my work, thank you so much for taking a chance on me. If I'm old news to you, thank you for continuing to support me. It truly means the world to me.

If you've enjoyed this book, or any of my other stories, please consider leaving a review. It doesn't have to be long at all. A sentence or two will do just fine. Of course, if you wish to elaborate, feel free to write as much as you want.

Acknowledgments

Thank you to my husband for being patient with me as I started a completely new series, taking up more of my time than I'd intended. I love you!

A huge thank you to my family and friends for your continued love and support. I don't know what I would do without you!

To the ladies at Hot Tree Editing, I can't say enough great things about you. You continue to amaze me and I can't wait until our next project together. You have been truly fantastic!

I would also like to thank Clarise at CT Cover Creations. Your work speaks for itself. I'm absolutely thrilled with each and every cover you've magically created for me. They just keep getting better and better!

To all of the bloggers who have shared my work, I'm forever indebted to you. You ladies are simply wonderful!

To all of you who have reached out to me to let me know how much you loved my stories, I am beyond humbled. Thank you so much, and I'll continue to do my best to bring you stories you can lose yourself in, even if for a few hours.

And last but not least, I would like to thank you, the reader.

If this is the first book you've read from me, I hope you enjoy it. If this is yet another story from me you've taken a chance on... THANK YOU from the bottom of my heart!

Standalones

Massey Security Duet

Addicted Trilogy

Knights Corruption MC Series

KCMC Complete Series (all 5 books in one)

Knights Corruption MC Series – Next Generation

S. Nelson

Made in the USA
Middletown, DE
09 October 2021